WHEN SHE'S GONE

WHEN SHE'S GONE

STEVE LUNDIN

GREAT PLAINS
PUBLICATIONS

Great Plains Publications
420 – 70 Arthur Street
Winnipeg, MB R3B 1G7
www.greatplains.mb.ca

Great Plains Publications gratefully acknowledges the financial support pro-
vided for its publishing program by the Government of Canada through the
Book Publishing Industry Development Program (BPIDP); the Canada Council
for the Arts; as well as the Manitoba Department of Culture, Heritage and
Tourism; and the Manitoba Arts Council.

Design & Typography by Relish Design Studio Ltd.

Printed in Canada by Friesens

CANADIAN CATALOGUING IN PUBLICATION DATA

Main entry under title:

Lundin, Steve
  When she's gone / Steve Lundin.

  ISBN 1-894283-53-8

  1. Title.

PS8573.U543W48 2004   C813'.54   C2004-904013-8

*This novel is dedicated to
Keith, Neil, Ian, and
Matt, Spencer, Keir,
who played for real.*

The game got in our blood when the Selkirk Settlers first showed up at the forks of the Red and Assiniboine rivers. Not hard to figure out why. They were farmers one and all and given land along the rivers, each allotment the precise dimensions of a hockey rink. Come winter the whole world froze up and there was nothing to do but skate and whack at frozen rubber discs with hickory sticks.

Those first leagues were vicious. There were two major ones, the Northwest League and the Hudson's Bay League. Serious rivals and it all came to a head when Louis Riel, left-wing for the Voyageurs, jumped leagues and signed with the Métis Traders right there at the corner of Portage and Main, posing with a buffalo hide signing bonus. The whole territory went up in flames–the Riel Rebellion–culminating in the slaughter of nineteen Selkirk fans. Redcoats came from the east and refereed the mob that strung Riel up and hung him until dead. The Northwest League got merged into the Hudson's Bay League shortly afterward and a troubled peace came to the land.

It was the first slapshot fired in anger, but it wouldn't be the last...

The beginning

We sold our soul. No point in complaining, no point in blaming anyone else, not the Yanks, not anyone else. We've done it ourselves and if you were a Yank you'd be saying the same thing. If your country was Italy, France or Belgium, if the city you called home was in England or Scotland or Wales, you're saying the same thing I'm saying right now, at least you'd be if you were thinking about what I'm thinking about.

Being Canadian I'm thinking hockey, I'm thinking the breath of ice and the hammer of the puck against the boards. But you could be thinking rugby, the muscle and pumping blood and the flow and ebb of human will. You could be thinking baseball and the expectation and tension and explosions of power that change the universe in an instant. Or soccer, a field of players trying to find the right pattern, turning motion into music with agony in your calf muscles at every near miss.

And I know you're all saying the same as me. What the hell happened?

Now if you got the guts you'll say, all right Mark, tell us what happened. So I will.

The arena

Jack always called it a temple, with ten thousand pagans on the seats, the ritual going on there on the ice below and the portrait of Queen Elizabeth, the distant goddess, looking down on the whole thing and by the third period the air's gone grey with cigarette smoke like a thousand torches burning low and the Queen's look has turned sly.

A temple. Our temple. The 'Export A' scoreboard and time clock hung suspended from the girdered ceiling directly above centre ice. It showed us the news of the cosmos, every detail precisely clicking away. Like an angel sometimes, other times like a damned demon. It was an altar in the air, unreachable and runnelled with divination and a secret energy coursed down to the players and back up for as long as it was lit with numbers. Down below sweat on brows misted into blood and rose up, soaking into that altar and we cursed and prayed in the same breath, living and dying moment by moment. It floated implacable, the hand of God.

We sat in our seats. Row on row, ten thousand watchers making their own sound like hornets in a nest about to be kicked. Thrumming to the taut ticking of that clock overhead, to the mystery patterns of men on skates, ancient heart of the game thumping a single beat that turned the temple into its own chambered world.

The family

Jack says sport and religion are the same thing. He says the game – whatever the game – is the contest between humans and nature, the laws of the universe struggled against, sometimes matched and when matched everyone gasps a breath as if to take perfection inside, down into the lungs, as if for that moment the universe has shown itself, every pattern realized, every dream possible.

Down into the lungs. Jack also says that's why the scoreboard is a giant cigarette ad. 'Export A' cigarettes, and there's more ads along the walls, ads everywhere, and before the rules were changed the walkways beyond the portals filled with spectators between periods, all lighting up like maniacs. It wasn't until we played against the Plains Cree one winter that I realized the connection between tobacco and religion, but I'll tell that story when it's time to tell it.

Sport and religion are the same thing. The contest between humans and nature. Life and death, quantum mechanics, the Big Bang, evolution. Jack can go on and on like that. I sit and watch and study his face, that half-smile that makes women melt, not knowing if he's bullshitting me or showing his truth and maybe sometimes they're both one and the same which is probably why the women can't resist.

Bullshit or truth? I wonder about it all the time. I'm wondering about it right now, sitting here on this mounded ridge of Scottish grass with the old ditch down below and the effigy's shadow crawling over us like it was a secret we weren't supposed to see. There's clouds scudding overhead, rolling land on all sides and sheep and hedgerows but summer's on its way out and tonight we'll be sitting here as frosted as the grass.

The effigy. It was a joke, it started out as a joke, for me at least. But with Jack you can never be sure since most of my brother's jokes are dead serious. So I'd laughed at first, but not anymore. It stands over us, squat and wide like some arctic samurai, a suit of plastic, leather and cloth armour, the equipment pretty much new but the damned thing looks a thousand years old, raised up out of some rock-lined earthen pit where priests once cut hearts out of babies.

We'd rigged up our stupid walking sticks, the ones we'd bought for no special reason from that farmer outside Edinburgh our second day over here, rigged them up along with a five foot length of pipe we'd found in the ditch. The pipe stood straight, the walking sticks made an X and we used hockey tape to join all three together where they crossed.

Just having fun, emptying out my hockey bag, all my goaltending stuff: the huge leather knee pads, the nylon-covered plastic plates that protected the chest, the clacking shoulder pads, all straps and plastic and cloth down to the elbow and wrist, the blocker glove, its leather-covered fibreglass board bent into playing shape, and the trapper, broken in and polished from countless hard rubber pucks. And my mask, fifteen hundred dollars worth of wire and fibreglass and straps and neck-shield and air-brushed paint turning the whole thing into the snarling face of a dragon. Hockey tape, bungie cords and laces all went into hanging that equipment onto its frame. The effigy.

We'd made ourselves an empty goaltender out of my equipment. It was that part that had begun bothering me.

The wall

Hadrian's Wall didn't seem much like a wall to me. Just a ridge of earth all grassed over, broken up by roads and other stuff, and ditches appearing here and there.

There's Scottish blood on the old man's side, along with Cree and Métis, a Canadian bloodline going back to the very beginning. The other side's pure Swedish, first generation immigrant. Jack says our Scottish blood belongs right here, on Hadrian's Wall; he says our ancestors stormed this wall fifteen hundred years ago, peeled it back like the lid of a sardine can showing underneath Romans in olive oil who we then ate with salteens.

He came here to find his Scottish roots, which explains or is supposed to explain him going and spending sixteen hundred pounds in Edinburgh to get himself tattooed all over in blue. Face all swirled, neck, arms, hands, chest, back and probably everywhere else. Seems extreme to my thinking but that's Jack and there he sits all blue and talking about growing his hair long then braiding it.

It's the middle of the day and it seems we're staying put to wait out the hours till midnight and then the hours till dawn, since it's some kind of Scottish or Pictish anniversary or something. Though I think Jack's just made that up but he's got a bloody expensive bottle of single malt and I'm looking forward to that.

But it's the effigy I'm thinking about right now. It stands facing south.

South, Jack says, *is the direction blood flows.*

What the hell does that mean?

Blood, Mark. Blood, dreams, life, all flows south. You know what I mean, brother, it's something Canadians understand and know as truth, down inside your bones like cancer. Blood flows south.

Jack says that all those savages who crossed this wall went south and became the very people they went to kill in the first place and it's all just the ebb and pull of history the world over. Grass is greener to the south fed rich by blood. But the point, Jack says, is this: those savages *wanted* to go south. Lured by riches and civilization, they went by choice and if they ended up rotted and soft and suffocating under mounds of gold, it was all their own goddamned fucking fault. And you know the worst of it is, the boys back home saw them off with cheers.

The city

The corner of Portage and Main, the official coldest corner on earth. Portage Avenue runs in a damn near straight line west and keeps going until it becomes the TransCanada Highway and that runs straight some more, across three provinces until it hits the mountains, then it climbs up and over and down again and stops at the sea, waits for a ferry, then goes on but angling south like a final flick of the tail to the city of Victoria on Vancouver Island. Twenty-seven thousand miles.

Main Street runs north forever up to the tundra and the frozen wreck of the Franklin Scouting Expedition, and south down into the French community of St. Vital. Where street meets avenue is the centre of Winnipeg, the prairie city, city of oaks and Dutch Elm disease, mosquitoes and street hockey, starved promises and empty buildings, festivals and woodticks, city of green from the air in summer and grey with thousands of tons of dumped sand and gravel embedded in packed snow and ice and sun-dogs overhead and air so clear and cold it cuts like blades in the chest in the winter. City with no spring but sometimes a long autumn. City of blizzards, thunderstorms, twisters, floods, heatwaves, coldsnaps, endless wind of frostbite and dryburn and aching ears and squint-line corners in cool seen-it-all eyes. City of Indians: Assiniboine, Ojibwa, Swampy Cree, Lakota, Gros Ventre, Chippewyan, Plains Cree, Blood, Blackfoot, Inuit, a lot of them still in the rough but something's happening there and you see Band jackets with crests worn like team pride and there's summer pow-wows in the city parks and chain dances and leatherwork and art and the old rough's mostly in white people's minds these days like memories that won't let go.

City of seven hundred thousand people and holding, city of farmers and immigrants: Chinese, Taiwanese, Cambodian, Ukrainian, Polish, Scottish, French, Mennonite, Hutterite, Luddite, Stalagmite, Termite, Jamaican, Haitian, Nicaraguan, El Salvadoran, Russian, German, English, Icelandic, Swedish, Finnish, Filipino, Japanese. City of bend-over-backwards governments and cold-hearted fuck-you governments. Broken-hearted city now and I can never ever go back and see it as it once was and it's just a shame, a sad shame.

The arena

Gold to red to blue to greys and standing-room only, we lived in the greys, the top rows of seats and with a good pair of binoculars you could scan the crowds below and find every beautiful woman there was to find. When we were thirteen we looked and shared grins and nudged each other a lot; a few years later things turned serious. We'd got strapping and muscled and predatory and laughably bold in a way that would get you arrested these days, or at least injunctioned. Jack had the charm but I had the mystery, although I was late to realize that's what I had and used to get all twisted inside at the way Jack got laid and I just dreamed wet frustration. The thing was, mystery would reel

13

them in but it took longer. Jack's conquests were instantaneous and that's what I saw and seeing it made me want the same but like in so many ways we were different and I was slow to appreciate that fact.

Caroline was the one. We saw her in the preseason, down in the golds. She was bored and who wouldn't be, it being a cruddy exhibition game with most of the premiere players sitting out. But her old man was one of the serious fans, the kind who took notes but only in his head and kept the details fresh by repeating them over and over again to his buddies as he shelled roasted-in-the-shell peanuts by the thousands, with the mound growing up past his ankles and then his knees and crotch until he was a pontificating head on a pile of peanut shells. A man of money and taste, Caroline in tow, hour-glassed like his peanuts and shelled once a month by his stubby fingers in a fit of insensitive lust.

She was Japanese but Canadian-born. She had breathtaking full lips painted red and looking sticky. Wore silver fox fur, had her hair long but wavy, blush on her round smooth cheeks, eye-liner and silvery turquoise eye-shadow flaring out under her brows. She wore high-heeled brown leather boots standing five seven in them and five feet three and a half in stockings and a fraction less barefoot.

Jack had that dreamy glaze in his eyes.

I'm in love, Mark.

Who?

Queen Elizabeth. Her portrait. It's huge, you could climb into her mouth. She could kiss your head and engulf it. Mona Lisa's got nothing on her smile –

She's looking down on a hockey game, Jack, of course she's going to look a little confused. It's the same look as on the dollar bill she's probably never seen a dollar bill just uses hundreds when she's over here. She's looking confused.

And we're all looking up at her. The goddess, Queen of the Empire, you know if she'd wanted to, she could have poisoned husbands, marrying one after another until she'd inherited nine-tenths of the world. It's the power, Mark, it's there in that smile, that hint of a smile that makes you confused so you think she's confused but you got it backwards.... Power is sexy, plain and simple.

Well, I'll take the Japanese woman Row 14, Section 6. You can have the Queen.

I'm thinking of dropping down on a rope in front of her, plastering myself against that huge painted mouth, then humping –

You'll bounce, that's canvas.

You'll never get near Row 14 Section 6, even in the last five minutes of a blowout, those seats never empty. Besides she's with her old man.

Not always.

Plan on ambushing her in the washroom? Get real.

Me? You're the one talking about coming all over the Queen's portrait. Probably against the law.

And adultery isn't?

Is it? Really? Can you get thrown in jail?

You can get lynched, brother. It's almost as bad as horse thieving. At the very least they'll run you out of town. Besides, you'll be damned for all time for coveting another man's wife.

I'm not talking coveting. I'm talking fucking. Fucking another man's wife isn't the same as coveting another man's wife.

You mean you can fuck without coveting.

Of course.

Well all right, then. Your soul's safe.

Hallelujah.

Amen. It'll be a cold day in hell you get her in bed, Mark.

You picked one out yet?

Row 39 Section 7, half-way along.

Gimme the binocs.

Blonde, with the tits.

Oh yeah I see. She's got a boyfriend.

I covet nonetheless.

Looks like he'd beat the crap out of you.

Then she'll cradle my bruised head in her lap all flattered that I'd take a beating just to get into her pants. Eighteen seconds left in the period.

They'll head out together, or just him and if she stays planted in her seat you're fucked.

They'll head out together for smokes. All I need do is angle myself behind him and get her to meet my eyes and if I stare long enough she'll sense it and do just that.

What makes you so sure?

Women always sense it when a guy's watching…

…You two, are you both going down?

Another coffee, Mom? No problem.

The buzzer sounds, thousands collectively sigh, rise up from their seats. I hold the binocs firm. She's standing now. He isn't, he's yabbering on to his buddies, giving them a rundown on everything they've just seen and how it doesn't look good for the rest of the season. They're puffing out their cheeks and shaking their heads in agreement. Looks bad, boys. Not good. Better get their act in gear. Won't happen. Won't, you got that right. She heads for the aisle, reaching into her purse.

Between periods

Life unfolded between periods. Kids in team jerseys lined up to buy hotdogs, popcorn, ice-cream sandwiches, chocolate bars. The beer booths were islands in small lakes of spilled brew with men in nylon puffer jackets and workboots holding semi-translucent plastic cups filled with Labatt's or Molson's or Extra Old or 50 Ale or Standard's, sucking on a butt with the other hand, the hands blunt and yellowed and scarred and these guys stood talking in grunts or not talking in winter-silence.

Winnipeggers know winter-silence. It's immigrant in a godawful bloody-minded land, it's the cool quiet of facing down numbing wind and watching livestock freeze solid where they stand and year after year after year of this thins the eyes to slits in hoarfrost wrinkles and weathers fingers blunt and burns fat for energy until by fifty a man's nothing but tendon and wire cable muscles and the women are pretty much the same. Winter-silence is facing the world, Russian peasant style, gulags escaped, pogroms avoided, Holocaust survived, '50 Flood waded through, June blizzard dug out of, politician bled and cancer bound. The Canadian who travelled once from a hellhole country and never again who isn't noticed by visiting Yanks because not being noticed is bone-bred, but they rebuild the frost-heaved streets every summer, they clear the tons of sand and gravel, they bake brown under the sun and drink gallons of beer and walk straight and drive wearing caps at a steady fifteen miles an hour. In their faces is winter-silence, the heart of the hockey fan, the father of hockey players, the volunteers at Dieppe weathering the slow murder of the game to this day.

Each break between periods we left our seats, my brother and me, and walked down the steps to the gates and out into our country Canada. Beer and smoke and colourless clothes mostly in dark shades, men, women and kids standing and milling and lining up to piss and buying souvenirs and united in the culture of hockey just like others in other countries united in other games, only in Canada opinions are muttered not screamed and drunk is quiet not loud, sad not in your face obnoxious.

In that country between periods stood my gentle Japanese, a flower in the mud, pulling on a Matinee Kings like nicotine was the only thing holding her up, her lids half-closed, the long black lashes sweeping down from straight lines below eye shadow all moon silver matched by the paint on her long fingernails.

I hovered thirty feet away. Her presence turned heads, drew gazes and she was bored with all of it. I was sixteen, six foot though I'd be six one by Christmas. Disco still covered dance-floors back then like nylon puke but I wasn't into that being a Jock, not a Greaser, not a Geek, not a Freak, not Flared, not Flouncy, not Fevered, but Levis' bootleg with solid goalie thighs and shoulders that made push-ups in bed damnnear effortless. I had a jaw, light green eyes, thick black hair, and all my teeth in a straight line.

Jack had gone off in his own pursuit. I acted nonchalant, beerless and smokeless but keeping my hands out of my pockets because girls liked my hands and someone once told me that hands in the pockets was a put-off. After a few minutes it started getting difficult staying nonchalant. Her ESP had sensed my attention and she'd coolly swept across me with her bored look, then swept back and my shifty study of her red lips had my pole stiff enough to push upright if I let it but that wouldn't do because though I wasn't as big as Jack it wasn't no mushroom and I'd still end up with a red knob over my belt buckle. As it was it went down along my right leg though I didn't dare look to check to see if it was obvious, I hoped not because she was looking my way again behind smoke as she took a drag.

I watched her draw her left hand across the front of her fur coat and figured she was showing me the wedding ring and studded engagement ring as if I didn't know or couldn't have guessed so I kept looking and she noticed that and got uneasy, dropping the butt and crushing it under one boot then lighting another.

Time was nearly up, though. I sighed, edged into the line-up at the nearest concession stand to get Mom's coffee.

The family

In 1960 Mom arrived in Halifax harbour with two trunks and a tiny coffin in tow. The Trans-Atlantic voyage from Stockholm to Copenhagen to Rejkavik to Gander to New York then up to Halifax had taken the life of her year-old daughter. Once her new husband escorted her to Toronto, he turned around and went back to Sweden unable to cope with a dead daughter and a new country. But Mom had a way of landing on her feet. She found a job as a seamstress and six months later married the floor manager's son which wasn't surprising since she was all curves and a stunner. He took her to Winnipeg a year later and she ended up managing thirty sewing machine operators in his new sportswear company.

She produced two sons who learned to walk on the factory floor surrounded by sergers and stitchers and presses and Catholic gewgaws and round honey-skinned women fresh from the Phillipines. When hockey jerseys entered the line, the Winnipeg Jets of the World Hockey Association, rival league to the National Hockey League that only found legitimacy with the signing of Bobby Hull, late of the NHL Chicago Blackhawks, but pulled aboard with the game's first million dollar contract which he accepted on the corner of Portage and Main in the summer of dreams, entered our lives though only in a business sense at first. But it wasn't until the Swedes, Ulf and Anders, arrived that Mom became the maternal fan, so in the end it was just national pride but that was enough.

Jack was four and I was three when we first skated on ice, there on one of the four outdoor rinks around River Heights Community Centre. Wednesday nights and sometimes Thursday nights and Friday nights and Saturday nights but only rarely and Sunday afternoons we went by taxi down to Winnipeg Arena since Dad was off somewhere and Mom didn't drive and we sat in the cheap rows because things were tight. There on the ice Bobby Hull roved on leftwing and the Swedes Anders Hedberg on rightwing and Ulf Nilsson commanded centre creating the Hot Line and blowing the turgid up and down style right out of the rink with wheeling symmetry, drop-passes, breathtaking stickhandling and blinding speed oh my they were something and they were the flag in Mom's heart.

The wall

The best ever?

Hard to say, brother.

They changed everything, they brought the European style into Canadian hockey. Drop-passes, crossing over along the blueline, Hedberg firing wrist-shots on his off-foot and on the fly, using the feet because in the summer they played soccer I mean it's one thing playing against the Russians but it's another when it's your team-mate playing that style and they pull you in because you keep finding you've got no choice these guys keep planting the puck on your stick when you'd thought it impossible and suddenly you've got a clear shot on net.

More than that, Mark. They showed us that skill could win games. Not intimidation. Pure skill. But they paid for it didn't they.

Mugged every night, jabbed, hooked, cross-checked, kneed, gouged, butt-ended, punched, and then there was the night when Steve Durbano of the Birmingham Bulls leapt over the bench, skated across the ice with twelve thousand horrified people watching and jumped on Bobby Hull's back and ripped his hair off, Bobby being one of the old guard who never wore a helmet but had used some of his million dollars getting a transplant but we all saw that night that it hadn't worked and his hair lay on the ice and shame and compassion and outrage filled the bristling air and made patterns of eternal memory in the arena's girders and pylons and in the brains of every man woman and child in attendance.

When Bobby disappeared into the dressing room and came back and stepped onto the ice with a helmet on his head we stood and cheered with tears in our eyes and sure it sounds funny but it wasn't, it was like a rape, rape of a man's dignity, rape of the game we all loved and this was what our game had come to and we all felt helpless and soiled.

Bobby owned a ranch. Spent his summers pitching hay, pulling wire and driving fenceposts. Bobby's wrists were as thick as a normal man's thighs and if he'd wanted he could have turned around and driven his fist to the back of Durbano's skull but he didn't and Steve knew he wouldn't, just one more coward thug on skates and back then there were scores of them, both leagues, and in the NHL they ruled the game but it was all too much, just too fucking too much.

Sheep crested the ridge opposite us and I wondered if we'd get trampled remembering getting chased from a field once near Dauphin by a bull, but of course these were sheep and up to my knees or a bit more and they didn't look mean or territorial, not that I knew much about sheep this being the first time I'd seen one for real but the thought of sheep got me thinking about sports fans.

My heart's broken, Jack.

Want me to show you the tattooing on my dick?

You got your dick done, too? Man are you crazy or what?

A filigreed screw, Celtic spiral, marching soldiers with their hair in braids and tied one warrior to the next. When the wall was seriously taken it was a combination of Picts and Scots on the land and Saxons from the sea. Saxons were basically Danes, old Norse, pre-Vikings meaning both lines of our European ancestry had a hand in taking this wall.

We got no Danish blood.

Who's to say? Sweden owned Denmark once, Denmark owned Sweden once, it went back and forth so why not? Same language root, Angles, Jutes, Saxons, Burgundians, Thuringians, Franks, Frisians, Geats, Rus, Vundal all more or less the same.

Did they tattoo their dicks, too?

Origin of the term 'bastard sword' and 'hand-and-a-half' which was a measure of penile length, as those red-cheeked English nuns well knew.

Bullshit, rape is rape even if you take it with a smile.

Spoken like a true Canadian hockey fan.

The city

The Winnipeg General Strike of 1919 was triggered by a six cent raise on ticket prices when the Winnipeg Warriors had a shot at knocking off the Stanley Cup Champions, the Kenora Thistles. The Royal Mounted Police showed in force and clashed with the strikers on the corner of Portage and Main, trampling thousands.

The real culprits behind the whole thing was a family called the Finians, Yank sympathizers who wanted to see the American Hockey League expand into Canada all because we'd sheltered Sitting Bull after the Battle of Little Bighorn and then hammered them in the War of 1812, burning their White House down, not once but twice, but of course they won in the end when the New York Rangers signed Anders and Ulf and the Hot Line was gone forever and I remember watching highlights and seeing a Philadelphia Flyer cheapshot Ulf against the boards and shatter his leg and welcome to the NHL.

The General Strike ended with the '50 flood, when everybody had to pitch together with sandbags to keep the arena safe but we almost lost it anyway so we voted in Duff Roblin who campaigned on a promise to protect the arena, which assured him a landslide and he then singlehandedly built a floodway now called Duff's Ditch around the city, which saved the arena for all time against forces of nature but didn't save it from greed.

Much later they built tunnels under Portage and Main, subverting our glory but only temporarily because things were destined to come to a head one more time and that would include Portage and Main again, along with the Forks, which was where the Assiniboine and Red rivers meet and was the site of the earliest rival hockey leagues from which the city was born and it's funny how Portage and Main rose again to give us a lie and the Forks was witness to the city's death. Betrayal lives in the city's cycle, an ever-bleeding scar that cynicism only scabs but never closes.

Ice rinks lived in their thousands every winter, in every neighbourhood, outside every school and in every park at community centres and on the river's ice. Wind-chills that froze sled-dogs into solid lumps couldn't stop a kid stepping onto the ice, couldn't stop the shinny games, the industrial league games, the double-A games, the sponge hockey, the Midget League Triple-A Junior Senior Old-Timers, the Native League games. We were red-faced ice-dwellers who'd be content with an ice age ten thousand years long and there'd be lights for night games and heaters under the benches in the dressing rooms and some of us wore our skates in barefeet. The community centres had indoor rinks, too, for league games and midnight games when twenty guys got together and each pitched in five bucks to rent four hours of ice-time.

And out in the countryside, out on the prairie in towns consisting of a main street, a rail line with grain elevators, a gas station, a cafe hotel and six houses, there'd be open rinks and a community arena and bus-trip games and six a.m. practices and pucks thundering against the boards like gunshots all hours, some quiet kid with the dream he'd make real skating alone under stars diamond sharp in brittle plastic-shattering cold and a few years later he steps out onto the ice at Maple Leaf Gardens in Toronto or The Forum in Montréal and it's for real, but those cold nights under the stars stay inside him, joy-filled, the memory of paradise and unsoured dreams.

The arena

Any luck?
I got close.
Then what? You come in your pants?
That's coffee.
Sure thing, whatever you say, brother.
And you?
Friday night at The Fireplace. Her boyfriend went for a piss and she reeled me in with her eyes I threw caution to the winds –
Don't you always?
The boyfriend, we know him. Number 15 North Kildonan. Remember last season that game before the play-offs? NK was out of it, it was a nothing game –
The guy that broke your nose?
That's the one.
Did he see you?
He saw but wasn't suspicious just gloating with his arm around his chick and I gave him a smile that's going to haunt him one day.
He'll fucking kill you, Jack.
It'll kill him when I fuck his babe, you mean. I'll have ripped his manhood right out from between his legs and me and his babe will dice and slice it into mincemeat and there'll be nothing left of him.
You hope.
I know.
Huh.
Who have you found for next break?
Same one. My Japanese widow.
Widow?
As good as.
Pack it in you don't stand a chance.

Half way through the game and the Jets led six nothing. I scanned the crowd with the binoculars. Every type of fan I could list them, lay bare their lives with love in the heart. The three teenaged girls wearing Jets jerseys all number 15 because Hedberg was a blonde god but two years back they wore number 9 because that was Bobby Hull's and in a few years it would be number 10 for Hawerchuk and finally number 8 for Teemu Selanne. Three girls, never ageing, always fifteen, always dreamy-eyed. Who needs rock stars when you've got magic on ice and smalltown stars-in-the-eyes memories, could be the pimply kid next door who spends seven hours a day out on the rink and that closeness is like holding hands in the playground or could be.

Scrawny quiet boy two rows down, comes to every game, no talent but living and breathing the game with stats cramming his head, the lightning rod of intensity and yearning for greatness, he's the silent core of it all and like everyone else he's about to be betrayed by faceless money-men and if it's done over and over and over again there'll be hell to pay in ways never imagined.

But right now this is the arena and we've all stepped in and out of the real world, the small rooms, the kitchen arguments, dying parents, dying children, alcohol haze, fists in the face, midnight tears, it's all pushed back and life's drama is down there on the ice, every fate hanging in the balance.

The Japanese woman rose in her seat. I tracked her with the binoculars as she made for the aisle.

She's heading out.

You'll have to move fast if you want to reach her, brother.

I'm off.

You don't stand a chance.

I handed him the binoculars, he grinned up at me, mocking and pitying. I edged past others in the row then went down the steps.

Section 7 was a quarter way along the concessions concourse. The area was almost empty, no one but ushers and security and the occasional latecomer to the beer stands. I moved fast, came opposite the ramp.

She'd made excuses, off to the bathroom but in fact she'd come out for another smoke.

I was balls and thick dick and hormones and fearless and she watched me approach, expressionless.

The wall

Do you work days, what about tomorrow, where can we meet, are you bored, do you dream, do you lust, do those lips smile, tomorrow under the clock at Eaton's ten-thirty a.m., your old man will be halfway into his morning busy at his office, we can go to the Maple Leaf Restaurant beside the Metropolitan, it's got booths and it's smoky and gloomy....

My back ached as damp crept up from the ground. *Where's the bottle, Jack? How long do we wait before you crack it?*

My heart beats to an ancient time, brother. No hurry.

I've got my try-out day after tomorrow, if I'm still pissed come tomorrow morning I'll be up shit's creek.

You'll be a walk-on, Mark. Don't expect to be lacing up the same day you arrive. You'll need to do the physical. Insurance rules.

I'll sign a waiver.

I'd like to inject some realism at this point –

You've tattooed your dick, give me a break.

I fully acknowledge that art must be seen to be appreciated.

Don't you go pulling out that dong you'll get us arrested or at least the sheep excited.

Then don't question my grip on reality.

All right all right, yeesh.

Why Cardiff anyway?

Why indeed.

Fifteen hundred years ago the Romans stood on the ramparts aghast. They were Internazionale kicking a ball around on the embankment but a wind was ripping down from the north highlands and the Orkneys and fjords and ice covered the moors and the Attacotti Marauders and Pict Pillagers and Scot Scouragers were coming across the fields, all offence with blades held high and on ice-sheets from the North Sea came long-faced Scandinavians including Finns with names like Seppo Reppo and Veli Pekka Ketola but with free agency in swing they were in the uniform of the Saxon Storm and there was hell to pay on Hadrian's Wall.

But the game was slow to catch on in the south, no open ice, not enough rinks, a different story from Canada.

The first wave of Vikings came down through the St. Lawrence. There'd been earlier attempts, on Greenland and in Newfoundland, but the colonies died out for lack of competition and leagues consisting of one team and one team only, so the first legitimate Swedish players, a gaunt defenceman named Salming and a leftwinger named Hammarstrom, made landing in Toronto Harbour and Hammarstrom didn't last but Salming sure as hell did, he wore a maple leaf for bloody ever even though every bone in his body had been broken at least once, but it was really the second longship that did the business, coming down from Lake Winnipeg after a six thousand mile, over the Arctic Circle portage, and a short visit in Gimli, then across the Lockport Dam and upstream on the Red making landing at the Forks.

Goalie Larsson, who had his moments, Lars Erik Sjoberg, a national team veteran defenceman, a doctor by profession who would die of cancer in New York after his playing days, and it was probably a broken heart that weakened him and that was a cue card we missed, Hexi Rihiranta, a Finn, and Veli Pekka Ketola, another Finn, who could fire wrist-shots hard enough to break plexiglass but never hit the net, and forwards Anders Hedberg and Ulf 'believe it or not, I only drink milk' Nilsson, who'd never played together before and in that first season the Jets became the Yets because Swedes can't pronounce the letter J, nor could Mom.

The family

We lived in a red brick house in River Heights. It was a heavy house, sitting on river clay that oozed like plastercine until the basement floor looked like a miniature replica of Lake Louise's black diamond run. There was a school across the street and a community centre, meaning two outdoor rinks with nets and boards, the one for league games fitted with lights.

We'd be out there all hours. Before the water was poured and became ice we'd use the driveway behind the house. Buddies from school joined in since even with league games and practices we needed still more. The street itself would, by the end of December, be packed snow as slippery as ice but softer, and we'd play with the guys who couldn't skate, using a tennis ball and moving the nets to one side every time a car rolled past. Nobody complained, nobody batted an eye, and the cars went by at five miles an hour and the driver would wave thanks and we'd wave or nod back.

In the house's living room was a TV and on the TV were hockey games, NHL games Wednesday and Saturday nights and rival league WHA games whenever, and highlights on the Sports segment of the news. There was a worn sofa in Swedish style with teak legs and wall-to-wall shag carpeting, smelling like our German Shepherd, the carpeting we laid on with pillows and sleeping bags to watch the games.

If the WHA Jets were on or the NHL Leafs Mom would sit in her easy chair, the kind that rocks, and watch because of the Swedes playing for both teams. Jack and I would argue and sometimes fight but you couldn't argue with her, a stubborner woman no man's ever known, and rules never mattered so much as the victimhood she draped on her favourite players, which wasn't hard since the Swedes got fouled and beat on something fierce and the referees had a way of turning a blind eye on it since nationalism was rife with the men in stripes as much as with anyone else.

We'd be sprawled on the floor and she was the matron behind us. Dad was off somewhere and never had time for our practices or games or much of anything else and strangely that seemed to suit everyone fine but we were young and didn't know yet that his fucking other women seared pain into Mom and she focused it all making the game of hockey life's game and resurrecting ancient bone-deep beliefs in Fate, but holding fast, the immovable rock we all clung to without even knowing it.

In all those city games I'd played in, the referee would collect the puck and skate for centre ice, opposing teams lining up. I'd give my back a last stretch, scour the ice with my skate blades around the goalposts and along the goal-line, building up snow in the hopes that it'd be enough to stop a slow-moving puck. I'd look up into the stands and there Mom would be, hands in lap, her face glowing but stern since that was the expression of her life.

I'd be on a bad team so I'd get a lot of work keeping the game close and I don't know what dreams she lived out or hoped for because even now I see Mom in silence because she was something without words, but she was there, she was always there.

Jack and I rarely played on the same teams, a year's difference in age meaning a lot, at least until we got older and slipped from draft prospects to hackers, Jack out of indifference and me because of injuries one after another. From sixteen onward I never played a full season.

Once late in the season, Jack's last, we had been blown out of the playoffs but were then invited to play some charity games in Saskatchewan. Couldn't afford to hire a bus so we all piled into cars and drove the TransCanada through blinding drifting snow in bitter 40 below winds to play a three game series against a team of Plains Cree.

It was an indoor rink, thank God, pretty well set up actually with fast ice and solid boards. The boys lined up along the blueline during warm-up and fired shots at me. The Cree down at their end did the same, dressed in yellow and blue jerseys with only a handful wearing helmets.

Jack skated in to stand off to one side of the net and send pucks back out to the others with a cool gauging look on his face.

Those guys are big.

Bruisers. Check out 18, a defenceman I hope.

Never played Indians before.

Me neither.

Expect they'll take out on us the last two hundred years of history.

I grunted, taking a shot above the padding on my left thigh, and made a show of staring down Aimless Aimes who'd taken the shot who smiled back sheepish.

What history?

Oppression, Mark.

They don't look oppressed to me, just big and mean.

The end of the second period, one period left, we sat in our dressing room bruised and stunned, trailing 8 to 1. Forty minutes of play and I'd had at least fifty shots fired my way and conjuring up a picture of my defencemen on their knees or sliding into the boards.

Jesus H Christ, Billy Konowalchuk muttered, a wedge of orange motionless in one hand.

You said it, Billy, Paulie agreed, sucking on a butt.

Custer's last stand all over again.

We were getting slaughtered, hammered, outskated, outgunned, scalped, and it was clean hockey, hardhitting but clean, these guys had shoulders of iron, didn't say a word, just grinding away, never out of breath, never letting up, my head was still spinning and I'd sweated out ten pounds.

We were scared. Of them, of the war whooping fans. Turned out 18 played centre. He'd already scored a hat-trick and had tried to drive one puck straight through my chest, my ribs still ached every deep breath I drew.

Thought this was an exhibition game, Mosley whined.

It's a playoff game asshole, Jack snapped. *A three game series, we were invited and it's a blow-out, shit is this the best we can do?*

Yes, everyone chorused.

We laughed then. It was just us, no coach, no trainer even. Jack was playing-coach and we sharpened our own skates. A team of grunters, a few ex-Juniors, a half-dozen old triple 'A' players. I'd had a try-out on the Brandon Wheat Kings, Western Junior Hockey League, pro, the draft pool for the NHL and WHA, but I'd pulled a groin and never got called back. We weren't a bad team, every now and then we shone but inconsistent. We'd never heard of these guys the Plains Cree, maybe some kind of Native League playing invisible across the prairies.

Third period we managed two goals and held them to one. Won the period, nothing else. The usual booze up at the motel never got off the ground and we got as serious and quiet as them and held them close the next two games and lost anyway but they'd let up the third one since the series was already won.

The last night we walked in a clump from the arena out onto the smooth-packed snow of the parking lot and 18, 6 and 7 stood by their equipment bags smoking Export A's, and our group got quiet and we eyed them warily and 18 might have done something like a grin, it was hard to be sure, it was there and gone in an instant. 18 had taken Jack out in the second period, a clean check right at centre ice, Jack had his head down – you do that when you're tired, the hit damn near dislocated his shoulder.

Jack set his bag down, walked toward them. The night air was still, quiet, winter stars overhead bristling and Jack's Pumas squeaked on the packed snow and when Jack spoke he could have been talking in your ear and we all thought there was going to be hell to pay as the Cree rounded on him.

You guys, Jack said, *are fucking good.*

The Cree didn't smile. One shifted as if nervous with the attention. Then 18 said, *You got back up.*

Jack shrugged.

Didn't think you would.

Me neither and I had trouble finding the bench.

Everything was quiet again until 18 tossed his butt away. *We're going for a beer.*

Jack turned to us. It got confused, most of the guys not interested since they wanted an early start back home tomorrow and were beat anyway and it ended up just me and Jack and Mosley, and 18 whose name was Lester offered to drive us so we piled into his four-door Ford and we headed down the highway.

At the town's outskirts the RCMP pulled us over. Lester rolled down his window as the officer came up.

Coming into town?

Yes.

Been drinking?

No.

You fine with a breathalyzer?

Lester nodded.

Swearing under his breath Jack leaned over. *We've just played a hockey game, sir. See the equipment in here?*

Is that equipment yours? I'm talking to the driver right now. Is it yours?

Yes.

I've seen you in town before.

Lester nodded.

Don't get drunk and try driving back to the reserve, understood? All right, move along.

Lester rolled the car slow onto Main Street.

That happen a lot? Jack asked him.

Two, three times a week.

No one spoke, what was there to say? A life like that, enough to make anyone feel a right piece of shit but Lester didn't say a word, it was Jack fighting down the rage, his face getting paler by the second – I knew the signs.

Easy, brother, it's shit, that's all.

We sipped beers in a crowd of Cree players and fans and family and got invited to a sun-dance in June and got shown how pointing lit cigarettes in different directions meant different things, who you honoured, and never ever point them down because that was a curse and Mosley and 6 whose name was Albert took turns selecting the

Beatles' *Revolution* on the jukebox and by the sixteenth consecutive time the waitress unplugged the box.

So, Mosley said, looking at Albert and Lester and Frank each in turn, *is it true you've all been hung by your nipples?*

That's Lakota, Frank said, *they're wimps, we get hung by our dongs, stretched nipples don't do a man any good but a stretched dong, well....*

Mosley gaped then he shook himself and said to me and Jack, *That's my point – us whites we don't have any rituals to take us into manhood, we're fucked because of it, we get nasty cry-babies in suits as a result.*

That's right, Lester said, *you whites are all fucked up.*

Frank cleared his throat, *Of course the last generation we were stripped of all those rituals, we were made Christians, that's what fucked us all up for a while there but we're going back to what we were. Reshaping it to handle the modern world. We have rituals hanging us from our dongs, hanging us from our balls, from our tongues, we hang ourselves from just about everything to separate the boys from the men.*

If those rituals are suited to the modern world, Jack said, *then you'd need to be hung from the buttons of your three-piece suits, you'd need to hang a briefcase from your dongs and hang from your silk ties.*

We do all that too, Frank said, *they're just barely worth mentioning and I haven't even mentioned hockey practice.*

What kind of drills do you do then?

We strip down, skate across each other's backs we take off our jock cups and take slapshots into our crotches, we wear all our equipment in sweatlodges.

You do sweatlodges? Mosley asked.

We do sweatlodges, hundreds each year, summer, winter, all year round, wearing our equipment or three-piece suits, why do you want to try one?

Yes.

Frank looked at me and Jack, we shrugged, then nodded.

It induces a trance state, Frank said, *and connects you with the spirit world. You all get hard-ons even though you're not gay, that's the spirits grabbing hold of you, they grab you by your dick. Of course none of you have very long dicks, being white, they might not be able to get a grip.*

Mine's ten inches long when it's hard, Jack said.

The Cree stared at him. *Bullshit,* Albert said.

Jack grinned at me. I nodded seriously. *It's true, guys. Ten inches, and I'm only nine but thicker.*

We had our own rituals, Jack said, *we pulled canoes across dry-ground with our dicks, walking backwards.*

That's a good ritual, Lester said.

We all nodded.

That's bullshit, Mosley said, *not how long their dicks are, it's true, from what I've seen in the locker room, not that I looked with interest, just checking things out, makes me depressed doing that too often, but the canoe bit is bullshit.*

Don't worry about it, Jack said, *there's plenty of bullshit going round right now.*

Frank made a face as if offended and that sucked Mosley in, *You shouldn't call any non-whites at this table liars, Jack, you don't know their truths, you don't know anything about their culture.*

You're absolutely right, I'm terribly sorry, guys, didn't mean to insult your intelligences.

That's all right, Frank said, *we can take it.*

Lester nodded. *Our dongs are long.*

We closed the place down and in all those hours Lester had maybe two bottles of beer and he drove us back to our roadside motel with a picking up wind that turned the world, white-slicked the blacktop, and on a slow bend the Ford got up on skates and made for the ditch.

Crunching into the snow bank sobered the rest of us quick. We piled out and settled and studied the car, working out how best to push it back onto the road. Blowing snow whipped in our faces, it was the middle of the night but somehow the snow-filled sky glowed.

We turned at a shout from Mosley and saw what he saw which was a pair of headlights burning into view, then a vintage bus, an old Flyer or Bluebird with sky-blue trim but otherwise white and all scraped with a crumpled front fender, and as it rolled past us without even stopping we saw boys and a hockey stick or two and then the bus disappeared back into the snowstorm.

Bastards coulda stopped, Mosley whined, stomping his feet to keep them from going numb.

But Lester and Albert who'd tagged along at the last minute were lighting up cigarettes and pointing them after the bus and both saying something in tandem which we couldn't quite make out but wasn't English.

God's truth the story came out, a bus in 1959 carrying a local Midget hockey team rolling in a winter storm, everybody killed, a tragedy, made the papers in three provinces. What we saw was a ghost bus, the boys on their way home but never getting there, just trapped forever in the white world of winter storms, I've no reason to lie about any of this.

Later that night back in our motel room Lester and Albert drank one last beer each and told us about Bigfoot and Lester's grandmother who'd chased one away from the cabin one night when she was looking after her grandchildren. It was a good story, I'll tell it later.

I could never look at the Export 'A' time clock in the arena the same way after that.

The arena

You're beautiful, can we meet sometime, maybe tomorrow?

She looked at me as if I was speaking another language, her eyes flat.

Downtown, at Eaton's say, under the clock. Ten? Ten-thirty?

No accent, a voice smooth and almost deep, a voice like royalty, a grown-up's warm momentary dream, a lifetime of yearning packed into that moment, a voice of possibilities and insatiable desire, a voice of the city, any city, all cities, oh such a voice it reverberated and grew inside me. *No.*

Is that too early?

No.

Is tomorrow no good, how about Friday?

No. Please go away.

I can't. I want to see you.

I am married.

I know.

Older much older.

I know. I need to see you again. Alone. I'll be under the clock at Eaton's tomorrow morning.

32

Her eyes widened as she studied me and I could see now she was nervous.

I won't talk hockey, I said. I won't talk about the office, I won't ignore you or check if you dressed well, I'm a good listener and I'll hardly talk at all and I keep my word about everything, saying nothing causing no trouble.

She looked away, dropped her butt and crushed it underfoot.

I smiled.

She walked away, back up the ramp, back into the game. Back to her seat her husband probably not even glancing over to acknowledge her, too busy with his buddies and the throw-away preseason game. But the woman who'd left that seat ten minutes ago wasn't the same woman who came back and sat down.

I went for a piss, then up the stairs to the greys, down the row with excuse me's and into my seat beside Jack, who handed me the binoculars, grinning.

What the hell you do, brother? She looks rattled, fidgeting. She's scanning the crowds like you switched her radar on. You talked to her, didn't you? I can't believe it.

I went right up and talked to her, I said, only now sweating. *Shit.*

And?

And ... I don't know. Maybe. We'll see.

Look at you. Not just fucking. Coveting.

So I burn in hell.

The Trail Blazer

He came from the Old World but nobody knew exactly where. If there'd been trading cards back then his stats would have said: 5'10" 185 lbs, Shoots Left, Centre, and there he'd be, metal-etched a true graven image, wide shoulders, wide hips the kind of hips that seemed genetically perfected for playing hockey. Low centre of gravity, you see, hard as hell to knock off the puck, tough as nails in the corners. He had long, greasy hair, tied up in braids, a handlebar moustache, small close-set eyes and a scarred jutting chin. Across his shoulders was a pair of shoulder-pads covered in wolverine skin. He wore a dented, pitted cuirass like some kind of conquistador, and mukluk skates. He was the first.

It was a time when the middle of the country was unknown to whites, and west of that was even more unknown to whites. He arrived in Montréal on the season's last ship from Europe, with autumn winds blowing leaves crisped by the coming winter, and there was ice on the shores of the St. Lawrence – thin transparent sheets that hovered above a dropping water level and cracked at midday when things warmed up.

He walked down the gangplank and set foot on the plastercine mud of the New World, a man with no name, no place of birth but with a far-away look in his dark beady eyes. Later the ship's crew would swear he'd never been on board.

A week later winter hit hard, with arctic winds whistling down from the vast flatlands of northern Québec. Everything froze, and the man was seen again, walking down to the river with a pair of fur-lined skates.

A band of Iroquois traders had just pulled their birch bark canoes up from the ice-laden pebbled beach, having lingered too long in the town and now consigned to a long walk overland back to their village loaded down with woollen blankets, pots and pans and gunpowder and flints and musket balls and clay pipes and ceramic beads and whale oil and a Bible the thin pages of which were ideal for lighting fires. In broken French one of the Iroquois asked "Where you going, white man?"

"West," he said, strapping on his skates and eyeing the wind-swept ice.

"How far?"

"To the Pacific Ocean."

The Iroquois nodded at that. Disbelief was a European notion they'd yet to acquire. "It is a long way," they told him.

Not replying, the stranger stepped out onto the ice. He paused to adjust his wolverine fur shoulder-pads and the Iroquois saw that the wolverine was still alive, lying draped over the man's broad shoulders with eyes like frosted musket balls and they knew then the spirit of the land itself had come to bless the stranger's journey and that the world was about to change.

He set off, his strides choppy because he was a mucker, and the Iroquois stood on the shore and watched him each of them silent witnesses with the certainty lodged in their stolid hearts that the white man would succeed and with that certainty they also realized that the

Europeans would conquer their land, their world, at least for a time anyway until the land in turn conquered them.

The stranger skated into the white unknown.

Over that winter in Montréal stories arrived from Indians, from voyageurs, prospectors, Jesuit missionaries, each story travelling a greater distance. The man was skating across the country that was not yet a nation, up rivers and across lakes, he skated without pause, not stopping for sleep or for food. Through empty lands and through hostile lands, he skated, a buffalo on blades, monstrous and unstoppable.

The last story to reach Montréal that winter came from the mountains on the other side of the Great Plains. It was told by the Blood to the Blackfoot who told it to the Plains Cree who told it to the Assiniboine who told it to a rum-trader in a post in Pinawa on the Winnipeg River and from the rum-trader the story was heard by a voyageur with the dubious name of Jacques Olat because he claimed Aztec blood and was hung three years later for killing the captain of an opposing team in a vicious lacrosse game on the Ottawa River. Jacques was heading east despite it being February 14 and 130 degrees below outside not counting wind-chill, and so he took the story with him all the way to Wawa, which at the time was a village of native orphans being tyrannized by an ex-Jesuit Black Robe named Juan. The instant dislike between the two men resulted in Jacques slowly roasting Juan over a fire whilst the orphans made a break for it. One of the orphans was an Algonquin boy who strapped on snowshoes and jogged to Montréal.

The story he brought was this:

The stranger was crossing a vast mountain lake. The ice was free of snow, a milky slick surface flat as a marble tabletop with a hint of green in its depths. The high-altitude air was brittle and crisp, the sky overhead impossibly blue and cloudless. It was midday and he was nearing the western shore. Beyond the lake rose jagged white mountains, and he knew that ahead of him was the difficult and dangerous task of skating up steep mountain streams on tumbled, ridged ice in search of a pass through the range.

He slowed his choppy strides, glided into a lazy circle, and looked back across the immense lake he had just crossed. A grizzly, roused from a long sleep and hungry, had been on his trail for days and he saw it now, a quarter mile distant, crossing the ice in that shambling, loping gait bears use for long-distance pursuits.

The stranger drew a deep breath of the frigid air, clawing the crusted ice from his moustache. His very small eyes fixed on the bear, and the circle he seemed content to skate he then cut short. He dug in his edges, leaned far forward, legs wide. Hiss went his left skate. Hisss went his right, hisssss his left, hiiisssssss his right, each stride longer, each stride the pump of taut bound muscle, explosive in strength. Faster and faster he skated, straight for the bear.

The grizzly stopped, rose up on its back legs, head wagging side to side, then it dropped back down, lumbered forward, the lumbering turning into a charge.

They closed the distance between them in seconds. At the last moment, as the bear roared and reared up its head – slavering jaws opened wide – the stranger dipped his right shoulder and bodychecked the beast.

From the top of a tree a half mile away, a Blood warrior watched as the bear, struck dead-on, sprawled backward, limbs splayed as it impacted the ice and slid spinning in circles across the surface. The stranger shook himself, shrugging once to re-adjust his lumpy shoulder-pads, then swung back for the shore he had just quitted.

The bear made no move to rise.

The stranger was the Trail Blazer, and hockey was born.

The city

It was the hottest day of the summer. The team was flowing south. I saw the scrawny boy with the dreams and the three teenaged girls in their jerseys and I saw old immigrants, grandfathers now with grandsons' hands buried in theirs, all that battered, blunted bone and calluses and weathered stains closed protectively around tiny soft hands that would've trembled on their own as they came in pairs up to the grandstand, the boy with a piggy bank under one arm or a plastic bag or glass jar filled with pennies and a few bills, all their savings, the dream toys or whatever set aside, and I saw women with children arriving in the carpark in Landcruisers, Landrovers, Cherokees, minivans, all wearing their jerseys. Musicians played on stage, there were people in their thousands, gathering bags of pennies, and impromptu collection areas, not a single receipt issued because no one ever imagined this happening, not this way and this was the Forks where the rivers met the heart of Winnipeg, and notaries made speeches and old performers came from across the country back to the city where they were born and under the newly manicured ground there at the Forks there was history before, and now again, and it wasn't till we sat on Hadrian's Wall that Jack told me all he knew about it.

The Forks. At the peak of immigration it was all railway property, though there was a shantytown squatting where the immigrants first stayed and a red-light district to serve them. But that went away and there was nothing but old trainsheds and cinders and clinkers and only a few years ago the land was given back to the city and a huge redevelopment project got underway.

In the days of the Selkirk fans who first settled, along with the Métis Traders, there were forts and then warehouses along with hockey rinks for each rival league and the city thrummed as the gateway to the West, the same as St. Louis, home of the Blues, down in the States and in fact river boats came up with St. Louis bricks that were used to line the rinks at their foundations, but the river bank was trouble so tunnels were cut through the floodsilt clays, fixed up with rail tracks and small mining cars and goods came from the boats along the tunnel then lifted up to the gleaming warehouses overhead.

The redevelopment scheme was incorporated and a site archaeologist was hired, this man knew everything there was to know about the Forks all its history and prehistory and when construction stopped in various places the news reporters came down and he explained things and looked good on camera with his cowboy hat and feather and cowboy boots and belt buckle and faded jeans as he squinted in the sunlight like a prairie farmer and talked:

We got excavations going on everywhere, got one crew from the University of Manitoba trying to find the first hockey rink ever built here. Got Parks Canada with a crew hunting for evidence of the first Native League. Got my own crew excavating the first dressing rooms and going through what the backhoes dug up, finding turn-of-the-century skate blades and leather straps and old gloves and wooden pucks and fired clay water-bottle shards and stick shafts and leather helmets beautifully preserved since the flood-deposited clay is anaerobic, meaning no oxygen, meaning no decomposition, and that was bad when we hit on a players' outhouse and all got skin rashes and hundred-year-old flus but we could read the newspapers they used to wipe their asses, the preservation was incredible and this is the city's history, the country's history, and once the landscaping comes in and buries it all again every place you step at the Forks is history underfoot.

It was summer's hottest day and Winnipeggers gathered in the thousands, all those toddlers and kids with bags of pennies. I don't want to talk about it right now.

Before malls in the suburbs gutted our downtown, it was the city soul mapped in old blocks. Two department stores stood like bastions on either end, both on Portage Avenue just west of the intersection with Main Street.

Those stores were Eaton's and Hudson's Bay. The second store, Hudson's Bay, had a direct history going back to the first League by the same name and Eaton's came from a business tycoon named Harold Ballard back east, Toronto or somewhere like that. In between these two huge structures there were cinemas, so many cinemas, the Capitol, the Metropolitan, the Odeon, The Garrick, the King which became the Colony which became the Eve, and stores for winter window-shopping. When we were small our Mom used to take us down like pilgrimage when she wasn't working and we'd meet Dad under the clock at Eaton's and my childhood memory of downtown Winnipeg is Christmas lights slush on the streets and the gust of hot air from overhead at the glass entrances into Eaton's.

The clock at Eaton's was on the ground floor, in the Lingerie Department and as kids Jack and I acquired early intimacy with female undergarments on busty mannequins, armless and legless and headless but everything we needed to know was there, chest and butt and crotch, and we used to wander off a ways and practise unhitching bra straps, reaching around not looking, at least until a clerk escorted us back to Mom and adult words were exchanged and Mom would settle a stern gaze on us as the clerk hurried off. But later Mom took us to a movie at the Met and Sean Connery made fierce love to a woman on a beach in some weird science fiction film that made no sense and had something to do with the Wizard of Oz and boy were we all shocked silent but Mom loved Sean Connery and God knows what she was thinking anyway, no one said a word about it ever afterward though I'm sure if she'd known about that scene she'd never have taken us to the movie but might have gone solo with us never knowing, who knows eh?

The clock was the traditional meeting place. It was a sacred place and standing there Thursday morning from 10:45 a.m. waiting for my Japanese woman, I thought about all the other times I'd waited here with Mom and Jack and surrounded by bras and panties and hosiery. I sensed a glimmer of continuity that I knew Jack would have sensed right away and clearer than me and he'd have laughed.

I waited till noon with the store detective circling me in a slowly closing spiral like a shark, then went down to the comic store just past the Capitol. Within minutes I was into this strange underground comic, all shadows and crummy gangsters, and a detective superhero with double-edged powers that made him depressed, a bottle of rye on his office desk and gorgeous blonde sidling in past the starburst glass door and lighting up once sitting opposite him and crossing impossibly long legs and the next page we were suddenly in a shoot-out and some thugs came down on the hero and it wasn't till I was ten pages on and the hero'd been beaten up six times by six different sets of thugs, not one connected to the other, that I realized this was a spoof and tossed the comic down in disgust and went over to check out Weird War.

The next morning I was back under the clock at 10:45 and at 11:15 she stood in front of me.

The wall

Life has its times – the ones you remember and the places where you remember them and the two put together make up most of living but it's not a simple thing. Shit times can come back to you when the place you're at is a place of beauty and wonder and a shiver ripples through senses unseen of fifty thousand years, echoing footprints, and sights and scenes unchanging in front of countless sets of eyes, each set with a different brain behind it and that shiver's as delicious as sex but somehow God-touched at the same time, but what you remember might be fierce loss searing pain. And living is the place between the two, the tension of contrast like blood in the vein hesitating between two hearts, each current tugging.

There is no more under the clock at Eaton's. Heritage is a hole in the ground, a memory someone dug up and stole away. When I heard about that I wept. What was done was wrong. Just plain wrong. The new arena? You don't drop a pearl into a wasteland of decay, economic depression and no residences and expect it to shine. Things don't work that way. You need people living downtown. Living, eating, buying food, shopping, what's so mysterious about that?

And hey, assholes, I thought we didn't have the money for a new arena. That's why what happened happened. You the same people? You lied?

Anyway, the Scottish sun was setting back over our right shoulders, swallows spun through invisible clouds of midges and the ghosts of savages were gathering beyond the wall, painted in woad and pissing curses up at the Romans manning the defences, darkness and death waited ahead, stretching shadows because when the sun set it set behind the wall.

We'd cracked the single malt and weren't saying much and I felt we were brothers again but dark gathered in my skull, the surly outrage of long-gone crowds at the joining of two rivers and I wrestled with visions of kids, faces full of hope and already haunted with fear of truth and this was cracking open foul brew.

What the fuck's gone wrong?

Jack tilted the bottle back, swallowed then smacked his lips.

Dreams flow south, bro. Blood flows south. We take the sacred blade and deliver our own cuts and everybody smiles and nods like it was the right thing to do, smiles and nods because some things are beyond even questioning, some prairie boy's got a chance to earn twenty-six million U.S. over seven years and we say 'hey boy you've done it now go for it.'

Can't just blame the players.

We've all made a virtue of greed and we smile and nod even as it kills us. Don't blame the players? Why the hell not? But I also blame the owners and I blame the fans who swallow all the bullshit even as their hearts break and I blame money that buys loyalty by the month, hell I blame the game and that's fucking that.

But it means ... well it means more.

I know that.

He drank again, passed me the bottle. This was a wake, I finally realized, for all that we'd written off and wasn't it a lot.

The city

Couldn't make it yesterday?
I needed to know.
What?
If you were serious.
Let's go to the Maple Leaf. You know it?
Not there. The Charter House.
The hotel?
The bar for now.
Okay. I was underage but it didn't seem a good time to mention that besides I'd been in bars before nobody asked for ID. She led, I followed.

I need an excuse, she said as we stood waiting for the light to change on the corner of Graham and Donald.
For what?
To see you, to take time. *What can you teach me?*
Teach? I was sounding thick but there didn't seem a way past it.
Lessons. *What can you teach me?*
Oh ... canoeing? Rock-climbing? Skating? Can you skate?
She glanced at me. Yes, that's good.
Can your old man skate?
She smiled and shook her head.
How come all the real experts on hockey can't skate?
She said nothing to that and we walked along the sidewalk, cars rolling past and he could have been in any one of them she couldn't get lost in a crowd up on those high-heeled boots, straight up, head held high, black hair tumbled down over the fox fur, lips bright red looking sticky, rouge on her roundish cheeks, gold hoop earrings, pearls around her neck choke-tight.

We entered the hotel foyer and she led again as we walked into the bar, found a booth and sat down opposite each other. A waiter showed up, she ordered a Caesar and me a Standard. She opened her purse and pulled out her Matinee's and lit up.
You're beautiful.
She shook her head. *I'm nothing special. My husband says without the make-up and the expensive clothes I'm nothing special. He won't look until I come out of the bathroom in the mornings. I'm nothing special. What is your name?*

Mark.

I'm Caroline.

Your husband's scared of you. He knows if you realize just how beautiful you are you'll leave him, so he cuts you down.

Her hand shook as it tapped ash, her lids were half closed as she studied the cigarette between her fingers.

I won't cut you down, I said. *Not ever.*

You're nice, Mark.

Did you get a room, Caroline?

Yes.

Good because I want to make love to you. Today. Now. Up in that room. Have you got the keys?

Yes. Let's finish our drinks.

Nervous?

Yes, very.

Scared?

Yes.

Me too, but I can't think of anything else.

She shook her head I didn't know if that was agreement or if she was fighting things. Then again she'd gotten us a room. I watched her smoke, I watched her eyes, I watched her lips, the white of her teeth, her hands, the lavender flash of her fingernails.

This is very wrong, she said.

I said nothing, watching her, filling my brain no room for talk.

This isn't what a married woman should do.

She was talking herself out of it. I struggled to open my mouth, struggled to think. *He doesn't love you, Caroline. He owns you. You know that or you wouldn't be here.*

She crushed out her cigarette lit another. *I'm twice your age, Mark.*

I'm old enough to make you forget that.

She smiled and it was a real smile. *What cheek.*

I shrugged, shifting in my seat, the bottle of beer cold in my hands, looking up and over her shoulder as a bunch of suits came in talking insurance.

You've had many girlfriends?

A few.

Are you a good lover?

Passable. Ready for lessons.

You teach me to skate and I teach you to make love.

Deal.

What do you know about me? What do I know about you?

Only what we want to happen here today. Let's see the keys.

She hesitated then slowly pulled them from her purse and set them on the tabletop. I shook my head. *Hold them. In your hands. Feel them, squeeze.* I watched her following my instructions, I watched as a deep flush blossomed her cheeks. *You see?*

See what?

No matter how hard you squeeze, they're still there.

What are you doing?

I don't know but it's like our clothes are off and we can finally look at each other.

Her breath had quickened and her knuckles were white as she gripped the keys in her round fist. She took a last drag singeing the filter then butted it out.

I'm finished my drink, she said.

The wall

Down on the bank of River Tyne, we stood across from the boat rental man. We were caught up and the idea started us here. There were dories and dinghys and sculls and kayaks and canoes and Jack was getting steamed because the Brits had got it backwards.

This one's the canoe, that one's the kayak.

Rental man smiled. *Y'got it backwards, mate.*

You telling Canadians what's a kayak and what's a canoe?

I'm telling ya how it is. Watched the Olympics?

Fuck the Olympics. Let me explain it linguistically. 'Canoe' is an Algonquin word and it describes an open craft with thwarts, made of birchbark traditionally and propelled by single-bladed paddles fore and aft; you do a J-stroke aft and you can paddle in time straight as an arrow. The word 'kayak' is Inuit – Eskimo for you – and it describes a covered craft, one or two seater, with either a single-bladed or a double-bladed paddle. Because you're wearing a water-tight girdle you can roll a kayak and pull yourself back upright. Inuits never used canoes and Indians never used kayaks. Canadians know the difference, you and the Olympics don't. You've got it bass ackwards and I'll be fucked if I'm going to buy into your goddamn ignorance.

You got it backwards, mate.

Jack pointed. *We want to rent this cedar ribbed, canvas, narrow-keeled canoe. Not the Kevlar one, not the plastic one or the fibreglass one, if you had a Grumman aluminum seventeen footer we'd rent it but you don't so we'll take this canvas.* He pointed again. *We don't want a kayak, we won't be nudging ice rafts, we won't be harpooning seals and any rapids this country can throw at us we can handle in a canoe with our eyes closed. We want it for two weeks.*

Two weeks? I'll want a full deposit on that, mate. Thousand pounds.

Credit card?

That'll do me fine once I do a credit check.

While you're at it do a dictionary check.

We'd checked the maps and concluded it could be done. We'd canoe from Hadrian's Wall to Cardiff. Nothing to it barring a few portages but back when we were just getting hairy crotches, fifteen and sixteen, we'd average 350 miles every two weeks three times each summer taking out trips for the YMCA and the Inner City Program. We'd done the Manigotogan and the Winnipeg River and we'd done Lake of the Woods from Kenora to the States, Shoal Lake to Kakagi Lake, we'd rigged sails and shot across Little Traverse Bay in two hours flat running ahead of a thunder storm.

My only worry was those short blue-skinned people who now followed us everywhere from a distance. Would they follow us all the way to Cardiff and who the hell were they anyway? You'd think they'd get arrested being naked and all.

Don't tell this guy what we're planning, Jack said to me as the rental man went off to run the credit card. *This ain't Hertz rent-a-canoe, this guy would go apeshit he had any idea.*

No kidding. I'm surprised he's even talking to you with those tattoos. He's probably off calling the men in white coats.

The card'll check out fine, won't he be surprised.

He'll figure it's stolen.

He's got my passport number.

He hasn't got a brain in his skull he rents to us.

That's his problem, I've already had enough of these Brits so goddamn fucking rude every act of kindness is so rare it hits the papers front page brings a tear to the eye, Christ. I bet you the guy's sitting at his desk in there lighting farts.

I don't like cedar and canvas. They gouge, the canvas rips, they aren't tough like a Grumman aluminum.

Aluminium.

Whatever, we're bound to take knocks this trip.

You've patched canvas before.

Right, it'll put him at ease asking for a repair kit.

Do you want to do this or not?

Paddle to Cardiff? Sure. Beats the train. Can we get there in three days? That's the maximum for walk-ons, the door closes Sunday Noon.

No problem.

We need better detail maps.

We got the rivers.

We got blue lines but what kind of rivers hell I can't even tell which way they flow, half of them there's no joining tributaries at least not on that map.

They all flow south, Mark.

How do you know?

Nothing gets past Hadrian's Wall.

The arena

The day after getting clean-swept by the Plains Cree a few of us hung around and went to the rink to watch them play against the Blackfoot.

The game took our breath away and while me and the others just felt wonder when it was done Jack seemed to be steaming up about the whole thing.

That, boys, was a lesson in loyalty. You're Cree you play for the Cree, you're Blackfoot you play for the Blackfoot. And then there's the history, the centuries of rivalry the counting coup stealing each other's horses a few nasty bloodletting tangles but mostly one-upmanship. Wearing the jersey means something, a goddamn second skin you guys understanding me? These people should be pros with a TV deal coast to coast, it'd be a lesson to stick like iron spearpoints in our throats. I blame money and fans and owners and this whole fucking culture of ours for giving greed a halo, how many times we smile and say way-to-go boy earn your millions then bitch at the ticket prices and guys jumping teams on the fucking money trail, how many times eh and why doesn't it sink in we've fucking gone along with it, made our bed, laid in it and the leeches sucking on our love of the game keep on sucking cause it never runs dry. But it does you'll see one day it does.

But what a game. Clean, hard, fast. Maybe the raw skill wasn't there but that didn't matter, you knew these guys played for keeps. Lester joined us at the bar afterward and grinned which was about all the emotion he ever showed and we played stripes and solids on the beer-stained table all night and it was a hell of a good night and by the end we'd decided to do the Manigotogan River come summer. Lester had two camo-painted Grumman seventeen-footers.

The city

Once the door closed I stepped up to her, framed her face in my hands and kissed her deep and long. Cigs, booze, Clamato, Tabasco Juice, her tongue dancing like a manic sprite on mine and like a shaman vampire I drank her in, brought something of her into my body slick down my throat I could have drunk her forever but we pulled apart, clumsy, getting our clothes off. Her bra was black, skin white as dusty marble, her tits big and round, her nipples dark and big and hard.

Sometimes life throws you a handful and I had mine. She crouched, then sat, both hands pulling my cock and I had no choice but to follow it, her legs spreading wide as she laid back on the purple and orange shag. Pulled me into her crotch, I saw doughrolls of fat that was her tummy then I was down on her kissing again her lips sticking against mine and I thought of how I looked remembering once eating a candy apple at the Red River Ex all red-smeared face then I was inside and her hands were up the nails clawing into my back and pain was lancing wet fire and I remembered a barely controlled fall down a granite cliffside, the ragged stone shredding my t-shirt then scouring fierce and suddenly gone as I dropped sixteen feet into tumbled rock, moss and rotted fallen black spruce not even a sprain though one branch gouged me six inches up one calf.

She rolled me over, sat over me grinding and the shag wormed into the bleeding slashes on my back and some old carpet shampoo left behind stung like hell but I had her tits in my hands and her hair was hanging down over her face all tangled and she sunk her nails into my pecs and I think I screamed before she leaned down and drove her tongue into my mouth and all her old man talked about was hockey and his hairy back was scarless except for the moles I knew this as certain as snow Halloween night.

There was blood on my chest and she was smearing her tits in it. So far it had been pain filling my brain no room for thinking about coming, though every dig of her nails brought me to the edge, the stinging aftermath bringing me back. So I was still there between her legs nothing yet to make her check my ID a display of staying power that was really only distraction but she didn't know that and she was out of breath above me now as she rocked, swivelled, ground her hips which were round and cool under my palms and with folds. Skinny high school girls drifted out of my mind, away forever, just girls not women nothing in excess except for one who I'd never looked twice at before but I knew come January I'd see her different and it's funny how everything changes all at once like you stood in one place and some invisible giant hand spun the world under your feet and when it stopped you weren't seeing things from the same perspective anymore.

She was breathing hard and sweat was in the blood.

Intermission, I said.

She settled above me and our eyes met for the first time since we sat opposite each other in the bar and I saw sudden fear there and a shock that widened her eyes and she was still taking deep breaths and her cheeks were red.

If we're going to do any skating we'd better get you into shape.

She looked confused, then said, *Oh that.*

Make things look ... above-board.

I don't want to get into shape.

Can't pretend you're having lessons, you never learn to skate.

I still don't want to get into shape.

All right.

She started up again.

The wall

I unscrew as I get bigger.

You unscrew.

Yes, it's a Celtic spiral winding up my dong. I get hard and it stretches dusty blue and unscrews.

It doesn't unwind, it just stretches.

It conveys the appearance of unscrewing, then. I'd show you but it'd be hopeless your ugly mug staring at it.

Glad to hear it. The single malt had made my mouth numb. Stars blinked dully overhead, all the sheep had left the slopes and the clank of armour from the Romans patrolling the ramparts behind came soft as chimes, the world getting cooler with night. Headlamps crawled on nearby ridges and from somewhere to the dark north came a scream like a man's heart was being pulled out from his chest, tied down on a rock slab, his brothers' eyes glittering and I remembered a dusk on a portage beside tumbling rapids the trail was ancient, early hockey teams having walked here, before there were buses only high-prowed Red River boats plying the Winnipeg River up from Eaglenest Lake and there were plum trees growing to either side from pits tossed a hundred fifty years ago and I had a hundred ten pound canoe on my shoulders an eighty pound food pack on my back with ten-year-old Rickie, a troubled kid, more troubled than the others. On this trip he was carrying the paddles and we were far behind the others when something cold slithered up my spine, I had the canoe down in the mud, the pack off and rolling heavily to settle on its side. The mosquitoes swarmed us as we stopped and Rickie, his sour face looking up at mine, unsure like he'd walked into one of his old man's invisible minefields and was expecting a fist in the face, but something was coming up the trail, maybe a bear but I didn't smell bear and my skin was crawling fierce and I eyed a nearby oak tree. *Let's climb* I said to Rickie and he dropped the paddles and went over to the tree. *Hurry.* And he did like a kid can do and I followed until we looked down on the trail from fifteen feet and everything was quiet beyond the rushing water and whining mosquitoes, it'd been a hell of a week on this river nothing but rain and leeches and mud and never dry and blisters from the paddles and our group was kids from messed-up homes, taken away and given something else to do, which was taking to the bush with two counsellors, me and Jack, and we'd pushed them hard into sullen silence but this silence was different, it was world-brought not in-the-head silence and our breaths caught as three timber wolves came like ghosts up the trail.

They circled and sniffed the food pack and the two smaller ones may have gone for it but the big one swung his head and the other two ducked their tails and continued up the trail. The big male paused below, then slowly lifted his massive head and met our eyes. The knowing look rattled me deep and I saw Rickie's thin lips peel back baring his teeth.

Then the wolf was gone and Rickie was a different boy, he buckled down toughened and three evenings later two left before the trip was done and we gathered the kids in a circle on the muddy bank of a swamp with old pottery underfoot and we spoke memorized French and had them repeat it and we handed out blue bandanas. *You're Voyageurs now, too young for this really but what you've been through has changed everything, you're not the punks me and Mark started out with. You know that, so do we and so we honour you here and that's that.* And how solemn can eight soaked-down leech-sucked bug-bitten exhausted ten year olds get, you'd be surprised.

Feel the night, Mark. A night for ghosts.

I nodded, not yet ready to speak, the old memory swirling up and around and over the now, twenty-four kids every summer made them a little less fucked up and we always thought about changing them never about how it changed us, that secret ritual over and over again, the different coloured bandanas that the kids tucked away as often as wore outright. How many were sitting in drawers now all faded and rag-worn or crisp, clean, never used and what did they still mean or had something cynical taken the place of what was earned, twenty-four million over six years with bonuses can eat like acid through damn near anything.

The governments that came to Manitoba in the last years of the Jets were cold and bloodless, making fiscal the holy word and if that social services canoeing summer program hadn't been axed there'd be fifty kids lined up for every one who got selected now but it's just the way of the world they tell us these days, and fuck that, the way is the way it's easy to be and those belts are tightening fiscal over tender bellies here and now and this heartless nightmare won't end.

Thing is we just took it, Jack said. We keep taking it like it's just the way of things. The curse of common kind. Selling out's not a one-off thing, it's forever. And that's where cheating comes in, in the game right now.

Cheating?

Playoffs. You've seen it. It's between periods and there on the screen are two commentators from hell. Slow motion scene on the ice, some hack talentless player has his assignment and what is it? Cover the opposing team's star player. Cover? Yeah, holding the guy's stick, hanging on him like a dead-weight, hooking, dragging him down and falling on him. Crosschecking him when he's in front of the net. We got it all, slowmo, and the commentators are gushing. Great hockey, one of them says. Who the fuck are these guys and who are they kidding? Hey, dodos, it's called cheating. Goes on all year, but come playoffs it's the team that cheats best that wins, and you call this hockey?

Well it's a rockem sockem game, ain't it just.

No. It's cheating. Some player gets suspended for turning on another player and whacking him in the head with his stick. Victim's coach does a press interview and he's all sputtering indignation and he's warning that somebody's gonna get that boy someday. Clips of the offending whack go on again and again, but run the tape back, fellas, let's see the three separate hooks that stick-swinging player had to deal with moments earlier, the last one around his neck. Around his neck. That indignant coach took the truth of things and shoved it so far up his ass it'll never see daylight.

I smiled, said, Nice going, coach.

Yeah, that was as fine a lesson in cynical grandstanding as any pro wrestling manager pulls off. You're teaching our sons and daughters well, aren't you just. Whatever happened to grown-ups taking responsibility for things, anyway? Why didn't the coach say, yeah, that was a nasty swing, but as you can see with the full replay, he was seriously provoked by my players who were playing like assholes. In fact, they were cheating.

And on that day pigs in frilly dresses will dance.

No kidding. Some Canuck cold-cocks another player to deliver vengeance against an earlier nasty hit, and breaks the guy's neck. Probably facing criminal charges and that he should, but let's go back to the earlier hit. Against a star player, all the commentators saying it was an accident, but hey, I saw the replay too, over and over, and man, that bastard leaned down to connect with the player's head. He leaned down. Cracked him good and left him concussed. Question. What if he'd broken the guy's neck?

Ask it again.

All right I will. What if he'd broken the guy's neck? Just luck that he didn't. On the street you hit somebody hard enough to concuss him you get arrested. You can say it was an accident all you want, the judge don't care. You did what you did.

All part of the game.

What game would that be? The game of cheating. At some point, we forgot what the real game was. We forgot that the stick is for handling the puck, passing and shooting. It's not for slowing somebody down, it's not for cross-checking, spearing, hooking, whacking somebody over the head, it's not for any of these things and guess what, the rules say so. In plain English, they say that stuff is not allowed. It's cheating, and it's not being called, and that has destroyed the game of hockey. Come playoffs one infraction in twenty is called, sometimes even worse. They're just letting 'em play, say the commentators. No, they're letting 'em cheat. One in twenty, one in thirty. And what's with all the whining? No matter how obvious the penalty the guilty guy's bitching all the way to the box, shaking his head – yeah, you know the camera's on you so what is all this, acting? Hey, hoser, try being an adult. Try accepting responsibility. Most other adults have to, unless they're politicians. Stop being such a suck, stop being such a liar. The trap. Doesn't work if you can't cheat. It's a system invented by bureaucrats, coached by bureaucrats and played by bureaucrats and the game has all the flow of a boardroom meeting. It's perfectly designed for mediocrity. But hey, wasn't this supposed to be entertainment? Man, hockey needs to be torn down to the ground then built back up. Infractions? Yellow card red card. Red card means your team plays the rest of the game one man short. The rest of the fuckin' game. Call the penalties when they happen – wow, what a brilliant idea, how come nobody's thought of it before? Stick is used to check stick-on-stick, handle the puck, pass, shoot and score. Does anything else and it's a yellow card, does it twice and it's red card and your team's in trouble till the final buzzer arrives. Can't think of many sports that allow so much cheating. No wonder people have started comparing it to pro wrestling – it's not just the fights, it's the cheating that's now part of the entertainment, just like in pro wrestling. What you do when the ref's turned the other way. But wrestling fans know it's all fake. Hockey fans want to believe their game is all real, all on the up and up. And maybe it would be, could be, if not for all the cheating. Oh hell, Mark, it's Harrison Bergeron all over, that's what it is.

Who? What?

The mediocre cry loudest for a level playing field. And that field is knee-deep in mud.

Savages moved through the starlit wildlands beyond the wall where sheep had once grazed, a shifting with coming night from sheep to wolves, a transformation. We all dream hungry dog dreams like pulling the mask off at game's end and the stone wall you were is stripped back, your sweaty human face exposed, and the other team's players glance at you over their shoulders for that one real look, the one they remember because next time they've got your face in their heads like a weapon and the stone wall is now vulnerable which is why I never took my goalie mask off, kept it on until I was in the dressing room.

The effigy glittered dull plastic behind us, creaking in the breeze that slid over the ridge riffling the grass. I was getting pissed my hands and feet numb. *What anniversary did you say this was?*

The falling of the walls. Night of blood spilling, blood rivers guttering the slope, the clash of leagues, the conjoining of games because everyone is desperate. For a change, a revolution, a new paradigm, the wholesale rejection of bullshit all the lies shovelled into our gaping mouths spewing it back into their faces. The night when cynicism's put aside and all things are possible. The fans say no more, you're killing us, you're killing our love you fucking vampires, here's your empty arenas the switched channels we've turned our backs we're facing the old gods.

Who's they?

They is the owners the players the fans each other baseball football basketball soccer twenty million franchise fees nauseating contracts bottom-line-team's-gotta-move bullshit, buying for the pennant, buying for the cup, the money frenzy the whole goddamn mess.

Right, the untouchables.

Forces of human nature, yeah, I know but you put a stake through the heart of myths what's left? Is loyalty so easy to sell?

You tell me.

The city

Thousands gathered that hot summer night, thunderstorms flickering to the west, a city gathered swollen with blood chilling the cynics making national news a bursting boil on the bubble of apathy and bastards and bitches with ice cubes for hearts voiced their disgust, *it's only a game we can do as easily without it, big effing deal why aren't we gathering for the homeless, the substance-abused, the victims of domestic violence, the cuts to social services, higher cigarette taxes, and prohibitions, why are you so heartless about so many other things? More important things?*

The game is yearning outside yourself. The game is all those things whatever the flag you're waving. The game is dreaming God's other face, you cut it off to spite your nose, break the heart once and it breaks easier next time around and easier still until it's a goddamn way of life and you live behind all those scars if you want to, if you're afraid of doing anything else, but not me not me, cuts in social services sorry didn't see you on those canoe trips don't talk to me about inner-city kids and things to dream about.

The wall

We dumped our backpacks and my equipment bag into the canoe and took our places. We did a draw to pull us away from the dock and into the flow of the River Tyne.

Upstream all the way but then we slipped into the rhythm and started making time well enough, people on the walkways and lunching on the grass verges watching us in our jack-shirts and bandanas, the perfectly in-sync flash of our paddle blades flipping vertical as they came out of the water to slice the air on the way forward before cutting back into the water. I started bellowing out a voyageur song, remembering cutting between two lakes – six canoes the kids singing and we were in shallows when Rickie and Josh's canoe ground to a halt as if hung up on a rock and me and Sims drew alongside and we saw a snapping turtle under their canoe one of the big ones easily a hundred years old and his head came out on his long neck and Josh started reaching down. *Keep your hand away! He'll take it right off!* and the boy suddenly pale snatched his hand back. *Reverse paddles butts to the bottom one-two-three lift and push toward us ready?*

Down in the silts under the River Tyne: old Roman breastplates and rusty clumps hiding spearheads and dagger blades and swords and rotted leather and old coins and broken-keeled rib-spread boats and anchors and round shields and horseshoes and mouldering bones and musket balls and shell casings and unexploded bombs and old docks and bricks and clay jugs, Roman plates of pewter and Roman glass and beads of amber and malachite and silver earrings, and brooches and torcs and chainmail and iron scales and wooden tool boxes with clumped-together tools inside, and nails with square heads, round heads, and bundles of wire and Jute axes and antlers and wolf skulls, cow skulls, sheep skulls, dog skulls, cat skulls, clinkers, rail-ties, old cars, cannon, ballestae, crowns, sceptres and awls of fish bone, all waited sealed in eternal mud along with cricket bats, rugby balls, golf balls, tennis rackets, football boots, field hockey sticks, ice hockey sticks, skates, roller-blades, old jerseys, old mouthguards, shinguards, knee-braces, wrist-bands, baseball bats, baseball gloves, muck-filled trophies, Olympic medals, steroid pill bottles, urine samples, stool samples, rock-hard hearts and broken hearts and bleeding hearts.

The river slid remorseless above it all and we plied its surface, me still singing against the current. Jack had his shirt off and there was suddenly a lot more attention paid to us from the banks including six hundred extras from some movie set all wearing wolf furs and covered in blue woad and with pigtails and swords and spears and axes and maces that they waved over their heads and Jack called me to solo and then he stood in the bow bracing his feet on the gunnels, his fleece shorts off now too and his rod at full attention as he spread his arms wide, held his shoulders back, and lifted his face to the heavens.

I ground down to it keeping us overriding the current, hooking my J stroke with a vengeance, no time for singing left in my lungs.

Shouts of awe from the crowds lining the banks, Jack's penis was still unscrewing like a coal-drill, I could see its shadow to the right thrown out on the swirling surface and young women stripped down in a frenzy and threw themselves into the river, hundreds of them converging on the canoe. I gave up the ghost and let us drift backwards turning slowly in the current.

The city

Couldn't hold back any longer, came in her like a bursting water balloon juddering away as she sank down over me her sweat-slick flesh sliding against mine more stinging from the cuts the shag imprint on my back feeling permanent. Then she rocked back and collected her purse from the floor beside us, drew out a Matinee and lit up with a shaking flame from a gold lighter.

I lay there gaping like a beached fish shivering as I cooled.

My dong was a thick soft lump still embedded and I groaned realizing she was waiting.

Three lessons a week.

Sure, I'll pitch in on the room.

Do you work?

Yeah, at the Y. I'm a counsellor. Problem kids, every weekend and most of the summers till end of August anyway.

I'm not allowed to work.

Lucky you.

She shook her head, flicking ash onto the carpet.

Oh, right, I get it. So what do you normally do ... with your time?

Nothing. Shopping. I get a hundred dollars a week. I need to show receipts every Sunday night.

I'll need to write one for you, then.

Yes.

Do you even like hockey?

No, I hate it.

Were you born here?

Vancouver. He went out, found me, bought me and brought me back here. Eight years ago. My family disowned me but they were probably going to do that anyway, since I wasn't growing up properly.

Why not?

She shrugged her round shoulders, the motion jiggling her tits and that was the only answer she gave.

I felt a tingle from down below and silently thanked the god of dicks whoever he was I'd have to ask Jack he'd have an answer maybe true maybe not he'd been getting fuller and fuller with bullshit lately reading all the time between getting laid.

I was hard by the time she leaned far back to reach the ashtray on the nightstand beside the double bed and she crushed the butt after a last hard pull and the thought of another round with my lacerated back on this carpet had me wrapping my arms around her hips, sitting up, lifting her as I pulled my legs under me and stood, her hands gripping my shoulders now and I felt something twang in my lower back, knew I'd pay for that later but I walked her over to the bed and settled her down shifting my own weight to my arms. Time for push-ups slow and steady and she was in for the long haul I looked down between us and saw punctures in my pecs to the outside beneath the fronts of my shoulders, christ I'm going to need tetanus shots, the insides of our thighs were wet and sticky we'd both leaked all over the place I paused, *What if you get pregnant?*

I'm on the pill, he doesn't want me getting fat. I'll get fat if we have children.

This guy's a serious asshole, Caroline.

Fuck me and shut up.

You want to go and go without coming you think of other things.

Not hard to picture businessmen and politicians, the businessmen with their cocks up the politicians' asses and giving instructions behind their ears money like sperm, the seeds of cutbacks and credit ratings and international pressures and stay-low wages and mouthing the you'll-all-have-to-tighten-your-belts-these-are-hard-times-restraint's-the-word-but-my-CEO-bonus-is-going-through-the-roof-meaning-restraint's-a-selective-force-of-nature-unaffecting-us-gods-on-Olympus-my-heart-really-goes-out-to-all-you-crawling-goofs-down-below-welcome-to-democracy-ha-ha.

Vote for A, B or C it's the pool that's skewed, they're all in the game. Money runs all things especially who you see and how often and so go the choices that aren't choices at all. Jack's gorgon of modern civilization. I guess I know what he means, cut one snakehead away get a hundred in its place but one day it's all going to ground to a halt this city this country this world the gnarled hard shell rising up from underneath, pebbled long tail, fleshy legs, long tearing claws and muscled neck with a massive beaked head rising hungrily and it's something Lester and his Plains Cree know all about, that snapper's got a cold remorseless brain and chopping off the feeding hand's as certain as season's end.

Oh hell, didn't work, I came anyway. She lit up again, looking down at me, waiting.

Tell me about the women you've been with.

What's to tell? Different kinds, everyone different.

You must have preferences.

No.

What turns you on?

Women.

All women?

Just about.

You won't be staying with me long then, you'll get bored.

No I won't. I'll stay with you as long as you want me.

Don't make promises you can't keep.

I'm not.

What kind of women do you like, tell me.

Big ones skinny ones athletic ones non-athletic ones tall ones short ones ones with red hair brown hair blonde hair black hair dyed hair natural hair long hair short hair.

Hair, you like hair.

No bald too, if that's what she's into.

Do you like eyes?

Yes dark eyes bright eyes one-eyed absolutely.

Are you a tits man?

Yes.

An ass man?

Yes, and upper arms and belly and thighs and calves and feet and hands and neck and the way she walks I guess the way she walks is important no matter how big they are, if they walk straight up and proud that turns me on.

You don't like weak women, then.

I scowled. She had me. *No I guess not. I don't like wimps, I have a wimpometer it rings alarmingly around wimps.*

You don't like needy women.

If they're needy they should just take.

Take and take and take?

Only if it amounts to something. If it's a bottomless well and you see no change in them then it's time to get out before she sucks you dry because that's what she'll do until you're sucked dry, then she'll find someone else.

So what does taking and taking amount to?

That's the great part, it's different every time.

I'm needy.

57

You take.

I'll keep taking.

I know, I see it in your eyes and what I see there is power just a glimmer like it's never been used before or even realized in yourself. It's new for you, you're excited by it and scared, you don't know how far it might take you that's scary but it also turns you on.

Evil's a turn-on.

Could be. See what happens how far, don't hold anything back sink right into it see how far, Caroline.

Tell me about your last girlfriend.

I just did.

The bottomless well?

I made a mistake but got out in time, well no not entirely she'd already moved on since I wasn't meeting her needs not that any mortal man or legion of mortal men could but she found a real needy guy they'll suck each other dry I guess.

You're not needy.

I don't know maybe I am tell me if I turn into a leech.

You won't.

Tell me if I do.

I will, are you ever going to wake up down there again?

Don't say anything just think about having power let's see it in your eyes just like those keys in your hands in the bar. Go with it all the way. I want to see in your eyes, something that sends chills up my spine.

So she did and lo there I was.

The arena

Willy Lindstrom was the only hockey player to ever win both an Avco Cup and a Stanley Cup, but don't quote me. He was one of the Swedes on the Jets and in the last year of the WHA he played on the Avco Cup winning team but after that season the leagues were merging. Only the conditions of that merger amounted to butt-rape of the WHA teams – the talent stripped away so we'll never know just how good the WHA Jets were – and that's how the NHL wanted it. The possibility of a first-year NHL team winning the Stanley Cup must have terrified them so they did us all in. Until the Edmonton Oilers won the cup and on national television Glen Sather said he'd modelled his team on the old WHA Jets which he considered one of the best teams ever. That must have stuck in their craw, especially the CBC our National Television Network who pretended the WHA never existed even though there were as many Canadian teams in it as in the NHL.

In the early days of the Selkirk settlers, so-named for Lord Selkirk brother of Lord Stanley, who with his own hands made the Cup, the settlers gathered together and stone by stone raised the arena. Masons with secrets designed it, stone blocks were brought from ruined temples the world over, plaster from the Taj Mahal, limestone from the Great Pyramid at Giza, limestone from the Pyramid of the Sun in Chichen Itza in the Yucatan, basalt from Machu Picchu, sarsen stone from Avebury, granitic feldspar from the Pre-Cambrian shields of Scandinavia and the Whiteshell Park in Manitoba, Tyndall Stone all packed with the fossils of extinct animals and plants, bricks from the Great Wall of China, Hadrian's Wall, the Wailing Wall, the Appian Way, Staines Street, dolmens from Brittany, adobe from Puebla ruins, frescos from Teotihuacan and Knossos, cyclopean stone from Mycenae, luckstones from Sanmarkan, paving stones from Ur, Ugarit, Sumer, Babylon, Aleppo, Antioch, Troy and Saskatoon.

All went into the mix coming out the other end as a yellowy mush used as fire retardant on all the walls. The girders were cast in Vienna – after the siege they melted down the Turk cannons left mired in the mud or so Jack told me, the arena was then sanctified by leaders from every religion including a tobacco and sweetgrass blessing from the local Ojibwa medicine-man. The arena was given over to eternity that even God couldn't undo, but mortals did in their cunning ways because betrayal is what we do best.

The city

Adultery. I coveted something fierce. The afternoon hours in the Charter House Hotel room I was buried in tits thighs belly, had my face between the cheeks of her ass, had my face up her what's-it drank her deep, had my fingers in there in here skin slick with sweat, blood-smeared fingerprints. I fucked her from behind and diagonal and holding her up and standing and off the edge of the bed and in the easy chair and in the bathtub with the shower steaming down. I even fucked her in the closet, the chrome-plated hangers clashing and rocking and sliding this way and that along the pole, the shuttered doors shut and the air smelling of mothballs and then she lit another Matinee and got dressed and I stripped her down and fucked her again and got a burn on my shoulder for my efforts. Still have it, round and puckered.

Took more out of me than any hockey game. I ached everywhere, I could barely stand and my cock was dry-burning till I pulled the foreskin back over and found blessed relief and all I wanted to do was sleep.

This will wear off, she said sitting on the bed.

Something will.

You'll get tired of me.

This is what happened on your honeymoon?

No.

Then how do you know it'll wear off?

She looked at me a long time before shrugging and looking away.

Can we meet again tomorrow?

No. This needs careful planning. Oh God you're so young!

Whatever you want.

If he gets suspicious he'll hire a detective.

We'll shake him.

Maybe I was followed today.

What would he do?

I don't know.

Divorce you?

No.

Do you two still have sex?

She shrugged which I took for yes but then she said, *He's afraid I'll trick him, stop taking the pill, get pregnant on purpose by accident.*

You want kids?

No, but it's his excuse for not wanting me very often. He counts my pills.

Wouldn't stop you from flushing them.

I don't want to get pregnant.

Jack says the teen years were traditionally the years of prime sexual activity. In tribes, you went through puberty you were then an adult. All this waiting till you're in your twenties is hogwash. I'm an adult, you're an adult.

Who is Jack?
My brother. He knows ... stuff.
Will he know about me?
No.
Do you have any sisters?
No.

The family

When we were kids, we were a family. Weekends came and we'd be on our way out of the city in our Chevy Impala, the whole bunch of us dog included, out to the sandy shores of Lake Winnipeg where we'd fish for walleye though mostly it was me and Jack a hundred yards farther down the beach swimming and body-surfing as the huge waves rolled in. You could walk out half a mile to where pelicans wheeled over the water sometimes dropping down to pick up a dead bullhead.

Stella Lake. God, there'd be every fish you could think of waiting to be caught. We'd walk a long rocky service road beside the lake's man-made rocky shore, the grass would grow high along this road filling the air with grasshoppers as we walked and frogs hopping away from underfoot and garter snakes slithering into the rocks, the world was alive and I guess this was how we thought it would always be. But just a couple of summers ago I drove out there with some buddies and there were no frogs, no snakes, no fish and it came to me like a large boulder slowly rolling over my chest and the heart in it, that we'd grown up in a special time in this province of Manitoba and that time was gone and I look back to see my mother sitting on the lake edge holding her fishing rod with assured patience. We'd stood inside an opened flower back then, long since dead-headed, and the vision wrenches me deep inside so I'm leaving it for now.

The arena

Ice crystals hang suspended in the air and refract the sunlight so you get mirror reflections to either side and these are called sun-dogs you look up and see three suns the big one in the middle and smaller ones to either side.

All I said was it's bloody cold.

Jack scraped the ice surface with the blade of his hockey stick, rolled his shoulders against the biting air and shifted weight on his skates. Ready?

I checked my equipment one last time then pushed my cold-stiff fingers into trapper and blocker gloves grasped the goalie stick. *All right.*

We had problems in the world, the game took us away from them gave us its own focus nothing else to cloud the mind. It was fierce cold, the kind that freezes sap in trees and they explode like gunshots, but cold without wind making everything fragile, swallowing sound and rasping in the throat.

Jack skated like fluid shooting on me from every angle, wrist-shots, slapshots, backhands, he'd come in and deke this way and that trying to pull me out of position but facing him like this over the years had taught me how to poke-check so he never brought the puck in too close or I'd slide my stick through my hand stabbing the blade out to knock the puck from his stick.

Jack skated hard, shot hard. I took the shots against pads, into my trapper, off my blocker, against my chest, my upper arms, off my skate toes, my stick and a few ducks as the puck went head-hunting. Dad had run off maybe with a woman maybe not the business was on the edge of receivership he'd sent a cashier's cheque for five grand no return address though the stamp said Vancouver. The money backed the creditors off for now. Mom was holding the fort running the whole show; she'd had her first ever meeting with the bank manager and had come away with double the overdraft and fifty grand to re-organize. We'd known she was tough and canny but this was impressive. Dad's note said the pressures were too much, he couldn't stop crying but he was coming back as soon as he felt able.

Winter-silence in the house. We were on the rink as soon as it got light every day this week just two more days till Christmas there were presents under the tree that wouldn't get opened and thanks to be said but no one to say it to.

Jack read his books and came out here and hammered me senseless with the puck and Mom read through the business ledgers and did the math by hand and a Filipino Christmas hamper arrived at the house from the girls on the shop floor making Mom cry though she'd not cried at Dad's running. At least not that we could see but thinking back I'd say that bad news never broke her. Just kind gestures. I wonder what that means what it meant then what it means now.

Jack took it out on me and I deflected what he gave me harmlessly away from the target though sometimes he got the puck through and I'd straighten up, eyeing him from behind my cage mask as he circled waiting for the puck back, and I'd shoot it out to his waiting stick and we'd start again.

I'd gone on my first canoe trip at the age of ten. In a drawer in my room there was a faded ragged blue and white bandana. Sometimes deflecting the bad is all you can do though it doesn't last. I think those moments of invincibility do a lot of good, every thudding save sending an echo into the future and back into the past too.

Out on the rink where the Furies played by the rules or paid the price.

What the hell does that mean, Jack?

In his cold-tight face I saw a downturn to his mouth then a hooked grin hiding it by half, this was the face of breaking inside though I didn't know it then and didn't for a long time. He'd always seemed immune to the world in the days of my worship. It's funny how things like that can still tremble you inside.

Where you been disappearing lately?

What?

Got a new girlfriend? Don't be coy, brother, who is she?

Can't tell you.

Why the hell not?

It's ... delicate.

She married?

Can't say.

You don't know?

Can't say.

There were days when I fought the puck, out of sync and letting ones in I shouldn't have. Those days came more often once me and

Caroline spotted the guy who had to be his detective. Always around, sitting in a running car near the rink where we did the skating lessons, and afterward she'd pay me and we'd head off in different directions he'd then tail her more often than me as she drove downtown, parked in the Eaton's carpark then head into the store to look at clothes and try things on and find new ways of shaking him. Old fire-stairs behind the trying-on booths, catching buses along Portage at the last second a few stops down, to the Hudson's Bay store into there then back up along Graham Avenue to the Charter House.

I had a harder time since the guy could follow me into bathrooms and I wasn't much for trying on clothes in department stores but I finally found my best route was taking my skates down to the river. Just like the guy that hired him, the detective couldn't skate and the snow would be cleared from the ice for a mile or more on the river and I'd take off in my white-capped goalie skates going full tilt and there wasn't much he could do. I'd be out of sight in no time then cutting in to the bank at Donald Street Bridge and up onto Donald and into the Charter House bar flushed and breathless. And there she'd be waiting for me halfway through a Caesar, a Matinee between her fingers two or three stubs in the ashtray and the bartender knew and the porters knew and the Cambodian maid knew and four or five regular suits coming in for liquid lunches knew and from those the web spread out in every direction who knows how far until my growing paranoia had me scanning the crowds in the arena each game night with the binocs convinced everyone there knew with the exception of him (maybe) and Jack and Mom and actually Jack sort of knew since he'd seen me stripped down after games often enough as I took razzing from the guys because of all the scabs and rakes and nail-punctures and bruised nipples.

She learned how to skate and skate well. I made her buy hockey skates, not those white figure-skating ones with the brakes and long blades and high heels I taught her to skate backward, I taught her cross-overs and power-skating and there's nothing sexier than a beautiful woman on hockey skates.

There was no letting up. The sex went on and on and the arena was full every game night as the Jets played magic on the icy temple floor, twelve thousand worshippers shelling peanuts, drinking beer, eating popcorn, smoking cigarettes, buying souvenirs, because we all knew the WHA was coming to an end, time never ever stands still.

The wall

Notice the use of vehicles here? This country's history entire social structure is exemplified in the rules of the road. You have to think back when only the rich folk owned carriages. Some poor bugger in the street had to get out of the way or get run down. It's the same today. In every other civilized country pedestrians have right of way crossing a side street intersection. Cars turning onto that street and cars coming up on that street are obliged by law to stop. But not here in the UK. Pedestrians take their lives into their hands, cars wheel into turns with a touch on the horn to let you know your death is imminent. National rudeness steeped in class consciousness I feel like I'm running a gauntlet every time I cross a goddamn street, doesn't matter if it's pissing down, no one stops not even at designated crossings. This is symptomatic of a fuck-you culture.

The naked women treading water around the canoe stared up at Jack in aghast adoration. As if criticism was oxygen. Or maybe it was just the wonder of his tattooed penis.

We drifted on the current toward Newcastle and I guess beyond out into the North Sea. This trip hadn't started out well or maybe it had and we were just fated to go farther than we'd thought at first. Canada Geese bobbed in the waves along with all the women.

Jack turned to me. *We can't buck the current, brother.*

Not with you catching the wind like that.

We need to go with the flow. We'll rig a sail, sweep down the coast all the way in around.

In three days?

Sure why not?

Look if we push hard we can do thirty maybe thirty-five miles a day. So a hundred miles in three days. Not enough.

Okay so we go up the Thames then hunker overland once we run out of tributaries.

Which is where?

Stonehenge.

All right.

Before the flight we'd read a statistic noting that British women's breasts were getting bigger. The first few days we'd picked a pair to stare at but they never got any bigger. Ha. Well maybe a bit but on average they left Canadian women in the dust probably a population thing. Jack said it was mammary nutrition. Edinburgh in summer was incredible and all these bobbing tits in the River Tyne had me gaping. You know, me and Jack had always prided ourselves on being crass on purpose but we were tame compared to British men.

You go to the States and people roll at you like tanks, men, women and children, it's kind of frightening but the ones into athletics are seriously good, it's amazing what money can do I suppose not to mention breathtaking egomania. I was starting to see where Canadians got the piss-on-your-own-head-it's-good-for-you mentality, a sharing of traits going back to the fur-trading days. There's no point in counting Quebecers, they're completely different and should form their own country. I'd vote for it on any referendum, not out of spite at all, go for it guys believe me you're not anything like non-Quebecers and why would you want to be?

Newcastle's old buildings rose up around us, most of them older than the country where we were born. It got me thinking about Canadian identity but not for very long and pretty soon I was bending the blade keeping us out of the path of motorboats. So much for Mariner's rules we damn near got swamped five six times before slipping under the last bridge and out into the North Sea.

A big trawler swept past us and netted all the women, which was a relief. They were off to Russia. Finally with a blank look Jack got dressed again, his dong like a seagull perch before he worked it back down under his Stanley gotch. He retrieved his paddle and helped me swing us about heading south along the shoreline.

When Hudson tried sailing into Hudson Bay they got ice-locked and looked to starve and freeze to death until a passing Inuit team playing shinny on the wind-swept ice skated over. Lines were thrown and they pulled the ship through to the harbour of Churchill though no one came down to meet them all being holed up while a gang of polar bears tore up the town.

Crap, I said. Hudson Bay wasn't even called Hudson Bay before Hudson arrived.

Had some Inuit name, of course. I was just simplifying. And when they found the arena there they saw it was named York Factory because the Northern League was a goddamn factory producing top players Bobby Clarke of the Flin Flon Bombers though he wasn't actually talented, he'd just been brawling black bears at the town dump all his youth and was fierce-mean. Imagine the frustration of a toothless vampire and you got Bobby Clarke. Anyway they all had Chippewyan agents. Talk about canny middlemen, contracts like 22 million beaver furs over seven years with scoring bonuses. But the plains Indians had a serious advantage, they got horses which meant road-swings access to rinks in the centre of the Great Plains. You can carry lots of equipment and sing-songs are easy from the saddle, you don't waste your breath trudging, made for excellent team camaraderie.

Why? We never sang.

We never won the big games neither.

We did in the industrial league. We hammered the masons.

You're a wit, brother.

What?

I gave up, got quiet at his laughing, hunkered down to paddle. The waves were a bit rough, some coast guard boat came alongside and megaphoned something about gale forces but we'd seen worse on Lake Winnipeg and there were no shallows here that could roll high a fifteen foot silty wave in knee-deep water toss up one end of the canoe and drive the other end two feet into the sandy bottom. The water was cold but not as cold as West Hawk Lake which was a meteorite crater and could turn you blue just looking at it.

Out to sea I could make out a few Saxon longships through the spray, boy were they lost. We flashed our paddles a hello but they never answered. Out in the northern tundra on the flat lands if you pissed in expanding circles day in day out you could make a skating rink. Not sure why that occurred to me but it did, then I was thinking about lacing on my skates again and stepping out onto the ice in Cardiff, feeling the cool air on my face and neck and in my throat, the magic sound of blades cutting ice edges, that liquid friction as good as sex. If only my back held out, I stood a good chance, a year contract with option for renewal. Another year in the cage facing shots, tracking the speeding dance orbiting the ever-moving puck the dancing flow of play, the bone-shaking collisions celestial chaos writ human, Jack once said, but look hard and the patterns come clear like revelation.

The family

I suppose if there was anything left to do Mom would have done it. The business teetered and no word from Dad, just another cheque. I was pulling in seventy-five dollars a week playing Major and another fifty from working with messed-up kids on the weekends.

Christmas at home was silent and quietly bleeding. Swedish decorations, most of them made by Mom, Santa Lucia, trolls, tomkins hung everywhere. We'd gone out to Sandilands Forest to cut down the tree, harnessed the old German Shepherd, she was game dragging the tree down the snowy trail through the forest to the carpark but she was getting old, her hips wobbling by the time she was done. And now the tree filled a corner of the living room swathed in angelhair and blinking star-shaped lights. We celebrated Christmas Eve, not the morning of the twenty-fifth, but the dinner was smaller this year, one end of the table unoccupied and me and Jack feeling more grown-up but in a way that felt like loss. We were protective that night but you know there's some things you can't do for a Mom whose husband has run off, the personal private hurt between two people, her sense of standing alone which is how I see her to this day. At the end of it all she still went to sleep alone and maybe she cried quietly, there's no way of knowing.

What a family. We'd been like muskoxen all facing outward but now the circle was incomplete and we were vulnerable.

Dad came back in the New Year with presents and he and Mom talked late into the nights and probably during the days too. I think she told him to keep his hands out of the business and that must have been a knife in his gut but she could stand firm, immovable and tough, and he buckled and went with it and after a week the circle had closed again but the trust was gone and one night Jack threw Dad up against a wall, the first violence ever in the house, shocking everyone. Was never repeated but didn't have to be, the muscle had shifted and Jack put himself between Dad and Mom in ways that didn't make much sense to me. Some days we lived out on the rink, me and Jack, and it may have been giving breathing space to Mom and Dad but it may have been cowardice too.

The house kept sinking, cracks rising between the bricks in jagged skyward lines. The dog's hips went; one day she couldn't stand up on them and lost control of her bowels. Me and Jack drove her to the vet's.

In the scheme of things it was a small death, putting the dog to sleep. But the word sleep's a lie and for us it wasn't a small death. It was the crack of grief in young stalwart walls and cracks get wider.

Always the good and the bad get remembered. I had carried the dying dog into the backseat of the Chevy on a bitter February morning. Jack had been warming up the car but in a Winnipeg winter that was usually an unwinnable contest, the tires were frozen clumping unevenly as he backed the car out of the drive. I rested a hand on the dog, remembering all the weekends when she'd slept curled up wet and smelly after a day in Lake Winnipeg, twitching dreams of chase like a wolf disdaining a food-pack and of course I remembered a solid family in that time too. The dog gave me an excuse to cry but not the whole reason.

The car clambered over crackling ruts of frozen slush, slid and jerked sideways all down the alley with a slow, barely controlled slide onto the street. Almost no traffic and what there was was going slow and steady. We once went out to Vancouver when a sudden snowstorm dumped three inches on the city and everybody panicked like it was volcanic ash and the world was about to end and cars crashed into each other all over the place but mostly people stayed home, schools closed. West Coasters don't know how to drive on ice and snow and each year Vancouver puts a team on the ice that's forgotten how to play hockey so it's no surprise.

The air outside had frozen invisible, solid car exhaust not moving just hanging where it tumbled out from exhaust pipes. No wind, just the heart of cold, the definition of cold made real and the frozen tires clumped unevenly under us and the dog's head was in my lap and I stroked it barehand, the chill biting deep and twenty minutes later she crouched shivering on the vet's examination table and a needle went into her hip and she slowly sank down in my arms, head drooping shivering falling still, the tension draining away. It's a fist in the heart when all movement ceases and life leaves the thing in your arms.

All the while Jack stood with his back against the door, his arms crossed and my eyes were too wet to meet his. If I did I'd lose it completely so I never knew the expression he was wearing and sometimes I wish I did so it would have warned me of what's to come.

I know now our childhood died that day. Put out of its misery because the world tells us when it's time to leave it behind. Every child's told in some way or another and I think of those kids we took on trips into the bush, most of them were old before their time, seen too much, felt pain they never deserved, but they were still kids and the two sides couldn't meet, just the flash and fire of anger and maybe we gave them a moment for their memories. That silly voyageur ritual wasn't so silly and meant more than we'd ever imagined, a place to point to, the time of permission making stepping across something earned, the opposite of some fist cracking the head from child into grown-up all at once. There's no excuse for that, is there?

The game of the living dead

October 31, 1901, in a small Canadian prairie town the seven brothers and four sisters of the town's smallest family went out to the pond to play a game.

It was a late start, almost sunset. They'd been busy with their father and uncles in raising a barn to replace one that had burnt to the ground when a silo's load of grain had spontaneously combusted as they were wont to do and the wind had carried sparks into the hayloft. The sky was the colour of carbon-blackened iron, a streak of red on the west horizon marking the dying sun.

The pond was just outside town, a coolie that had once been a watering hole way back and had been the place Plains Cree buffalo hunters camped as they followed the herds north into the forests. Gnarled leafless oaks enclosed the pond, lightning-blasted and wind-twisted.

Winter had come early and the pond was covered in ice thick enough to hold a horse. The brothers and sisters laced up and pushed clods of earth onto the ice to make goal-posts. Using a dog-gnawed rubber puck they began playing.

The cold October wind moaned through the oaks as if the gathering darkness had lungs. Heedless of the growing gloom, the boys and girls played on.

When another team showed up at the pond's far end, the siblings gathered and discussed challenging the newcomers to a game of shinny. Some of the younger ones were a little frightened. The skaters across the pond looked ... strange. They skated stiff, their faces were white as snow, with dark smudges for eyes. Their hair was long and straggly and they all seemed underdressed for the weather. But a game's a game, and games weren't easy to come by even with all the other kids living in this area since for just about everyone else it was a long, long walk to the pond. Besides, it was almost dark.

So the oldest boy skated over to the newcomers. As he got closer he began to understand the trepidation expressed by his littlest brothers and sisters. These players weren't just strange, they were dead.

Belatedly he realized that it was October 31. Hallowe'en night, and that a bunch of zombies had arrived and were now watching him like the staring corpses they were as he skated up to them. Being the eldest boy it was unthinkable that he should wheel and skate away screaming his head off. His brothers and sisters would scatter in every direction and there'd be hell to pay if one of them got lost. So he nodded politely. "You guys want a game?"

They stared at him, then they all nodded.

"We've got the puck to start, eh?"

They nodded again and jostled and stumbled into a 3-2-1 formation.

The boy skated back to his brothers and sisters. "They said okay. Who's got the puck? Pass it here, Walter."

"They're zombies!" Suzie complained.

"So? C'mon, we're starting."

They played. The moon rose overhead, casting a pallid light down on the pond, and the hours went by, and by. The zombies had the desire and endless energy, but they basically sucked. Twenty minutes before dawn and the score was 771 to 1, the one goal against having been scored by little Billy who, being only four, had yet to comprehend the concept of sides or Us or Them and wouldn't have cared if he had since all he liked doing was whacking the puck any which way and one of his finest whacks sent the puck past his sister in their own team's goal.

Five minutes before dawn the zombies started falling apart. The game was hastily called and the siblings shook those hands that were still attached to arms and bodies, collected their puck and hurried home, knowing they were going to be canned for a week at least for staying out all night.

As it turned out, they weren't canned, because no one could help but believe their story, since from that night on and for every generation since, the Stapleton family has been white-haired.

As everybody knows, when a team of zombies wants a game of hockey, you play.

The arena

Everybody talks about the Russian game but not me. The night the Czech national team came to play, the big world out there arrived at Winnipeg Arena and took us all by the throat and intimidated the hell out of everyone for half the game, the Jets down 5-nothing skating confused and scared. Those Czechs played on another level and the mighty Jets looked humbled and us with them until something fierce took hold, some pagan god, all teeth and claws rearing up its head, blood spreading under its pebbled skin and this was the holy ground under the arena, some New World beast poked and jabbed awake by ten thousand restless immigrants and maybe a hundred Natives feeling what was coming a split second before everyone else.

The Jets rose on the back of that beast, matched level for level then surpassed it all, rattling the Czech nationals until they buckled under the pressure, goal after goal came, some like that tying outside-the-blueline Tommy Bergman slapshot that should never have gone in but was willed in by ten thousand fans on their feet, that blistering breathtaking moment between the puck leaving the Swede's stick and the netting behind the goalie billowing out a spread of time as fast as a blink but ten thousand minds bent collectively guiding that puck and the goalie seemed to wilt under that surge and that was the greatest comeback the arena ever witnessed and then absorbed into its iron bones.

Walking out of that building that night all things were possible to all of us. We were all winners that night against every odd riding high, god-touched the ancient way of being god-touched. We moved in a trance, faces shone, smiles plastered until muscles ached, every sports fan on the planet knows this feeling and the assholes who sneer and say none of it's important got empty places inside and their anguish in knowing it turns to bitter lashing out, souls that never stepped over, just ask the true sports fan and this is known, a seared badge of honour on the heart.

That night we were immortal, every man, woman, child who was there remembers that moment. It lives on ageless and pure under the crap that's been dumped in the time since, just pull it free some spit some polish and it's all back, a single memory of glory each time personal and held close.

The wall

We canoed into a wall of fog. Most things I can handle but fog's a new one on me. In the third week of one trip, eight kids, me and Jack, we'd cut from Lake of the Woods into Shoal Lake, the water changing under us from algae-flecked to dark clear between dips of the paddle and we'd rounded the point on the left and were making for Deadman's Portage when a thunderhead rolled in fast over the water. Me and Jack yelled out to bear down hard, make for the shore. Lightning flashed at our backs, the sky bruising, a green and gold tint coming to the air. All went still and we pushed, muscles creaking on bone, the kids showing what two weeks of twenty-five miles a day paddling can do. We shot up alongside bedrock, quiet lapping wavelets, the buzz of tigerflies closing in to circle our heads. We hustled the kids out of the canoes, pulled the Grummans up on the rock, made for the woods and had turned back to face the lake in time to see lightning shoot skipping on the waves a hundred fifty yards out. Then before a breath could be drawn up onto the canoes, it was dancing from one to the next, popping pebbles into the air and sizzling one foodpack's buckles, fusing two forks together inside and scorching the summer sausage inside its burlap wrapping.

But fog I couldn't handle. Everything just plain disappeared and even sound bounced like demon voices. Jack was saying something about cock-sucking mermaids when the prow of a Roman trireme sliced through the white damn near on top of us. Gallic faces scowled at us through oar-ports or whatever those holes are called and some guy in plate armour looking like Rex Harrison studied us enigmatically as his ship slid across our bow.

You'll lose it all! Jack shouted. *Beware the ides of April! Hah, mark that day on your calendar!*

Wait a minute, I hissed, *isn't it the ides of March?*

I know. Won't he be surprised. I wouldn't play the fiddle for him if you paid me.

You're insane.

The game is a country. It's not just what's on the field, what's on the ice or in the stands. The night I went to bail Jack out for what ended up a misdemeanour, even the cinema dropped the charges, he was brought out to the sign-out desk by a corrections officer and his face was calm and pale so I knew he was seething. But the arrest wasn't the reason, he'd been caught trying to break into the projection booth with the intent of stealing the film reels, not for profit but to burn them on the steps of the U.S. consulate, it was the year of the Mighty Ducks, the final humiliation of Canada's game, the theft of our myth nearly as horrendous as some Canadian blathering on about baseball.

Everything's in reduction, Mark. Pare away the crap and you come down to a single word: money. The world's poison rotting every soul there's no beating it. Some Hollywood execs got together and walked all over another country's heart, nothing new in that but they stole it from us and we take kids to the show, line up to buy tickets, are we stupid or what.

The Roman galley was past, the world of white closing in again and Jack was bending to the paddle like someone possessed.

It's not just sport, Mark. Money's poisoned everything. It bids for dreams, turns them into euphemisms for greed, every aspiration these days is just another facet of greed and success turns the soul rotten. Small-town prairie boys from Saskatchewan head south, become multimillionaires, have kids now living in some desert city. They don't grow up on wind-swept rinks, eight month winters spent on skates, they don't ever realize the game is a country where the dream started out pure and true. Now their Dad's a naturalized American. Goes to work, earns seven million a year and the money is what it was all for. It's all the kid sees and understands and takes inside and packing up and moving to the next desert city is just part of the chase for even more money. Dad wears padding, not a tie but it's still the same thing. There's no room for the myth in that picture. Dad reels out the old clichés of heart and desire and the rest but they're words you can just pick up and put elsewhere next year. If hockey was a game of individuals there'd be no reason for teams, just turn the whole damn thing into a tennis circuit one-on-one in tiny rinks. Loyalty's another product but the truth is, it isn't just another product. It's the fucking opposite of product and so is the game. We're in a world of poison, Mark, get used to it.

Fuck that. I just want to play.

If the pro players felt that way they wouldn't be holding out half the season in contract disputes. You can count on one hand the players with that kind of spirit.

Teemu Selanne.

Yeah absolutely, and maybe Brett Hull but for real Steve Yzerman and Joe Sakic and Paul Kariya and The Dominator and most of all Ryan Smith, the heart and soul of hockey right there in one decent man, but think of all the wussy stars who sit with their thumbs up their asses, faces turning blue because they want more money. And the team owners play their own game shelling out money they don't have then raising ticket prices to pay for it. You can't even go to a game unless you got money to burn. The players and owners think this bullshit can go on forever. Pretty soon corporations will own every seat in every arena that's where it's heading and you remember I said that because it's coming. The game belongs to the working stiffs and it's been taken away from them. Just one more rape in a lifetime of rapes.

Don't see any way of solving this, Jack.

You don't think radically enough. Canadians never do. We swallow up getting pissed off till the whites of our eyes turn yellow. We've made cowardice a national trait, getting stepped on a way of life and if no one else is doing it at the moment then we do it to each other. There'll be a lockout soon. Greedy players on one side and stupid owners who've been paying into the players' greed for years. Players want the owners to stay stupid so they can keep getting stupid big salaries, and owners want to stop it all and cap the salaries to make up for how stupid they've been for years. When that lockout comes, that's the chance, the final chance for the fans. To tear it all down and build something new. See that coast on our right?

No.

It's the same over there.

Wait a minute, what's that?

The Millennium Dome. It was built for the year 2000, a commemoration to longevity with a lifespan of seventy-five years.

That's stupid.

Well, it commemorates that, too.

Let's pull in and trash it.

Nah leave that for the Yobs in suits.

England has Yobs, Canada has Yahoos.

And Americans have Fox. We'll head up the Thames, pitch a tent in London for the night and that way you can see the youth of today roaming the streets consuming things. You notice how they're all litter dispersal units? One day they'll be wading through the stuff on their way to the corner superstore to buy more candy bars and green belts will be something you wear around your waist. Money is the momentary made material. Comes goes in seconds you want, you get, you had, and the wind sweeps up behind you and you go on to the next get got had.

I just want to stop pucks.

You want the impossible, brother.

The city

Road-trips were hell in the old days. Teams had to go by York boat along treacherous rivers and stormy lakes lugging their equipment on their backs, fighting off raiding agents. People were dying out there in the bush so the government decided to build a rail line right across the country east to west sixteen thousand miles, ten thousand of them through solid rock. The line was built single-handedly by some guy named Pierre Berton. He drove the last spike through his own foot off the coast of Tofino before drowning when the tide came in.

These days the NHL is more sacred than Canada itself. People in Alberta talk about seceding from the country, people in Québec talk the same talk but no one says hey why not secede the Canadian teams from the NHL, then get more Canadian teams like in Hamilton and Kingston and Saskatoon and leave the NHL to the American businessmen and their Napoleon president who runs it. It's a glutted empire anyway, the talent spread stupidly thin with expansion teams popping up anywhere there's cactus or alligators or both.

Besides, the game's gone rotten, this new defensive style which is mediocrity in action, if you can call it action. The games are pure dull, the players might as well play on their knees and the ones with skill got huge lumps on their back hanging on for dear life, these being talentless players whose job it is to slow down the good players.

Who cares if Burger King sells more hamburgers than McDonald's? No one frets, no one loses any sleep, no one cares if employees from one defect to the other. Hockey isn't Safeway's, isn't 7-Eleven, isn't Chrysler.

The game isn't a business. The game is a country.

One Wednesday we were in the bathtub in the room at Charter House, me on the bottom, Caroline lying on me, my soapy cock lodged up her ass as she rested her head on my shoulder, smoking Matinees, lighting one from the butt of the other, six down nineteen more to go in the pack, the talk turned serious.

This isn't right, she said.

Well I told you it was the wrong hole from the start.

She did something with those muscles and I groaned. *I want to be with you all the time none of this is right, Mark. I'm thirty-five and you're seventeen. I think he cries at night.*

He should've appreciated you from the start now it's too late that's why he cries.

Even if he had. Even if he was perfect in every way, I'd still be here. I'm evil.

I love evil.

It's a serious word, Mark. Look at the way I hurt you when we make love. Is love even the right word for the things I do to you? I made you drink me and it was terrible and I loved how terrible it was.

Nobody can explain what turns someone on it's not a thing for explaining there aren't any reasons the body just reacts.

I bought a vibrator and I take it with me everywhere.

Really? I started getting painful hard inside her and she squeezed back. *Where is it?*

I don't bring it with me when I meet you. I carry it inside. I pretend it's your cock and most of the time it's all I need. Just your cock, that's all you are to me most of the time it's all of you that I need. I carry you inside me while I'm shopping and sometimes I go into the bathroom and do myself. I'm almost always wet even sitting beside him at the arena. You're inside me, your cock anyway and I know you're watching with your binoculars and I'm so wet I need panty-liners.

Cool.

No it's evil.

Cool evil. Evil cool.

She lit another cigarette then started grinding me slowly up and down. The soap had all dried and the water that slurped in between just pulled at my skin painful and my fingers sank into the soft flesh padding her hips which had gotten bigger, she was putting on weight everywhere and liked pushing my face into it so I couldn't breathe, holding me there till I actually had to struggle free. I was cool with that but then the dryness was gone and things went smooth.

Lift me. Lift me up and out.

Yeah. Easier said than done. Damn near slipped, broke my back maybe both our backs, a crowd of police and ambulance attendants cramming the bathroom door, two corpses in the bathtub a hell of a way to go. Got enough pictures, Bill? I'll take one for my wallet, but I managed it finally, gasping, my spine crunching as I balanced with her in my arms then on one leg to step over the side of the tub onto the bathmat, her head thrown back on my shoulder, damp hair on my face, smoke in twin streams from her nostrils we stood there dripping under the orange heat-lamp and its buzzing timer. *Just glue me here,* I said after a few minutes as we dried in the heat and then she was sliding me up and down again and it was hot and raspy in there, I could feel the ringed cartilage of her colon. If I went any higher my dome would be swimming in her lunch. I don't know, I didn't see anything evil in it, well not much, the most common crime in sex is lack of imagination I figure.

The family

A surveyor came to the house and made official the fact that the house was sinking into lacustrine clay, flood silts, pockets of windblown sand, all on a bed of slimy loess which he explained was left behind by glaciers back when Gordie Howe was just a kid. The point was everything was shimmying around down there and our living room was a sunken living room now, the bay windows looking out on the stems of bushes.

Dad was trying hard, not that he had much to do since Mom ran the business now. He was around more though me and Jack weren't, and this slow spreading of a family, new, private worlds spinning off seemed natural, though we still orbited Mom in the old ways. Even as those ways compacted there wasn't a sense of a ticking clock, nothing overhead like the ledgers of God, the season was nearing the play-offs and it was pretty clear that next year at least four WHA teams would join the NHL, the end of the WHA had arrived. One last Avco Cup to win. Who would win it us Winnipeggers had no doubt at all, the team was simply playing on another level compared to the other WHA teams, hell, they played the game like demigods. We were all in a moment that would be remembered as a golden age which Jack says even Homer knew, he needed as a place for Greeks to look back on when sighing about the current sorry state of affairs. So in my head I've got The Iliad and Odysseus and the Jets in golden echoes and looking now on the state of the game I don't just sigh, I weep.

Mom took a day off work, went with Dad and when they came back everything had changed. She had a blood disorder, the first stage that would go through to a fourth stage which was leukemia and incurable. The specialist said she could live as much as ten years if she responded to the treatments. I lay awake that night trying to make sense of elevated white cell counts, rbc's, and other words I'd heard for the first time and the clock ticking beside the bed was fate's intrusion. Mom was acting cool about the whole thing, Dad was distraught I guess is the word.

Every family stumbles every now and then. Ten years was a good long time and she responded well to the treatment, cutting back check-ups to every two months then every three. We watched from the greys the Jets pounce on every team in its path, devour them like a tiger a rabbit chomp gulp who's next and the Avco Cup parade came to the corner of Portage and Main on a hot spring day. The Jets were champions. The city had lived through its best and under it all was a fear for the future. No one knew for sure what was coming, would the Jets management make deals, give up draft-picks to keep its team intact? No one expected the management would lose its nerve, fail every confidence in what the team had been, sell out, let go, get butt-raped smiling all the way through, descended on by vultures who only months before had scoffed at the WHA's dubious talent pool, then turned around, closed in on the Avco Cup champions, taking damn near everybody including the stick-boy. Leaving what, three players left?

After it was all said and done the NHL had pulled off its biggest swindle in hockey history and if it wasn't for canny Sather in Edmonton trading draft-picks to buy off the greed of the NHL teams, keeping most of his team, signing Gretzky and playing coy about just how good his players were, the NHL would have won hands down on all sides. But the Oilers and Sather had sights set on the Stanley Cup, the NHL's holy grail, and before long they were rolling over everybody on their way to getting it.

I finished high school that spring. Jack had gone the university route and I considered it only because of the Bison hockey team, a chance to play alongside Brett Hull, but I never got around to applying for admission. It all seemed pretty complicated so in the end it never happened and before long Jack hung up the skates more or less, and our lives split, each going different ways. When he was only months away from the NHL draft, professional scouts eyeing him at local games, he just went and dropped it all, didn't even try out for the Bisons, said he'd play occasionally, industrial league but not much else. I was pretty confused around then but got used to things eventually, even the sinking house.

One day Dad came and found us. We were packing gear in the basement getting ready for a week-long canoe and fishing trip, Bird River and Bird Lake. He was never one to say much, show much, but we could see he'd been crying and our packing got uncomfortable.

For me working's been everything but I want you to know I'm proud of you two. Both me and your Mom worked hard so you could do what was in your hearts to do and that was play hockey but I'm wondering, well, I guess I'm wondering now if it was the right thing to do.

Jack looked ready to explode at that. He went pale, that half-smile twitching, but Dad went on looking at us. I recognized courage then.

You haven't experienced struggle, you see. It's the way the best of intentions backfire, it's the work ethic I'm talking about I guess, the desire in parents to make it easier for their kids but maybe we missed the point. You only value what you've worked hard for.

And what, Jack said in a low voice, *do you think practising is all about?*

Dad looked down for a moment then nodded. *You have a point there, Jack, I guess I didn't think much about that. About what I was thinking to say here, you see, the few times I've watched you two play, the play-off games and such, well, you've been so damned good as if it was all natural, as if in paying for your equipment, the league fees and all that was all it took but I can see what you're saying and maybe that's the value of sports, something I never realized before. It prepares you for adulthood, dealing with loss and victory but it's also the working hard bit that teaches you that desire for something is not enough. You have to work damned hard to get there and that's what you've done. I guess it puts me more at ease but I still don't know if we did enough, if you'll be ready when it's time.*

I shrugged, not much I could say really but Jack shook his head. *This crisis of faith is yours, Dad, doesn't have anything to do with us or how we feel.*

I guess you're right in that but I should tell you that my strongest memories, my warmest memories, are of all those weekend fishing trips. We used to walk a lot once out there I used to carry both of you one in each arm. I think those times were the most special the most magical times of my life and it's funny how that realization doesn't come until it's past.

You're not alone in those memories, Dad, Jack said, *you showed us the wild and it stole our hearts and that was a good thing.*

You know, Dad said and he was crying again, *we went fishing every weekend to stock up on fish for the freezer for the winter just to make sure we had enough food because things were tight.*

We nodded, knowing that.

Doesn't take anything away, Jack said.

If we'd not had the need though maybe we'd never have gone out every weekend.

But we did because escaping was important, escaping was valuable, you taught us that, too, and that knowledge makes life easier to bear, we'll carry that truth with us.

Sometimes escaping isn't escaping.

You've showed us that too, Dad, I don't think we'll get mixed up in the same way as you did.

I hope not. Well, we're together again anyway. I won't make the same mistake twice.

All right, Dad.

He turned around then and went back upstairs, we went back to packing gear not saying anything. Life's full of surprises I guess. That memory returns to me from a hundred different angles, I still don't know if I understand it or even if it's important that I should understand it. Sometimes just holding pieces of someone else's life inside you is enough.

The wall

The fog lifted. We paddled up the Thames and found ourselves in London. Jack stayed dressed so we didn't attract much attention except after we'd landed in some park and without any way of securing the canoe we decided to take it with us. Before long, canoe on our shoulders, held high to see every now and then, we were pushing through crowds of German tourists taking pictures of Japanese tourists taking pictures of Dutch tourists and cars and buses honked furiously at us, Jack waving back, some suit with a briefcase and yabbering on a mobile phone walked his head into the prow of the canoe, fell flat on the pavement knocked out cold, turned out the phone wasn't even turned on and for some reason a paramedic took off the guy's pants which are called trousers in the UK and there was a banana taped to the inside of his leg but the paramedic wasn't a paramedic at all just a homeless ex-nurse who ran off with the trousers. Then some other homeless guy untaped the banana and ate it. Meanwhile everybody else just walked past the guy so we put the canoe down and dragged him to a plastic chair at a streetside café, propped him up, re-used the tape to fix a hand to the phone and the phone to his head and left him there, a big red lump on his forehead but otherwise deep in important conversation. If he's dead he's still there.

We kept looking the wrong way down streets when crossing but though people honked and one guy drove up on the sidewalk and buried the nose of his car in a store windowfront, no one seemed inclined to challenge us. I guess the canoe confused them though we cleared some guy from his mountain bike clean, knocking us only slightly sideways, the guy's air-filter crumpled on his face, his mirror shades all twisted, his alien helmet pushed high up on his forehead. Me and Jack paused for a good laugh then continued on our way and minutes later we saw a pub for Canadians, apparently the only one in London. We pushed the canoe through the doorway, set it balanced on a nearby table then stopped. All conversation, and there wasn't much of it, was muted, almost whispered, nobody at their lone tables saying anything or looking at anyone else.

Good God, I said.

We've stepped into Canada, Jack whispered, a look of horror and dismay on his face. *You'd think some energy would seep in from outside, some semblance of life. Anything.*

I went to the bar and asked for a Standard and got a blank look. I scowled. *A Canadian, then. Molson Canadian, one bottle for me, one for my brother here.*

Can't bring a kayak in here, mate.

Jack threw up his hands. *Canoe not kayak. If not here in this pub where else in London can two Canadians bring their canoe? Tell me!*

82

Nowhere, I guess.

You got that. Mate. What's with this 'mate' thing anyway? We can't mate and if we could the progeny would be terrifying but we can't and I wouldn't sleep with you if you paid me.

I damn near choked paying for the beer, talk about overpriced for two plain Molson's. We decided to ignore the bartender and found seats to watch the game. Two more Canadians came in, thought the canoe was a prop, were chuffed as the locals say and after that no more words were wasted trying to get us to take the canoe away. We drank our beer, ate nachos, watched a bad hockey game on bad ice between Dallas and Detroit. Hockey seriously sucked that day and we felt dragged down by Canadianness and Jack started moving from table to table talking to the loners, more beers were bought, then he dragged tables together and dragged one woman in her chair over to another table. She looked outraged but true to form didn't voice a complaint and before long Jack had one big table full of Canadians, none talking to each other.

We got more disgusted, drank down our beers, picked up the canoe and left. Twilight Zone that pub. Down the street we got stuck when a line of Japanese tourists filed under our canoe which we didn't even have to hold it high, but they were all smiles and took snapshots, some old grandmother with one hand on the hull of the canoe and Jack got excited and invited them all down to the nearest park along the river so we could take them out for a paddle and the grandmother sat like a queen between us as we moved upriver the thirty or so members of her family following us along the bank. We thought about kidnapping her and something tells me she wouldn't have minded but then I remembered we had to start some serious paddling if we were to get to Cardiff in time so we swung about, pulled into shore and dropped her off and got twenty Japanese business cards for our efforts and a digital film diskette and a couple memorable Polaroids, which put us in a better mood after the pub fiasco.

Finding a place to pitch a tent in London isn't as easy as it sounds but we found a stand of trees in a park, carried the canoe in, climbed a couple trees and hoisted the canoe into the branches and we stayed up there too, our backpacks and all the rest, until after it was dark and whatever park security there was had disappeared before we climbed back down, pitched the tent, set up the gas-stove, cooked a Mallard duck and drank grape-flavoured Koolaid till our piss turned purple.

We decided that we liked London, Jack calling it a new Constantinople, I suppose he meant the Turks which made me crazy hungry for a donair so we camouflaged our campsite and headed off, walking until we found ourselves in Soho and at this point we decided that we didn't like London, we loved it.

The city

The great march of the Redcoats brought peace and order to the leagues in the west. The rough small-town games with their shoot-outs and massacres became a thing of the past. In Winnipeg immigrants arrived by the trainload, a thousand accents, the pouring in Mennonites, Hutterites, Stalactites and Termites changed the face of the prairie, its towns, its cities. Sod was cut, rink-walls were raised and the ancient arctic winds swept unceasing, sculpting dunes of fine snow and all across the land the sound of pucks on boards and the scrape of blades on ice cut through the air like industry.

Those rinks became factories of legends. Slow-talking farmboys with piledriver hands and bale-pitching traps, all slope-shouldered, skated out from the prairie whiteness and into the Hall of Fame. Carving tattoo memories in the soul of a nation, they'd bent into bitter winds all their lives and all those open-to-the-sky sacred temples were changed for roofed-in Art Deco monuments in cities, stepping out into the cool echoing air windless and pure at ice-level, the ice smooth and fast, every kid's dream circling the rink in sliding magic.

What's anything worth these days? The answer is a price-tag and nothing else, all the words clustering the idea of worth, words like heart and pride and success and grit they all have price-tags these days. Used to be a farmer broke his land, faced down blizzards and floods and droughts and making it through was worth itself, now it's compensate me for this, for that, I'll whine louder if you can't hear me, dump every kind of pesticide and herbicide, increase the yield earns more money a whole way of life nothing but a price-tag. And if you don't want to play that way the GMO companies will screw you over big-time and call it Saving the World on TV.

Those hockey boys were green and naïve and the team owners shafted them again and again until the players formed a union so they could shaft each other. They'd forgotten their roots, decided the owners' game was the only one of any value, any worth, and so they learned to play it too and somewhere along the line the fans were forgotten until the fans bought into the same game and everybody sighed and nodded when greed became a right worth fighting for, but it killed the real game, every real game, television brought Hollywood into professional sports and professional sports went rotten. The core of worth got bought out, never stood a chance against money but the myths kept them alive for a long time, struggling against the tide but now even the myth's dead, the withered roots of a starved tree.

There are no dynasties in sports anymore, it's all payrolls. Players with real loyalty are rare. You listen to their vapid interviews and that's what they keep saying, it's a business, ain't it? You do what you do and that's that. But fans are loyal. That's what it means to be a fan. Loyalty. They live and breathe it and once there were sports players living and breathing the same damned thing and the fans understood and appreciated that down in their DNA. Try finding a real dynasty. They're gone and that's no accident. Win everything one year, bottom of the heap the next, nothing's more cynical than professional sports, nothing's more corrupt, nothing's so bloody heartbreaking.

The wall

The effigy squatted, plate-shouldered, the black of the cage-mask gleaming like water on bedrock, the jolt of its bones showing through the ghost-cloth of the perforated jersey. Jack had come back from Jerusalem in some poem he was reciting, down to the woad savages moving grainy and fuzzy in the darkness of the wall's ditch and I was drunk, cursing hearts that don't follow talent when talent is destiny promised, like slapping God in the face. Jack just shrugged his eternal answer when I bring it up, says faith died then sports died so God was gone from the world and all the worship left in a soul had a price-tag tied on with string and the confession booth was a house of mirrors and then he went on about living life out of time, spread-eagled on sarsen stones while briefcase crows picked out his eyes and slivers of descending venous walls down to legs that skate no more, he was drunker than me then someone screamed and from the darkness as we

85

sat straighter three women appeared, they'd dropped E then lost the dancefloor it's here somewhere innit, the effigy rocked and clattered in the hilltop wind scared them silly and we said no we're not Americans we're Canadians you can tell by our dicks and Jack peeled down and showed them his tattooed dong, one of the women or girls maybe hard to tell how old when you're drunk and it's late and chilly and you're suddenly thinking about pressing against something warm, one of the girls reached out and took it in hand not hard to guess what happened then even with Jack piss-drunk it unscrewed, she held it like the Queen her sceptre, Jack said he was ready to annoint the night then she had her leggings down pushing him laughing flat on the grass and mounting him, I gaped, another girl was getting ready to go at him next the third one wanting to see my tattoo I said mine got rubbed off with all the work it's been getting and she reached down to check me out, don't believe any girl who says size doesn't matter she got seriously excited as I got bigger and if I'd had a party-weiner down there she wouldn't have got excited, we rolled around on the grassy slope fucking and grunting and sliding wet until things blurred. I think me and Jack were fucked in turn by all three of them, they talked, comparing the merits of tattooed dick with untattooed dick, sure Jack's was bigger but mine was like a snake, seemed to move around all by itself then the girls got dressed and sat in front of the effigy sharing a spliff, arrayed like a Frazetta painting Jack said, whispering surreal over and over again and then they left and we decided later it was all a dream or maybe ghosts three girls with team jerseys ageless unchanging with Gascoigne or Ince or Beckham on the backs of their shirts moaning with distant desire or maybe the moaning was us drunk Flashman-would-be's, Jack said, who the hell would come out here looking for a disco, or maybe three witches glamouring us and we'd left our seeds in demon sirens, new antichrists all going in the first round of the draft, signing with the Lucifer Covetters, the night was still again, motionless, Jack dug a hole with his hands dropped a bluestone in buried it then spat on his hands to clean the dirt off, we decided we were hungry, Jack said we should kill a rabbit there'd been enough of them earlier, said Norman the Conqueror brought an army of rabbits to England in 1066 and beat up the Wussy or maybe Wessex Saxons, I said bullshit nearly as bad a lie as Hannibal the Elephant who crossed the Alps to wage war on the Romans but he was the one with the degree in history and I couldn't argue with that, I could believe that the Romans had a hell of a time chasing that elephant around all over Italy, Jack explained Hannibal hid in a crowd of Roman grandmothers and only his lack of a moustache gave him away and I said if he'd sat doing nothing saying nothing he could hide in a crowd of Canadians but Jack said he couldn't be saying nothing, he'd have to be apologizing every few minutes to really blend in, sometimes we get nasty and unlikeable but never in company, we'd killed the single malt which was a shame because it was getting colder so I asked again about this anniversary we were celebrating and Jack went all quiet and I was slow but it finally crept up on me and I was silent too, when memories come around it's like switching channels on the world.

The family

Dad's family-line went back to Lower Canada and the battle against the Yanks in Windsor. Some Scottish Highlander with hairy legs and a forehead like a clenched fist on his good days, swinging a claymore like Conan, bits of Yanks flying everywhere, the last stop before a battle is the latrine trench.

The Scotsman had himself a Micmac woman who'd come from an Iroquois village after being stolen from a Huron village, just a slave most of her life until the red-haired giant took her to his own. They built a house in the aspen and birch forest that would one day be Don Mills, a suburb of Toronto. The Scotsman had a cousin or a brother or someone like that who died at Balaclava of dysentery or maybe syphilis, anyway hundreds maybe thousands of children were produced in that house in Don Mills, populating most of southern Ontario except for the Voyageurs and from that family was born the Toronto Maple Leafs, the archrivals of the Montréal Voyageurs who would one day be called the Habitats after the furniture store I guess, then finally the Canadiens, and from this rivalry was born the Separatist Movement in Québec that formed an underground hockey league named the FLQ who played for keeps until the Redcoats marched back from Saskatchewan and restored order, at least until Maurice Richard was benched during the playoffs and the whole city of Montréal went up, riots everywhere, a city in flames, people in Winnipeg could see the red glow at night, the only thing from the East we cheered about.

Was Dad a hockey fan? I don't think so, he was a fan of himself and that's about as far as it went until after the diagnosis when something changed and he worked to make sure Mom enjoyed herself.

She was small and had to sit at the edge of the seat to see the game, her hands folded in her lap and when the Yets scored her face would light up, she'd be on her feet with the rest of us clapping and if I'd been less of a boy more of a man I would have hugged her every one of those times, wishing the Yets would score a hundred thousand goals. I think of those players down on the ice, all the lives surrounding them, focused desire, ravelled threads of destiny, small lives unfolding into the drama, did they ever realize all that hung on their shoulders, cancer-ridden construction workers one end at ice-level, all the kids and grown-ups in wheelchairs, Hedberg used to dip his stick as he wheeled past during warm-up, stop and give someone a puck and say a few words, what kind of heart is that to be ignored in the annals of Canadian hockey according to the CBC. I don't understand, most lives hang on gestures, nine-tenths of the sports stars these days seem to have forgotten that, locked their humanity in their locker in the dressing room, how many visit the children's wing at hospitals these days maybe more than I think, doesn't seem likely though. Sure there's Teemu Selanne, the Jets traded him as if Teemu and Winnipeg were strangers to each other. Jack talks about the rot of cynicism; I guess that's it in a nutshell.

Sometimes the last hugs you're left with are the ones in your head, invented and played and replayed but that's the way of families isn't it, those personal pockets crammed with coloured stones, gewgaws and tidbits, dig your fingers through the grit along the bottom seam find life down there somewhere, wrapped in emotion thick as wool, the hardness underneath is only a reminding estimate, the wool thickens with time, the pockets packed solid as the years pile on.

I don't know what broke Jack. He'd always had his hidden unsmiling self for as long as I can remember. He always sneered at my boyhood demands for justice, constricting joy to those unreal moments on the ice and the heart of the game when he left everybody choking on the snow of his skate blades, those moments in some cosmic dance leaving us mortals gaping in his wake, his gift of humbling everyone, the only times I ever saw him humbled himself was when he listened to a piece of music or looked on some old painting and a few times when we took the canoes around a promontory and the lake opened up in front of us even the kids falling silent, the lichen-skinned bedrock shorelines, the water calmly awaiting our gliding entry into a scene perfectly at home without human beings.

I'm coming with you he said one afternoon as we paddled across Crowduck Lake. *Where?* I asked him. *The United Kingdom. I need a break from universities, buried up to my neck in all that crap and all the other crap besides.*

What other crap?

National identity.

What? Who the fuck cares, Jack?

Do you identify with being Canadian and if you do then what does it mean to you?

God I hated questions like that one, so I paddled unspeaking for a couple minutes, Jack staying silent too, knowing I think slow when I think at all and I try not to most of the time but I finally shrugged and said, What makes me Canadian is what I'm not.

Right, he pounced and I knew I'd stepped into it, his thoughts getting to this first, *right you got it what you're not you're not American you're not Scottish you're not Swedish, it's all an argument of elimination. We all know Americans, loud, friendly, naïve, self-centred, talented, ignorant, cheering too loudly at the wrong things like when Paul Simon sang* Sounds of Silence *at Central Park and everybody cheers when he gets to the line about seeing all the people and he's basically calling them ignorant and they cheer anyway, or like calling the movie* Forrest Gump *the feel good movie of the year when it's probably the saddest story ever filmed, when Americans miss the boat they do it big-time, you gotta hand it to them, they never do anything by halves. So how are Canadians different...well they're too nice too quiet too modest too apathetic, the point is I feel no connection at all but the UK has five hundred thousand years of human history so I've given up on Canadian identity, I'm looking to identify with the species and that's what I'll do in the UK.*

How?

I was thinking of getting tattooed over there.

What kind of tattoo, how's that gonna do anything?

Not sure yet, this island looks good for smallmouths.

Yeah all right, was all I said, getting worried about Jack for the first time, he'd tilted his brain or something but we'd had a sad July anyway and conversations between us had become rare so I left it alone. How can you moan about Canadian identity on the one hand while choking the life out of the myth of hockey with the other but that's Canadians for you right there both the question and the answer and neither sits well in the gut.

If I was American I'd weep on baseball's grave. Same difference.

Winnipeg was falling to pieces, a fuck-you government in for yet another term. Anybody down was kept down, single mothers grew horns dripping evil from their fangs, raising children isn't worth nearly as much as waiting tables, not really work anyway and exorcism was government policy, that was Jack ranting on but you could feel the coldness seeping into the bones. Money buys indifference and self-satisfaction, Jack's girlfriend at the time was waging war against cuts in social services, her name was Luanne and she had a two-year-old boy, was thirty years old and sold sweater-wearing voodoo dolls of the Premier on the corner of Osborne and River, the Welfare people wanted her back working but wouldn't pay for a telephone for her cockroach-infested apartment which was all she could afford to rent with the money allotted her for renting. Who can get a job without a goddamn telephone, what anal puckered bureaucrat decided a phone's a luxury, for fucksake. Jack got thrown out of the social worker's office for ripping the woman's phone from the wall and there was a chance of Luanne losing her son because of health-risks in the apartment they lived in, welcome to despair but nobody batted an eye in Winnipeg, the city had joined the rest of the world, the global economy had the ring in the nose, joined the parade passive and near comatose.

This country's going down the tubes, Mark.

You think England's any better?

No. Farther down the tubes by half. Maybe ten times more fucked up but the point is that makes them that much closer to the brick wall, so the crash will come first there, not in Canada, too much room left, too complacent, don't expect a new paradigm arising in Canada.

What's a paradigm?

A still-folded parachute. Besides England's not my home, the trip down the tubes won't break my heart the way it's doing here.

A friend had just come back from Cardiff, said if you took Winnipeg got rid of all the trees and put it beside the sea you'd have Cardiff. With one big difference. Cardiff was on its way up, Winnipeg's on its way down. Winnipeg's only hope being if the Natives make it their own and even then it may be too late. Jack said the Natives should take over Winnipeg, said it to Lester and he just smiled, what to make of that who knows since a minute later the mall security came over to our table and checked the receipts in the bags of CD's Lester had at his feet. That smile never left him, Jack got loud talking about entering charges of harassment so all three of us got escorted out. Who knows maybe the Natives wouldn't do any better running Winnipeg but they sure as hell couldn't do worse.

I decided on Cardiff when I heard they had a hockey team and an arena and screaming fans. I planned on flying right into Cardiff but Jack talked me into Edinburgh, the distance didn't seem much by Canadian standards, about as far as Calgary to Winnipeg. Never occurred to me there were no straight lines in the United Kingdom or that there were six hundred million cars buses lorries all traversing the wrong side of the road just the driver no passengers.

The wall

One day the monolith will begin to shake. One day the lies we swallow we won't swallow any more. Every bullshit scam we've had shoved down our throats. We'll say no to it all, we'll face down CEO's and the governments fronting them, we'll sneer at the fusillade of words they spew at us, we'll pick sides, put on skates, pick up sticks, drop the puck on centre ice and we'll play, Mark, we'll play our hearts out. We'll play oh we'll play.

Some porthole slid back, the light of joy my brother showed me took my breath away, blinded me, then it was gone, the half-smile punctuated irony or curl of pain fended off to one side and the dark night was back sweeping in from all sides, cold luffing wind swaying the spine of the ridge, the tawny mane silvered colourless now under moon and starlight. The hard bones of Roman industry only hinted at beneath that rumpled command of lines of sight. I was suddenly hungry for history, for the beaten weathered stone fist to inevitably come crashing down, stagger dust into the air, topple the self-satisfied the contempt and wariness on their faces shifting into mortal fear, I wanted forests growing over the ruins obliterating it all, memory and ruins all one.

Some other breed rising from the muck ready to give it a try, do better this time around couldn't do worst.

Savage ghosts gathered at the foot of the ramparts, ready to flood over the wall, they were destruction tearing it down, defilers, the bared filed teeth of old gods, their gods, the promise of armageddon and I understood them then. Knew them in my soul, my silent joining to their war-cries, their triumph in bringing the curtain down into darkness.

Ever loved a woman, Mark? Really loved?

Yeah I guess maybe not sure yeah.

You're expecting her aren't you? In Cardiff. You're expecting her to come and meet you, be with you at last, it's your last, your only faith, you want something anything that one thing in this world to make sense. To work right you want that answer to every question you've asked. Those questions about yourself that you ask without putting into words. Those questions you know the ones.

Yeah I know the ones.

But what if she doesn't come, what if she bails out, too big a risk, too many years difference between you, all that security she has to toss away, it's more to ask than you probably realize.

What do you know about it?

He sighed, turned his face away. Ghost flames rose along the two-street-deep seventy-mile-long town that was once the south side of the wall. Somewhere a baby cried, somewhere a girl lost her virginity, a starved toddler closed its luminous eyes one last time its soul a momentarily hovering cocoon of futility around a withered body that money-men decided wasn't worth feeding, boys oiled guns, death floating in front of their young eyes the way it once floated in front of their father's eyes, their father's, their father's, their father's, and on and on for bloody ever. What we come to each time is what we were every time, the same rules, the same crimes, I understood then the Picts, the Scots, the Attacotti, the Vandals, the Huns, the Magyars, the Saxons, the Vikings, the Apaches, the Mongols, Ostrogoths, Visigoths, Alans, Frisians, Danes, Geats, all of them a single vengeance dream what I understood now was winter's arctic blood in my veins.

Birds started peeping small and uncertain in the greying light. The battles of the night were cooling ashes and dust, history asleep in the mist once more. I dreamed canoeing, cutting still water, dark, clear, rock-bottomed silence, the flitting shadows of fish beneath sliding passings, turkey-vultures circling, lifting in the morning sky overhead. I dreamed anticipation in the arena, the moments before the ritual starts unfolding mystery, the hard painted wooden seats, the sticky floor underfoot, spilling coffee on my hands as I handed the cup over into her hands. I dreamed skate-edges firm on the ice inside the crease, the sensed awareness of the goal posts framing my back, the netting slack. I dreamed watching dawn rise on Hadrian's Wall, swifts taking to the air, the chrome glint of distant traffic, the snapping stones of tires on gravel in the country lane behind us, columns of foreign soldiers trooping into view with spades to dig a ditch and cut stones with African graffiti, the Sixth Legion who marched out into the wildlands and vanished or maybe it was the Fourth Legion, Jack told me but I've forgotten like they're forgotten. What we know passes into what we knew, each moment worth cataloguing desperate. I watched an old woman crying in a cafe once as she went through photos just collected from the chemist's, smiling and crying all at once she had no secrets then, I knew her then for that moment who wouldn't. She in the past me in the present a chain's link closing briefly but forever, these are the chains holding us here on mortal earth, the reminder of sanity in a café. Questions and answers without words, maybe the only ones worth a damn.

The city

I played games, I taught kids in hockey camps the science of minding the net and faith in fluke, I taught kids rock-climbing and cross-country skiing and canoeing and kayaking and bush-survival, making snares, collecting water, I taught Caroline how to skate dreaming of sex on blades in some private arena. The Jets were in their play-off run, the prize was in sight. I guess you could say I was happy, in a way.

But it couldn't last. One morning winter was over, summer had arrived, the machines rolled into the streets collecting sand and gravel, the trees went from bare to leaved and the game subsided. The autumn to come would be in the NHL. The WHA was gone and the rape consummated. The Jets management held onto the wrong players, waved goodbye to the best and drafted a thug on skates to herald the team's entry into the NHL. Mom's interest waned, our family wandered in different directions, the era was past.

These are grey memories. The team's history – failure, mediocrity, bad management, great players, broken-hearted past glories crushed down into dust, only a few names to mark brilliance. Hawerchuk, Zhamnov on his good nights, Teemu Selanne, then some better than average players, some loyal, most kneeling before the dollar, too many losses, quick exits in the play-offs, the team going deeper into the red as player salaries climbed. Rich American teams buying stars but still failing to win the cup but pushing ever higher the salaries, then the ticket prices, then Mighty Duckism like salt in a much-lacerated body twitching the limbs. The myth was being crucified – just one more professional sport up on the cross bleeding its own sins.

Caroline pulled us into pain, her delivering it, me taking it, we were spiralling down into a dark world that was its own crucifixion. She said guilt drove her, guilt turned her on, one night she stood naked before me, called her cigarette butt Conscience, dropped it onto the bathroom floor and crushed it under her heel. Poets call that eloquent though a better word might be scary. I probably should have run at that point but I didn't and I paid for it that night and afterward she broke down in my arms. I didn't know what to do, never had to deal with anything like that before. She wept, her whole body shuddering, kissed my wounds, said she loved me and was punishing me because she'd fallen in love but it had stopped turning her on and I sighed with relief, the only thing about it turning me on was her being turned on doing it, and she said the sex was over, making love had taken its place or rather was about to, and she spread herself over me kissing and stroking and caressing and we fucked slow almost gentle, and hell's fires turned cool, snow melting soft under us. I actually felt safe in her arms. That was something new, damn near strange, that moment of change is usually a threshold stumbled over like clearing a set of rapids, gliding out on smooth water, you end up setting sights on the next set, just trying to catch your breath, arch out the ache in your spine, before the current tugs then yanks you into the next set. I didn't understand any of that at the time, I thought the calm would just deepen, carry us peacefully ever onward.

Jack says civilization's exactly the same, stumbling over those thresholds, fooling itself that the next calm will be forever. Youth doesn't apply, leaving stupidity plain and simple. Jack says each human condition is just a microcosm of the species condition, which if it's true is kind of depressing but that's all history anyway, there's not much in

WHEN SHE'S GONE

the way of calm these days, it's all speeding up, no time to take a breath, the night on the wall celebrated the last night of peace before the storm of war, before the wall was overrun. I'm slow but that's what Jack meant, I'm sure of it sure of it now.

The arena

Mom slowed climbing the stairs to the greys. We were reminded of sickness and it made us quiet as we took our seats. Both teams were on the ice warming-up, skating, taking shots on their goalies. I raised the binoculars found Caroline's husband in his seat all alone. I knew Caroline was in the concessions area chain-smoking in new clothes since she'd become what Jack calls Rubinesque but I called all curves, rounded everywhere you could think of. Her husband, whose name was Michael but he used Mack, a buyer and seller in commodities, no kidding what a surprise, made more money in a month than I did in year. Him just sitting there all alone reminded me that I'd never thought about a career, something beyond hockey and taking kids canoeing or leading them up a cliff-face. Jack was going into law or history or medicine – he hadn't decided, so I tried thinking about my future but all I could think of was Caroline's round belly, the folds on either side, the usual problem when I tried thinking, the story of my life, I end up hanging on something, working it and working it again, always swinging round back to it until my mind is exhausted, and I wondered what I'd been trying to think about in the first place.

Besides, Caroline was standing out there flicking ash, numbing her lungs with a vibrator up her snatch, four AA EverReady batteries humming my name slick in a sea of desire and she was working those muscles, God could she work those muscles, the ones inside, she could take a drag on a cigarette with those muscles, exhale slow, she was working those ones now and as the crowds gathered, line-ups at the beer stand, hotdogs, popcorn, Cokes, ice cream bars all bought and consumed around her, she'd wait till the anthem was being played before heading into the bathroom into a stall and make herself come sitting on the toilet.

I watched her take her seat beside her husband after the anthem was done. Saw or maybe just imagined the flush on her cheeks, her

Mack was disgusted these days, the extra thirty pounds on her an investment gone sour. I watched her sit knees together, hands folded on her lap waiting for the period to end, when she was off again. I didn't go down, too risky, besides I was keeping Mom company while Jack went for coffee, for her popcorn, for me and himself two Cokes and ice cream bars, me and Mom discussed the game, the team, all that had been done to the Jets. She really didn't have many words in that discussion, just nodding to my heated analysis and I wondered what it was like, exchanging seats exchanging bodies looking out from her eyes, the game her two big sons, the country she still saw as foreign after all these years, her blood going wrong inside her body, the business having gone into receivership, equipment sold off, saying goodbye and sorry to all her workers, her two sons, her two sons taking her to the games, her husband back working and making enough to meet ends, and I saw from weariness the life behind the life ahead and I didn't say much for a while. It was years before I turned all that over, her two sons that were her love, her pride, the sheer survival that was worth something, worth more than you'd think, the solid promise of lives and family. All that she knew and all that she thankfully didn't know, and all that she knew that we never knew, and how a life's tapestry makes new patterns once you start folding it up.

The Jets scrambled everywhere on the ice in hopeless pursuit, another game down the tubes, a dance of pathos Jack said his half-smile tightening. Frustration was steam in the air, twelve thousand Winnipeggers in Greek masks of dismay memories sniping at them in heartless malice. I went down to buy Mom a cup of coffee, got in line at a concession and there he was beside me, his eyes flat chips of slate eyeing me up and down then locking them with mine. Mack standing there in his Italian leather brown winter coat hands in his pockets.

The wall

We wandered back into our camp near dawn. Jack had hooked up with a fluorescent-orange-haired Jamaican in seven-inch spike heels. I wasn't even sure she was a woman though Jack assured me she was. Either way she was beautiful beyond belief. *Fully accoutred Mark, as you can see she's a princess of Constantinople, her name's Sophia.*

When she's old and withered I'll call her Hagia Sophia. We're getting married. Do you think it'll last? She loves my accent, I love hers, she says her brothers will beat my lights out but together we'll shake hands with the Queen, pose for snapshots. That'll make everything all right. What do you think?

She into tattoos?

That's what caught her eye in the first place. She had to see if they were just painted on or for real now she knows there's this luminosity in her eyes.

That's because she's stoned, Jack.

No another luminosity behind that luminosity.

What if she's a man has her dick wrapped around and taped up won't you be surprised.

It's the heels got you suspicious. She's all woman I'm besotted all aflutter with amorous desire best of all she's never been to university couldn't afford it her intelligence is natural and sharp as a whip she reads more books in one month than you've done since Grade 4.

That's not saying much.

You're right. She's erudite and intimidating and she's got huge tits, an ass perfectly designed for water-retention in tropical climates, day-glo hair and pierced nipples. What more could a man ask for and if that's not enough she prefers Alice Munro to Margaret Atwood any day of the week so there.

What she's bi?

Munro and Atwood are Canadian writers.

Are they bi?

I could have found my own day-glo nipple-pierced water-retentive bi if I'd wanted to or anybody else if I'd a mind to the big city's nightlife knew how to live. I could probably even have found an Atwood fan though I had no interest in doing so. God what would we talk about? So Jack led Sophia into our camp, her spike heels skewering worms and slugs and she tottered about muttering *gorgeous* as the sky lightened revealing mist on the heath and Black Death victims dancing ring around the posey though they dispersed as sunlight burned through the park. I crawled into the tent while Jack and Sophia fucked on his spread-out sleeping bag under some bushes with hanging red flowers that looked like women's private parts. We all woke sleepy-eyed when a file of uniformed school girls trooped in to study Nature, the teacher arriving gape-mouthed to hustle them away. Sophia had more twigs in her hair than a beaver lodge. Jack said he liked the effect so she left them in laughing saying she had a hedgerow head and should move out into the country. I asked do they sell spike-heeled wellies and she said yes which shut me up so I moped groggy packing up camp needing to pee awful bad while Jack talked about the planned visit to the Queen. But we had to take a detour to Cardiff first in this canoe and she said *fab when do we leave?* just as I started emptying my ballast tanks in the bushes.

Back on the River Thames we rode a tide that threw us inland. When we crossed some mudflats a shopping cart ripped a fifteen inch gash in the canvas. We pulled in to shore, upended the canoe and eyed the damage.

No repair kit, Jack. What now?

I see pine trees.

I see birch.

Problem solved.

I'll build the fire.

Jack walked off, Sophia staying with me as I gathered deadwood and lit a fire. We were in someone's backyard. We watched the curtains moving for a while then an old man with a green jacket and war medals on the breast came out, taking ten thousand inch-long steps to reach us, *Good morning I see you're in a bit of bother fancy a cup?*

Oh yes, said Sophia showing a third kind of luminosity in her eyes, and that old man showed us a fine set of false teeth in a bright grin and eyes glinting like a wolverine's *I'm laughing* stare and she sat him down on his lawnchair, took charge of the tea-making. Alma his wife was inside and would help. So off went Sophia swaying sensuous incarnate and Major eyed her openly then grinned at me and winked saying *You've done fine there, lad* and I shook my head said she's with my brother Jack. Mine's waiting for me in Cardiff.

That's a fine canoe you have there, cedar ribs if I'm not mistaken.

Dead right, Major. You're the first Brit to call it a canoe not a kayak.

Spent two years in Canada, training your blessed volunteer army. There was a full-blooded Blackfoot in my regiment, not that he knew much about canoes being from Alberta, but he knew the difference between a canoe and an Eskimo kayak.

Bet he knew about horses.

Indeed he did and it's all he and I talked about. How do you plan on fixing your canoe?

Pine pitch and birchbark. Trim the tear heat the sap slap on the birchbark let it cool and that's that probably the only advantage to using a canvas it takes the pitch. We prefer aluminum though they're more of a sweat to fix.

How on earth could you damage an aluminium canoe?

Run rapids, plough into a rock can turn the canoe into an accordion then you have to hammer the folds flat fit a new thwart and your seventeen footer's now a fifteen footer. Sluggish because you've had to flatten the keel where it snapped but it's serviceable enough. The worst is when one flies off the roof-rack at seventy miles an hour on the highway gets all twisted around the prow bent to the left the rest of the canoe bent to the right. That's a hard pig to paddle.

I can imagine.

Sophia came down with Alma on one arm, planted her in a chair, went back up, came down again with tea, toast, marmalade and biscuits – what a Canadian calls cookies. Jack showed up in time to dig in with the rest of us. Then I scraped pine sap into a small pot from our campkit, put it on the fire, roughed down the edges of the gash with a river rock while Jack got Major to tell the stories behind each medal. Alma had probably heard them a thousand times but she smiled and nodded a real trooper. By the time I'd finished patching the canoe Major was ready to adopt Jack and had listened carefully when Jack said he wanted to shake hands with the Queen. He said quietly he'd see what he could do about that. Jack shook Major's hand, the only one he had left since 1944. We loaded up the canoe again, a big white patch on its hull surrounded in dark brown pitch and off we went with them waving from their yard.

The city

I'm getting fat so he won't want me anymore.

Is it working?

I don't know but I've started enjoying being fat. I don't get stared at as much anymore and I like that.

Everybody except the detective, he still stares.

His name is Ralph.

You talked to him?

I found his weekly bill, on Mack's desk in the study. Ralph Anderson. Anderson, a Swede, perfect for a private investigator.

Why is that perfect?

Unnoticeable. National Lampoon said Canadians are just like Swedes only more boring. I think they were joking but you see I'm Canadian with Swedish blood and maybe Ralph is, too.

You're not boring.

You're not fat.

Overweight, then.

Dull, then.

You're not even dull.

Are we having our first spat?

We were walking through Assiniboine Park, the huge pavilion rising above leafless branches. The place looked glorious from the outside but was nothing inside but two cheesy fastfood concession stands inside a vast waste of space. The promise on the outside not delivered on the inside. It was a Winnipeg landmark just like the park itself, its sweeps of lawn in summer mosquito-free; Malathion-soaked grass where children played and probably started down the road to MS, is there a connection, no one knows but I'm suspicious, and dogs crapped, but now fresh snow had fallen, hardly a soul in the park this was before the toboggan ramps were set up. A year before maybe more or maybe I just don't remember them being there, don't remember any one else in the park, I was walking with Caroline. I was playing a game that afternoon industrial league had just given her a skating lesson the equipment in my car parked in the zoo parking lot it was a gutless Chevy Vega I used to time it running out of gas as it rolled into our drive then next morning I'd be in our garage finding something anything that smelled flammable pouring it into the carb firing the car up clouds of various coloured smoke backing out and labouring via back alleys and quiet streets to the Esso station on Academy usually making it all the way before gasping silent, though sometimes I just left it wherever carried the gas can to the station bought five bucks of gas trudged back and off I went wherever I was going.

The bison and musk oxen were in their paddocks at the zoo standing around looking bored, the caribou skittish. We circled around went in through the gates watched the polar bears swimming in their pool; I guess this was something lovers did walking around in the zoo. Used to see couples all summer wandering holding hands and staring at animals in cages. What's the fascination I wonder, couples and caged beasts eyeing each other, the jabbering monkeys playing chase the tail. Well, anyway, there we were walking holding hands talking.

Ever heard of the Cardiff Devils?

No.

A hockey team. In Wales. Ice hockey's taking off in the UK, draws more fans than rugby, lots of Canadian players head over, sign up, ones that couldn't make the NHL. Lots of European players too Finns and Swedes and Germans.

When are you going?

I was thinking for next season, trying out.

I got fat for nothing. I got fat to just end up alone.

I want you to leave him, come to Cardiff.

How can I do that? I would have to go as a tourist I wouldn't be able to stay.

You would if they signed me because you'd be with me.

How much pay would you get?

Don't know for certain but enough for us.

What if you didn't make the team?

I'll make the team.

What about your back?

It's been fine, all season. Just fine. Money's not a problem you know that.

Cardiff. What would I do there? What language do they speak?

English mostly and you could do what you want there, anything you want.

I have no hobbies no interests nothing.

You must have some, you just haven't mentioned them yet.

You tell me, then.

Birdwatching making driftwood furniture silver jewellery tie-dyeing collecting fossils gardening having babies.

Babies?

Why not?

You want to get me pregnant?

Sure.

When?

Whenever you want.

Are you serious?

Sure why wouldn't I be?

We were standing outside the Tropical House and I was thinking of iguanas, not sure why. She lit a cigarette and stood thinking looking around. If we went in to the Tropical House after she'd finished her cigarette we'd get crapped on by some tropical bird.

Mack doesn't have sex with me at all anymore.

So stop taking the pill.

I've thought about it already.

We got back into the car, drove to the Charter House, went into our usual room and fucked like the world was ending. I came in her like I was firing bullets from my cock to challenge fate. We didn't discuss babies afterward while she reclined sprawled half across me smoking and I did her slow with my fingertips until she came shuddering. After that we still didn't mention babies, the conversation was left behind as if it had never happened.

The city

Each day Winnipeg looked smaller to me, all the movers and shakers just big fish in a tiny pond. Jack said it was even worse at his university. He was taking English courses at St. Paul's and he was sick listening to hack academics, would-be literary stars, dreaming world fame. All those professors hanging on modernity's edge with their nails dug in, the observers of trends not yet dead, they don't just observe, they dissect and dissection kills.

The city is a string of days and nights in my mind each one grinding up against the next in line. It creates the illusion of never changing except for the accumulation of ground-up dust that the clean-up machines never quite take all away. Scenes wait like postcards in my brain tacked onto corkboard. So much of our lives now locked unlit unmoving in diesel-stained clay with fresh days and nights grinding away one after the other in the life of this city.

On the Rideau Canal

"Well folks we're coming to you tonight from the broadcast booth overlooking the Rideau Canal in the heart of the nation's capital. At ice-level it's a balmy minus 6 degrees Celsius this evening – a perfect night for the final game in what's been a hard-fought contest."

"Hard-fought, Foster? Most folks would say downright vicious, I think."

"They just might at that, Eddie. Folks, the voice you just heard was that of our guest commentator, Eddie Broadbent, who's here with us tonight to offer his insight into the game. Well, Eddie, the teams are lining up around centre-ice for the drop of the puck. Arm raised, referee Rene Levesque faces the goal-judge to his right, awaiting the signal ... and there it is, now it's to the goal-judge on the left.... The lights flash. The puck's in Rene's hand, the two centres face off ... and away we go!

"The puck's fired into the Liberals' end and wily Chretien collects it ... rounds the net and headman's it to Trudeau ... the clever veteran crosses the centre line weaving right weaving left ... and there's a nifty drop-pass to Pearson – whoah what a hit by young Mulroney! Pearson had his head down, that's for sure, never saw it coming....

"Mulroney passes 'cross ice to Clark he's trying to work his way along the left boards but Trudeau's all over him ... and the whistle goes.... Whew, Eddie, that was some bodycheck wasn't it? Glad you're not down there, eh?"

"Well I'd gladly face a hit or two if it meant playing in the final, Foster."

"Of course you would, Eddie, we all know that. There's some delay here, it seems.... Coach Diefenbaker's looking to be pulling one of his usual stunts, slowing the game down, that's quite a tirade he's on with Levesque. Any idea what it's about, Eddie?"

"I'd guess it's who gets last change on the lines, Foster. That's Deef's usual beef."

"The linesman have joined in the discussion now. Al the Eagle and Kenny Dryden – two veteran mediators there to give Rene a hand. It's Al's last season, as you know – well now Trudeau's joined in the argument, too – will we ever get back to the game? Is that a restless crowd down there, Eddie?"

"Sure is, Foster."

"I see Joey Clark's keeping his distance – he really has lost confidence since he was stripped of the Captaincy, wouldn't you say, Eddie?"

"Confidence sure is a tricky thing, Foster. He should've stayed at centre, I think. That move to right wing did him in...."

"Well you *would* say that, Eddie, hah hah – oh my Trudeau's just made a rude gesture at Rene and that could result in a misconduct penalty! Tempers are high down there that's for sure! Not an auspicious start between the Progressive Conservative Pirates and the Liberal Longshots, we'd have to say, eh Eddie? Do you think your New Democrat Ne'erdowells' could have managed the Pirates' intimidation tactics any better?"

"We're there for the fans, Foster, not for any of this kind of grandstanding."

"And there goes Pierre Elliot Trudeau, off to the sinbin for the next ten minutes. What will that do to the Longshots' chances of jumping into an early lead, Eddie?"

"Shouldn't hurt them at all, so long as they keep the play in centre ice – you can't beat the Pirates by working up the wings, as we well know. You've got to take command of the middle ground, but you can be sure they'll do their best to usurp that position. The real bone of contention is Martin, of course. I mean, buying the captaincy was a bit rich. And then there's Harper up in the stands – see him, Foster?"

"I sure do."

"On the sidelines as always."

"Well now, Eddie, he has a healthy following, and if they know what's good for them they'd better *stay* healthy!"

"The rich ones will do all right, you can count on that."

"So here on the ice … two teams. How do they match up defensively, Eddie?"

"Both surprisingly weak, I'd have to say. At the same time both teams have a virtually identical defensive strategy –"

"Which is?"

"Basic fear-mongering. Pure intimidation. Strong positional play on occasion, and a lot of dumping it out to relieve the pressure. Once you've got them scrambling and reeling, they're vulnerable."

"If only the Ne'erdowells could have *capitalized* on their chances, Eddie, hah hah."

"We don't like that word, Foster."

"Well while Rene tries to re-establish some order down below, why not compare the teams' offensive abilities?"

"Both are very offensive. They play emotionally, Foster –"

"Same for Harper's Reforminists or whatever they're called these days out in the wild west. Meaning momentum is everything. Who do you think has gained the momentum as a result of this fracas?"

"I'd have to say the Pirates, Foster. Clark's come out looking like a level-headed and reasonable ambassador of the game. Mulroney did well under his guidance for a while there."

"The Longshots still have Chretien, don't forget, or at least his legacy, and anyway he was riding the pine for a long time before he got his chance to shine. Had he earned those years of Captaincy, I wonder?"

"Does it matter? Martin's here now with all the greenbacks and unbridled ambition. He's got the C sewn on his jersey these days and that's what counts. Can he lead the team to victory the way Chretien did? We'll –"

"Oh my a fight's broken out! And now the benches have cleared! What started out as a tussle has turned into a full-scale brawl! And Trudeau's back on the ice – he has Rene in a headlock! Mackenzie King's pounding Pearson into a pulp! And there's Chretien and Mulroney going at it toe to toe! Good Lord!"

"Hey! Isn't that Don Cherry?"

"Yes! Don Cherry's come down out of the stands – he's wailing through everybody with his sights set on Trudeau! Harper's down from the stands, too, but he's slipping all over the ice, and there's Preston Manning, trying to mediate. And Joey Clark – oh my isn't he confused – he's jumped on Mulroney's back and looks to be trying to scratch his team-mate's eyes out! What old wounds are being re-opened there, eh? Eddie, can you believe – Eddie? Eddie! My God, folks, Eddie Broadbent's down on the ice!

"We're now taking a station break, folks, to give time to our sponsors. Let's hope that when we come back some order will have been restored – I now think the only man who can stop this fiasco might be Elijah Harper, and we'll tell you all about that Manitoba star when we come back. This is Foster Hewitt, the Voice of Hockey on CBC Radio...."

The family

I have these dreams, Mark. Scary ones. I'm skating and skating faster and faster my legs aching I'm gasping don't know if I'm trying to get away or going to I'm flying over the ice should feel like magic but it doesn't everything's white on all sides I'm just skating.

We sat on four billion year old bedrock beside the cool motionless dark water of Crowduck Lake, our last trip surrendering our hold on this forested scraped-rock lake-filled place we were on an island the stars burned overhead a moon rising slow over serrated treeline bats flitting over the lake.

I dream making saves.

Do you make them or does the puck get past you?

The puck never gets past me.

That's a good dream brother hold onto it.

Yours sucks.

I know. Mom's in Stage 3 you know.

I'd guessed. That fever those bruises on her arms what the hell are those?

Cell walls are breaking down blood seeps under the skin it's not good.

It's been a bad month.

It has.

Dad was dead, massive heart attack car into a tree, we were coping. Mom had flown back to Sweden her first trip back since she'd come to Canada she had things to do she said. We didn't know what but it was good she went. The sinking house was a cave full of memories, the mix of good and bad confusing stirring unease in my head. Must have been worse for her I'm sure it was. For a moment there Jack and I were like kids punched into adulthood face to face with absence a presence we'd taken for granted though never entirely not since the time he'd run out on us but the habits of expectation easily slip in when you're not looking and now the presence was suddenly gone.

We'd done the portage in the morning the up and down one from Big Whiteshell Lake to Crowduck. Jack found a stone arrowhead at the Big Whiteshell end I collected wild ginger in the swampy bit at the Crowduck end we'd pushed hard crossing Big Whiteshell against a headwind water-skiers on all sides but there was no road access to Crowduck no cabins except for the fishing lodges the lake was clean the only sounds natural ones we'd head up to Saddle Lake climb up onto the ridges of bedrock where a past forest fire had scoured the granite pink there was a high fire risk going on the park was officially closed in the interior but that crap never bothered us we could slip the Norsemans wheeling overhead never get spotted and have the lake to ourselves.

It was a good time to be away from the city from the house from everything a good time to be paddling smooth waters not saying much just paddling the steady dip pull and curl the sky clear except for hawks eagles and turkey-vultures we'd seen too much of it go away to take it for granted all the childhood haunts full of people now fake beaches set up trailer-park fine-weather campers with their CD players and televisions and beer cases, sitting in lawn chairs, the end of the wilds was a growing plague. We knew what we had there on Crowduck Lake and Saddle Lake, climbing up onto the ridge, seeing for miles, pinpointing the greying haze.

There's a smoke like we figured, Jack.

More than one. Spot fires. If those three link up we're cut off our return route.

Unless we go back to Eaglenest then head north we can go the Winnipeg River down to Sturgeon Falls and reach the highway from there.

A hell of a lot of paddling we've got three days worth of food not enough.

So we fish.

Either that or we let ourselves get seen by a spotter plane.

Do we wait for Lester and Frank? They may have turned back with the closing.

Give them till tomorrow morning and if they haven't showed we'll mark the camp and head on north. Fuck spotter planes.

If we push any at all chances are they won't be able to catch up not many people can out-paddle us when we're pushing hard.

We go our usual pace if they can't catch us they can follow us or maybe paddle an extra hour or two.

When boreal forest goes up, the heat comes on the wind, the tiger flies go wild biting big chunks from your back and shoulders everywhere you can't see. The sun turns copper even midday there's a grit at the back of the throat and eyes sting and the heat builds as the wind builds. Air's sucked in mile-wide curling swaths the forest goes still wreaths of smoke roll in at dusk and at night you can see the orange glow the reflections against the underbellies of clouds and smoke you start eyeing the skylines the high ridges for the lick of flame the new smokes the world turns into hell.

Late that night camped at Saddle Lake the water calm Lester and Frank swung their canoe into our tiny inlet the Plains Cree had arrived grinning and cool and we met them grinning and cool and nothing more needed to be said you see Hollywood Yank cool on TV the shades the skateboards the baggy pants well forget it we were powdered ice under a glowing red sky we were Londoners during the Blitz the four of us sitting on the bedrock the water lapping beyond our boots watching the world burning we'd caught and cooked four walleye sat drinking instant coffee with Amaretto not one of us hadn't fought a forest fire there in the front lines with shovels and chainsaws and water-tanks strapped to our backs sweat and ashes and a new pair of hiking boots to show for it at the end when the decision was made *we've beaten it its beaten us* and it was time to pack up and go.

Chances were we'd be facing down this one before long, once we were spotted maybe airlifted and for our sins we'd be there dancing on glowing coals the primal battle renewed one more time we all knew it were ready for it and appreciating this time before it happened which was that night beside the black waters on Saddle Lake.

They're thinking the fire will jump Winnipeg River. Lester was big and hulking in his faded jackshirt a dimmer grey in the darkness his voice low casual far apart.

Bad news if that happened. Jack was lying flat on his back staring up at the grainy clouds reflecting red. *We'd have to turn back make for the east shore of Eaglenest.*

What about Whiteshell River? Sure some of it you have to drag your canoe through the rushes but we could make for Grassy Lake. I mean there's nothing but bush on the east side of Eaglenest.

Not a chance, Mark.

Lester and Frank were shaking their heads too. Lester said, *Fire on both sides of the Whiteshell. I say we should still try the Winnipeg River, it's a wide river even if the fire jumps it we can paddle down the middle.*

Fuck, I said. It sounded reasonable but weird things happen to air close to forest fires gets hard to breathe.

The oxygen would burn out, Jack said. *If the fire jumped it'd be a river of death.*

Find a swamp, Frank said. We all looked over at him he was tall thin in some seminary school training to be a priest played pool like the devil he shrugged *Four feet down in the peat let the fire roll over the burning down there goes slow won't come till after knew of a guy did that in Yellowstone.*

Say goodbye to the canoes and our gear.

The canoes might survive, Jack. They might.

Annealed. Brittle. Anyway I don't think the fire will jump. So long as the wind stays westerly if it turns comes up from the south we'll be in trouble but I don't think it will hardly ever does unless there's a thunderstorm.

We'd have trouble seeing a storm coming in all this smoke.

True but we'd hear it.

We decided to try the Winnipeg River. The hours went on, I told Lester and Frank my wolf story they just nodded, we then talked hockey, the games we'd seen, the games we'd played, and for ten minutes the smoke spread in a tear showing us the moon full and red as blood. We talked omens Frank had been dreaming of hell since he was a kid taken from his grandparents who'd been raising him, had his hands rapped by his white guardians for speaking Cree, burning tobacco on flat rocks in the prairie giving thanks to the spirits and now he feared God, *no surprise there* Jack muttered, and dreamt of hell and a moon like a ripped-out heart in a mist of blood, *what's to come*, Frank said, *has already been. Dreams live outside time, we've sat here before under this crimson light but before was just the now, the now just remembered before it had arrived.*

Jack asked Frank, *What the hell kind of priest are you planning to be?* and Frank grinned and said, *My Grandfather's but it's important to know and understand the white god, he was born of tribes, too, you know, some tribes in a desert with goats and God was heat and fire and fate like He Himself had twisted under the sun, gone mad with thirst and paranoia and God's eyes were on you as you tiptoed on hot bedrock, everything bleached, He likes scouring things clean, the white God, like a bucket of bleach on an ant nest.*

God doesn't play pool, Jack said and I wondered what that meant but Frank seemed to know, grunting agreement and saying, *Gambling's a sin. You gamble in the desert you usually die, greed and coveting are anathema to tribes that need to share and co-operate to survive, pretty much the same with our people, but you take away the need to co-operate in survival and you end up running casinos, fighting the taxman. God's gone soft, rewards greed and coveting now, just ask the televangelists.*

Mark enjoys coveting.

Fuck off.

Mark does what Dad did only Mark thinks it's different but it isn't it's the same he just won't let himself see it true.

Her old man's an asshole.

That make any difference?

Does to me.

Lester and Frank stopped saying much they knew it was none of their business Jack knew that too he was just being a prick and yeah he had a point it's funny how things just come on you when you're not thinking and before you know it everything's changed in your life the goalposts keep moving but at night I dreamed making saves nothing but saves.

The arena

You're the one. I've known it was you for a long time. You've ruined my life, you know.

Wasn't much I could say to that, just nod, it was true I suppose. Joni Mitchell sang a line in my head but I just nodded, meeting Mack's thin-slit eyes, the flicker of something in them for just a moment then nothing again.

You've got me thinking. About when she's gone. I've seen you play, son, playing in goal. Been in the stands watching you. Been to every one of your games, watching you watching your every move all season. He went silent now watching me. I was amazed I'd never seen him in the stands hardly packed arenas the games I'd played in but I didn't doubt him. *You've ruined my life.*

I nodded again.

He shifted weight, his hands still in his pockets looking up at me. *I've got some advice for you, son.*

All right.

Your glove hand drops. Gets lazy. If a shooter picks the top left corner the shooter scores because you can't bring your glove up in time. Keep that glove higher.

The way I figure it, if a shooter can pick that corner he deserves to score.

Generous of you.
Maybe.
Well. He looked away. *Treat her well.*
I do my best.
I know that, I see it in your game.

He walked away back to his seat. I went to the concession stand, bought Mom a coffee two cream one sugar. Mom said thanks.

The wall

The ghosts came down from the north in the thousands milling taunting cursing below the wall, our goaltender effigy facing them from the rampart, clanking armour mask snarling down on the enemy, darkness was promised and a sword waited in answer.

The south waited trembling, exposed, the empire rotted from the inside, the legions taken by a would-be Emperor to Gaul, the wall was the only barrier the only defence. Roman citizens in villas in Surrey and Kent buried coins in their yards, in the fields at night, the darkness was coming, nights of fire murder and rape. The end was nigh wasn't it just.

The city

The word was out, the city wouldn't cough up for a new arena, the Jets were leaving: they were off to St. Paul, who'd already lost an NHL team and didn't seem much interested in getting a new one, the Jets were off to Jacksonville, off to Phoenix wherever the wherever being to the States, being leaving Winnipeg, the threat long talked about talked about again this time for real. In the city a groundswell had begun, the media, then the politicians slowly joining the fray, the Québec Nordiques were gone too off to Colorado, the Hartford Whalers soon to leave down to Carolina, the Edmonton Oilers talk of selling the team, the old reminders of the WHA eagerly awaiting burial and gone like it never was now. Like it never existed, but the story wasn't just the ex-WHA teams, it was Canadian teams, the low Canadian dollar, the high U.S. dollar the reluctance to subsidize, establish sharing schemes on profits, the south tugged at our myth. The NHL was delivering to Winnipeg its message: *Winnipeg you're nothing in the scheme of hockey, nothing in the eyes of the NHL, your fans are a drop in the ocean, who gives a shit about your loss, who really gives a shit. Face up to reality and reality is the face you're looking at, and that face belongs to us, just transfer your allegiance, nothing to it, you'll still buy our league ... its products, you'll still watch the games, the play-offs, you'll still live and breathe our game because it's the only game left. You won't walk away, you'll bite it down and play along, it's the way of the modern world and you're fucking nothing, fucking nothing.*

Winnipeg, you're fucking nothing.

It's just the way of the world, Jack said. Was it any better long ago, who can say but these days the lesson is clear, cynicism takes us all in the end and the end is only a stop in a series of ends going on till you're dead. With history you can look back cool and detached, you can be patronizing and cynical, reading the story of the species as a succession of surrenders a list of failures blind stumbling false promises every lie revealed in due course but what's the point reading history like that if only to prove that present misery is par for the course and should be swallowed by one and all why? Well because it's just the way of the world.

Round and round the city goes, up down down up this side that side, just a collection of buildings, a mass of people each in their own cars, their own houses, their own lives, each competing against each other and against some faceless mass, some thing without a name corrosive like acid eating at your insides day in day out, that's all a city is and ever will be, the mass never rises up, never shakes its head, shaggy, shaking sleep from its red-rimmed eyes. The city dwells in restless slumber for all eternity, sly leeches sucking blood from its exposed flanks.

Massive forces with offices in LA, in New York, in Geneva, oversee a herd of cities legion in number, the herd in a global field, and so long as the cud gets chewed the teats get yanked the occasional throat gets slit, the herd goes where it's driven, does what it's told and the offices get redecorated twice a year hallelujah *it's just the way of the world, friends, that's all it is.* Two cities get in a scrap, sell them both guns, sell them an arena, a few cities get uppity isolate them till they starve, a few starving cities ask for more, give it to them then bleed them regularly, call it *interest payments.* And if a city wants to play, sure thing so long as you got the cash. There's no lie in this picture, hearts and souls mean nothing children's dreams are auctioned off along with the children themselves those that don't die anyway, and it's too bad but lots of them die, it's the way of the world. Easy to say when you're sitting on a mountain of food, selling stamps no one can afford to buy.

The Jets were leaving Winnipeg, just one more kick in the balls. Used to it yet?

The Man who stole New York

It's an old story now and the older stories get, the less they mean, really mean, I mean. But here it is.

The heart of hockey straddled the border of Canada and the States. Six teams: Montréal, Toronto, Detroit, Chicago, Boston and New York. The great teams of old, the giants of hockey history. Cities that knew all about winter, the snow, the blizzards, the ice. The pure heart of hockey.

The New York Rangers were once giants in the game, but so many years had passed since they last won the Stanley Cup it seemed there wasn't a fan still alive who remembered the ticker-tape parade down Fifth Avenue in those old days of glory.

Until one lone Canadian arrived in town, walked Madison Avenue to the Garden and there donned the jersey of the Rangers' Captain. He was a huge man, wide, muscled, his eyes like chips of obsidian. He could skate. He could score. He could command respect, take team-mates under his wing, and lead like a demigod on skates. And he promised New York a Stanley Cup within four years.

Quite the claim for a prairie boy.

But he had been honed to perfection in the jersey of the Edmonton Oilers. Glen Sather's dynasty. When the Oilers joined the NHL Glen had hidden his best young players, he sold off draft-picks to keep the ones the NHL scouts really knew about – he did what he had to do to keep his team intact, and the wide-shouldered boy was one of those gems in the rough.

The Oilers swept to Stanley Cup after Stanley Cup, and they turned the game into a form of art, wonderful to watch, breathtaking. They were so good the NHL changed rules to slow them down. And in that team of astonishingly talented players, the boy led with his heart and his soul.

When he came to New York he didn't talk like a Canadian. Nothing modest in the boy. He made a promise to a city that chewed up stars in every sport and spat them out. He spoke like a Yank, then he went out onto the ice and gave truth to his words.

The Stanley Cup final that year between the Rangers and the Vancouver Canucks was one of the best series in recent history. Went all seven games. Had a penalty shot in the last game that had it gone in would have given the Canucks the cup. A series of raw, sizzling nerves, supreme courage and relentless desire.

And the boy delivered. The ticker-tape parade through the streets of the magic city, the Stanley Cup held high in a storm of confetti, the Canadian prairie boy sitting like a president in the back of a convertible with his wide grin and obsidian eyes, he delivered it all.

Then, like a gunslinger disappearing into the sunset, he moved on, west, to paradise.

But as everyone knows, you can't play hockey in paradise.

And came back but that's another, maybe more sordid kind of story.

The wall

Paddling up the Thames as far as it would take us back into the stone age dragging the canoe through swamps thigh-deep in muck and peat only pausing to rest when we found footing on bodies below with nooses around their necks. Finally we decided to kick overland south a bloody forever portage across farmland hills through forests herds of sheep down country roads on footpaths getting confused with all the road designations: A-roads, B-roads, M-roads. In Canada it's simpler: there's paved roads, gravel roads, mud roads, and uncleared roads – you can tell those because of the trees growing in them.

We got lost a hundred times, the canoe was looking rough, especially when we had to portage. People gave us strange looks, asked where's the water mate, what's with the tattoos, like the hair lady especially the twigs, until finally we were crossing the Wiltshire Downs. Though why you'd call hills Downs, why not Ups. Next thing we knew an army of riders were thundering on all sides dogs barking horns tooting red jackets knobby helmets quips and shiny boots. We raised the canoe high for a look-around, saw the quarry – one of those eco-warriors from the camouflage jacket and paint – but it was touch and go, the hunters had sighted him and the dogs were closing in fast.

Not fair, Jack said.

We eyed the slope, then each other. We flipped the canoe, loaded the packs, stuck Sophia in the middle, jumped in and were sliding down the hill. Would've gone faster in an aluminum canoe but the ground was greasy except for the occasional bit of chalk and before long our eyes were watering, the scene blurring, bumpy as hell but we were on an intercept course.

It was obvious that our arrival was unexpected and that neither the dogs nor the horses had seen a charging canoe before with a tattooed Canadian hollering at the bow swinging his paddle like a baseball bat. People screamed, dogs yelped, horses bucked, flinging red-jacketed riders in all directions. Anyway this was how we met Axel the Eco Warrior. He was new to the cause and had mixed things up by painting a fox fluorescent orange. The poor fox had been chased by every hunter, every dog in the south counties. In a fit of guilt Axel had followed, desperate to make amends. Hadn't seen the fox in days.

Axel was from Bristol. He was tall, lots of yellow hair, unshaved, a narrow face with a huge red nose, two watery blue eyes and bad teeth. He normally wore glasses but he'd lost them a day ago climbing through a hedge, we'd thought he was a mass of pimples but that was nettle stings and bramble pokes and scrapes. Some hedges, he said, had walls hidden in them, quite the surprise running full tilt into them, he might have broken his nose how did it look?

Axel had a degree in Engineering which explained a lot. He re-set the snapped cedar ribs, said they would heal in time, me and Jack exchanged a look, righto we said. We were sitting on the bank of the River Avon, it'd been a long portage from the River Thames. Why do Brits put the River first before the name, River Winnipeg sounds stupid to me. Axel said we could follow the river down the Salisbury Plain which got me thinking about a Big Nip at the Salisbury House on Pembina Highway in Winnipeg. Axel said it would be a short walk to Stonehenge from the river's nearest point. He'd never been there but it was the spiritual centre of Eco-Warriorism, the first such Warriors being Druids who fought the forest-clearing practices of the Romans five thousand years ago. Jack said you've an engineer's grasp of history, Axel, and he nodded, rolling a cigarette.

Sophia said her feet were tired.

The family

We slipped out onto smoke-wreathed glassy water breathing ashy air. Saddle Lake seemed to have shrunk overnight and the sun's light was dull and coppery as our two canoes slid to the far shore and the portage trail which was all downhill from this side back into Eaglenest.

Lester and Frank handled their canoe well, like us without much talking. It was comfortable travelling with them, no chatterboxing, a steady pace. We had no idea where the fires were. Visibility was nil, the air warm and sweaty slick and unmoving, but we paddled on to the portage.

Planes droned back and forth overhead invisible behind the smoke. Water was being scooped up from lakes then dropped onto the burning forest. Most of the sound was coming from the west and south which was good. We walked east, then came down to Eaglenest Lake which was really part of the Winnipeg River system. We took to the water heading north – the river would swing west eventually – and that was when we knew things would heat up.

We paddled steady and silent each alone in his own brain. It was a difficult place for me because our family was falling apart. Every morning I thought of Mom who'd lost most of her choices, the big ones anyway. Did it leave a person calm or impatient and frustrated, I don't know. I was stirring the bottom with my paddle as we slipped between two closing shorelines. The air was breathing hot in quiet short gasps, a blue heron stood watching us we swung into the west, then into the ashes…a curtain of ashes. Nothing for us to do but paddle into it, paddle through it looking for sunlight ahead, but for Mom there was only darkness.

The city

I sat with Caroline at a table in the Maple Leaf Restaurant. The space between us was full of smoke. She sucked so hard I could hear when she pulled the filter from her lips. Her dark eyes were fixed on mine, she'd just told me she was pregnant, not actually saying it but telling me anyway without speaking. I simply knew and she knew I knew and was facing me down now to see what I would do. But I didn't do anything, not anything different anyway.

I wanted to fuck her right there, throw her up on this table hike up her skirt rip off whatever she wore underneath if she wore anything underneath rock her on the table the salt and pepper shakers knocked onto the carpeted floor her head thrown back my fingers digging into the soft underside of her thighs pushing them wide as I ground deeper and deeper people all around standing shocked the manager phoning the police Caroline crying out and writhing under me I wanted to fill her up a nitro come juddering us both then I'd climb off she'd straighten her clothes climb down resume her seat light another cigarette and ask the waitress for a refill.

What are you thinking? she asked.

Teaching my kid to play hockey. It's not that hard thinking two things at once.

What if it's a girl?

So what I'd teach her too.

I'm not pregnant.

Yes you are.

She shrugged, looked away, pulled fierce, tapped ash, took a sip of coffee. *He wants me to move out. He's giving me fifteen hundred dollars a month, that's the arrangement. He's started divorce proceedings. He says if I ever need money he'll give it no questions asked. He's worried about you, says you'll never get drafted, your back's ruined. You'll need to do something else, he thinks you should go into coaching because you're great with kids.*

I can still play. I'll think about coaching later when I have to.

You should think about it now.

Yeah all right.

Will you move in with me, will you stay with me at least until it's time for you to go to Cardiff?

I have to stay at home right now, my mother's dying.

Oh I didn't know that. You know you hardly every talk about your family. I wish you would, Mark, I'd feel I was more a part of your life. Why don't you ever talk about your family?

I've told you about Jack.

What about your father?

What about him?

Well I don't know.

He worked. All the time. Late hours.

Does your family know about me?

They know I've got a girlfriend but right now our minds are on other things. Meaning we're giving each other lots of room I guess. They don't ask but I'll tell them if they do, it's just that nobody's asked right now. I'm sorry does that hurt you?

No, it's understandable. Besides what could you tell them that wouldn't make them hate me. I'm almost thirty-eight. I'm married. I'm bad for your health.

No you're good, it's just a matter of attitude. What you are for me is good, everything good.

I used to hurt you.

There are hurts and there are hurts, you've never hurt me in a way that really hurts.

I wouldn't hurt you that way ever, Mark.

The other kind doesn't even count. You were going with what turned you on that's all.

I know I still think about it, it still turns me on sometimes. I know it's because I have no belief in myself. I don't know if I even like myself so I punish you and that punishes me. Why should punishing us turn me on?

I guess because what we were doing was wrong.

Was it just that?

I don't know, I didn't think about it much. Only the look in your eyes when you were doing it, a dangerous look that had power in it and you were exercising that power and that had to be good for you.

I don't think I feel any better about myself.

I think you do, you just don't trust it.

I trust you.

If you did you wouldn't be worried about the future. I'm not running away. I want you to come to Cardiff. I need a place to make a new start we need that both of us I think.

What about your mother?

I wouldn't go till next August. I don't think I'll have to ask that question then.

I'm sorry, Mark.

I'm having to think about when she's gone. I have to prepare myself.

That sounded straight forward but there's no real way of doing that is there and everything else was going to hell the city the game but people were getting ready to make themselves heard. Would it matter would any of it matter? Is reshaping the world ever anything more than just fooling ourselves that we matter?

The wall

It had been the summer of the World Cup of football or soccer or whatever and the newspapers were still stirring the ashes of English shame. We'd bought inline skates, put on our equipment, stood at one end of a long street. Fifteen dipshit yobs rowdied at the other end throwing bottles stomping on people's heads. Fifteen yobs, a collective IQ of 4, we'd just met their seven younger brothers and said hi how's it going eh, they said:

Fuck you
Fuck you
Fuck you
Fuck you
Fuck you
Fuck you
Fuck you

Whatever happened to respect, who's in charge of raising these weasil-faced twots? Anyway we threw them all in a pond, lucky they knew how to swim and now we circled at the end of the street while the older pub-yobs beat up some quiet student and terrorized his girlfriend we circled one last time adjusting our shoulder pads our elbow pads then we picked up speed serious power-skating it's impressive what clean shoulder checks can do to a stationary open-mouthed yob we sent bodies flying everywhere circled again came back in and hammered the rest of them clean hockey checks hip checks shoulder checks thump crack sprawl here ya go yobs we do the same to Canadian yahoos just having fun mates just a couple Canucks got sworn at once too many we don't like pricks plain and simple so we dislocated a few shoulders cracked a few ribs the difference being we did it in style this nation is pretty sick if you ask me sometimes, never mind the excuses there's some inner rot showing itself here better cut it out or drown in the shit of your own nest. The Age of Communication is past says Jack, it's now an Age of Fear and hooligan tyrants run the show.

Three strikes and you're castrated, that's what's needed Mark, three convictions and you get your balls cut off, who wants their progeny anyway just perpetuates the stupidity, letting these guys breed is a crime against humanity against future generations they learn nothing. They think not. They teach violence as their only expression of frustration to their kids and it goes on and on. Put them on prison ships then sink the damn things in the Channel who'll miss them we'll all breathe a sigh of relief. Shame and embarrassment from everyone else isn't enough, they still rule the streets day and night the power is theirs what kind of life is it to live in constant fear?

The ghosts beyond the wall dreamed of tearing it all down. Nothing's turned out how it was supposed to, nothing's turned out right, tear it down start all over again. *Eugenics, Mark, it's the only hope for our species. That and Maltheusianism. We need to push genetic manipulation all the way, as far as it goes, we need to isolate the yob gene then start wholesale screening to weed it out from the gene pool, there's a yob gene I guarantee it, it's big and ugly, a stupid grin on the DNA strand with a seven-word vocabulary once it's gone we'll all be happier.*

Me and Jack once went to a school just a couple years ago we were there to teach a session of wall-climbing. The teacher in charge said she didn't need to learn, she'd been climbing the walls for years. It was a gym class – ten-year-olds – about thirty of them, they had one hour of gym a week but there were no games played because competition was suddenly bad for kids it singled out the clumsy ones, traumatized them for life. So here were all these ten-year-olds with no way of letting loose, all that aggression, not surprising they busted windows or roved around after dark beating up clumsy kids, traumatizing them for life.

Back when we were in school we had gym three times a week. We formed up teams, played games hard, competed like hell. I've never busted a window for kicks not once, never stomped on heads neither, same for Jack. This new system sucks, doesn't help the clumsy kids either. I remember one game in grade eight touch football we were stalled ten yards from the goal-line, all the hotshot jocks were too well covered so the quarterback singled out one of the clumsies, one of the kids always picked last, said to him, *you run straight ten yards turn around and wait for my throw you catch it you understand me you catch it and you run like hell for the goal-line got it?* and the kid pale and silent nodded and play started and he ran ten yards, nobody on the other team paying any attention to him, and he turned around and the quarterback threw the ball into his belly. He caught it, turned and ran like hell for the goal-line and he got the touchdown and we won the game. It was just a nothing game but if you'd seen that kid's face, the shine in it as we gathered around saying *you did it, Stanley, fan-fucking-tastic!* you'd realize it wasn't nothing at all. It was everything but now even a chance like that is taken away from the kid who'd be picked last if teams were being picked and even when they aren't being picked everybody knows he'd be picked last and he knows it too. You can't pad humiliation or step around it with stupid rules you can't cushion kids and think that's a good thing. It isn't and now its made things worse. So what happens? Well, take a look around. The day schools dropped real physical education was the day grown-ups sold out the next generation of kids.

Well maybe you've got a point, said Sophia, *but I think yobs are a backlash against Feminism, they're all being boys and boys have to be loud obnoxious brainless and full of attitude, nothing but aggression because they're all in crisis.*

Crisis? Jack laughed. *The only crisis they're in is the struggle between their two functioning brain cells. The point I'm making is it's just an extreme manifestation of a national characteristic.*

Well that's my point too.

So why are we arguing, my love? I'm not a Brit. I'm Canadian I've got nothing to prove.

Axel just stared at us. Being an engineer, he'd never heard of Feminism.

Anyway, said Sophia, *it's all Thatcher's fault.*

I thought it was a backlash against Feminism.

So was Thatcher. She gave everyone the legitimacy to be self-serving bastards and everyone took to it like ducks to water. There's nothing worthy of respect in Thatcher's world no institutions no society no culture the only authority was money.

Hey, I've heard this before.

It's no secret everybody knows everybody's aware but everybody's too scared to say anything or do anything. The sword over everyone's heads is the implicit threat to take it all away from you, stability, security, we're all clinging to the edge by our fingernails.

I just want to play hockey.

Not a chance, said Sophia and Jack. It pissed me off, made me feel like a kid, all dreams and hopeless ambition. We'd done with the yobs, re-packed the canoe, Sophia and Axel duffing as we paddled for Stonehenge.

The city

Women who think that men spend all day thinking about sex don't realize that men can think about other things while they're thinking about sex so it's not a problem really. I can stand in goal under fire during a penalty and think about sex, I can shoot rapids in a kayak doing rolls just for the hell of it and think about sex, I can tie my shoelaces, fill out a tax form, drive through a snowstorm, watch Kentucky Fried Chicken commercials, debate Canadian Identity, anything at all and still think about sex. So in that way women don't understand men at all. The other thing is that men think about sex even when they're not thinking about sex and this is how you can hold off coming for an hour but still stay hard.

I was thinking about all this when Mack came to our table, Caroline not looking surprised at all as she lit another one. Mack started questioning me like he was a father about to give away his daughter. I looked around at people at the other tables and knew they had no idea that here at this table was a wife her lover and her husband discussing future plans all matter-of-fact like sanity was something we'd all selected on the menu thank you very much. We set to and it all looks normal no cause for suspecting anything strange from fifteen twenty feet away. I sometimes think the whole world's like that. You just don't know, can't guess at what's going on down the street behind that door, behind those curtained windows or in that car beside you. There's simply no way of knowing unless it explodes out into the open draws attention to itself in some obvious way that turns heads pulls you out of your own little world with all its own little and big problems and it's like a jarring of perspective the sudden measuring of relativity an instinctive gauging of personal risk physical and emotional all at once, then if you think about it you realize that there are big problems out there and yours aren't as big as you thought they were after all and even grief which is personal becomes universal, making you feel better at least for a little while or maybe you just think are those people fucked up or what?

I want to invest in you, Mark he said all earnest leaning forward on the table waving Caroline's smoke from his face I wonder if he knew she was pregnant I guessed not he went on, *you need certification as a coach which means training. Courses. I'll pay for them. You're good with kids I don't know how you do that. To me kids are aliens as far as I'm concerned.*

It's not hard really you lead by example treat them like people you don't push winning on them you make them want to win by themselves for themselves. You're just there to guide them to say you did good, kid, how does it feel? That's all there is to it and you stand by them when they lose because that's when they teach themselves about themselves the most. You just stay solid nothing to it, kids need someone solid that's all.

Sure whatever you say, Mark, I've signed you up for a course next month you won't have a problem with that will you?

No I guess not.

That's what I want to hear. Pro-active. That's what counts in this world it'll get you far, son, very far indeed what do you think, Carol, didn't I say he'd do well? You know I did. I'm satisfied that's what you're seeing a satisfied man.

Wasn't what I was seeing but I kept my mouth shut I sat with my lover he sat with his wife she sat with her lover and her husband he sat with his wife and her lover I sat with them both a single table seating three at the Maple Leaf Restaurant.

Are you happy with your apartment, Carol? She wants you to move in with her, Mark, you know you should. That's only right. She deserves that much you know.

I will, Mack. We're going to Minneapolis first. I've got a three-game exhibition series to play there next weekend, we're driving down.

Not in that Chevy of yours you're not. I'll rent you two a car. When do you leave Friday morning? I'll have it delivered nine a.m. Friday morning. I could hire you a driver but I know you're a good driver, Mark, you're an exceptional driver surprising since you're so young.

If me and Caroline stripped down right there and started fucking he'd be offering advice, I guess it was all he could do, I didn't begrudge him much but Caroline had a different kind of expression on her face, one saying get out of our lives Mack but Mack dealt in commodities he made it his business to make sure everything's right everywhere. He wanted everyone happy and if he sat alone in his living room late at night staring at nothing well that was his business and his alone.

The family

Sometimes you can guess what's coming, sometimes it's more than a guess with the smoke thick, not a foot above your head, and heat that's not the heat of the sun pants against your face and the water to either side. As you ride the current is grainy slick almost oily, its surface sucking gassified sap from the air and it's a race against time. Your knuckles white, the muscles of your neck tight iron, the call came the trip blown a world in flames no chance to say goodbye or maybe one last chance if you can get there in time, the memory sits like a painting dark and gritty and in the style Jack calls superrealism it's the style of my memory, every picture I pull into the light to look at again, maybe that's why paintings in that style make me go quiet when I look at them, someone's memory and it's haunted, right there in front of you, we bought tickets to the last Jets regular season game and we bought tickets to what we figured would be and what turned out was the last Jets game ever played at the arena the playoff game against the Detroit Red Wings when we were eliminated and it was all over not just for this season but for all time and Mom stood beside us clapping mechanically along with everyone else, our only gesture to reflect all we felt and could not put into words, all those super real memories, the thank you to the team, the goodbye to the history, the end we were told. We should have left it there that unsatisfying sense of finality the patient got raped seven years ago the patient struggled on had its bright moments but the patient was finally dead and she stood and clapped with us this terminally ill woman immigrant of winter-silence small now, thin, her skin sagging and folded, faint purple blotches on her arms, her mouth set in a thin line, blinking back tears all that's past all that's been taken away all that will never be again folding the tapestry in time for the yard sale that disperses the pieces of a life's puzzle never to be reassembled, the clothes, the knickknacks, souvenirs, paperback books, but there was still the chance to say goodbye that much at least. Eight hours from Minneapolis to Winnipeg on a cold winter night doing the speed limit and with snow and ice on the highway it's a risk doing even that so eight hours that can't be shaved down not even to seven Caroline sitting beside me chainsmoking my knuckles white on the steering wheel my neck bands of iron. I'd been called out of Game 2 Jack hysterical on the phone from the hospital. She'd handed him her jewellery she knew she wasn't coming out of that bed she was bleeding everywhere inside I got out of my gear sheathed in sweat had the stick-boy bring Caroline down from the stands she took charge I said I'd drive it'd keep my mind occupied but it doesn't not really it's the opposite but it would have been worse had I just sat there in the passenger seat the car was full of sweet American smoke the road rolling under us grainy and slick we stopped for gas and snacks and cigarettes when we had to but otherwise we just drove the land unchanging flat stretching out into darkness on all sides except for the halogen glow of farmyard lights reflecting copper on grain silos the yellow perforated line stitching the distance in fast ticks the semitrailers their big headlights and cab lights climbing up your tail until they swung out to pass the ghosts of York boats surged past us on the river as we all raced through the smoke for Sturgeon Falls before the flames on the south shore leapt across if that's what was coming we couldn't be sure of anything right then just pushing on the old fur-trading route the one that took the first Europeans out into the uncharted west those York boats kind of a cross between a small Viking ship a dory and a Polynesian canoe all loaded up with hockey equipment and furs and food-packs and winter clothing the journeys one after another that laid the groundwork for the myths of the country those York boats would do Sturgeon Falls no portage for them they'd ride that overwhelming drop of water in the narrow cut between two lakes one seven feet higher than the next one and sometimes the York boats went down, the currents pulling everything fatally down to the mud-roiled bottom bodies to return to the surface two lakes farther along limp and lifeless to be picked at by crayfish and all those leather and burlap packs are still there at the foot of the falls buried in mud with sturgeon and walleye bones we reached the border Caroline explained the situation and were waved through inside ten minutes back in Canada now a final stretch through flat land the highway narrowing to single lane either way the burning lights of oncoming traffic blinding for a split second as each went past it was an hour before dawn so there wasn't much just the truckers driving into those lights each time is like a little death but then it's past. Caroline was passing me her cigarettes I didn't realize I'd been smoking them no wonder I felt sick my throat raw my lungs numb but I kept accepting the offer ahead was the glow of the city we stopped in Fort Richmond the Salisbury House Restaurant just inside the Perimeter I phoned home got no answer I phoned the hospital got put through to Intensive Care talked to a nurse who said *your brother is here would like to speak with you* and he came on crying such pain through the phone the sound not anything I could match with my memory of his face *she's gone she's gone just now she's gone,* she was gone.

The arena

There were the goodbyes, more than one, more than two and there was the *wait not so fast,* and it was that *wait* that did the real damage – the damage that went beyond the threatened loss of a professional sports team that took lives and taught them just how meaningless and irrelevant they really were. It wasn't just money men ten thousand miles away, it was money men in Winnipeg itself who even at the end, even as the gasp was being drawn, launched their egos at each other and made a cynical mess of things. There's no forgiving them that. The city's movers and shakers sniping and nipping and bearing sharp little teeth over a paltry feast but the only one in town. If I get down to hell before them I'll prepare their suites as only a servant of evil can. I have no problem in hating what's worst in people even though that may be hate itself. There's different kinds of hate and the ones who hate the good things in people because they don't have those good things in themselves, well that's the worst of the worst kind of hate and my hate for them is a clean thing in comparison. Start talking bottom lines to me and you've earned your ticket to hell as far as I'm concerned.

In my memory dreams, the arena haunts me, the temple of all things, a church or a cave that our species still calls home. A place where our representatives, as mortal as we are, show us the game we're all in. Not a fan on this planet doesn't understand me. Not one not a single goddamned one.

The city

When the team's gone some part of a city's life is sucked away. It dies a little bit more for some than for others sure but the absence is felt. History, Jack says, is the death of myths in succession. Each myth sustained its world for a while, then it died and if you were lucky you had a new one ready to step in take its place but sometimes that wasn't a lucky thing if the new myth was rotten at the core. You know, cynically excluding whole swaths of people, people of the wrong social standing, people of the wrong skin colour, of the wrong religion, people speaking the wrong language. If that happens real bad, you get genocide, concentration camps, gulags, you get the fierce zeal of fanatics bowing to the myth but reality's messier than any Golden Age of Heroes the poets dreamed up, meaning people die but that's history. Then there are myths the fuck-you governments of today are busy creating, new myths, they start small picking out lowlifes and unemployed, mostly defenceless people because it costs them nothing. Cheap and easy, just like the antismoking bylaws. That committee the government put together is like getting twenty misogynists to decide policy on women's issues. And so the puckered twits can feel all virtuous, but try taking away cars, the most polluting, filthy invention ever, and suddenly being virtuous gets painful. So that'll never happen. Hypocrites. But hey, Jack says, there's a long tradition in North America of lifestyle fascism, and fascism is inherently pernicious, so none of it comes as any surprise. If pernicious means what I think it means, small-minded and mean.

The day the self-righteous finds him or herself sitting in their SUV, filling their face with super-sized french fries, engine idling for the past twenty minutes, and their children, the ones they're waiting for outside the school, have just been diagnosed with asthma, maybe that day they'll realize that they and their lifestyle are direct contributors to the future suffering of their kids, maybe on that day, some demonic finger-pointer will rise up and nail them squirming to the wall of blame. In the meantime, of course, they can just go on kicking minority groups whose habits offend them and, of course, feel good about it. Why not? Let's go and drag some war veterans out of the Legion into the snow and bitching cold and tell 'em it's good for 'em and did they really think they were fighting for individual freedom? Did they really think they've actually earned a right to a quiet smoke in comfort with their friends? I mean, who are they to think that? Get uppity, bud, and we'll run you over in our guzzling monstrosity and that's that. But hey, we really care, in fact, we'll drive you over to our very own government-run gambling establishment, where we can tax you and feed your new addiction all at once. You see, the smell of panic and debt isn't nearly as unhealthy as cigarette smoke, right?

So they start imposing restrictions they themselves wouldn't dream of living under but the secret underlying it all is bigotry, *we don't have to live under those restrictions but you do because we're better than you and we're running this game we're running every game what the fuck are you going to do about it?* and the myth here is that's the way of the world, it's how things have to be, it's the bottom line, for the changes that really matter sorry, we just don't have the money. *Bullshit.* But the painted savages are growing in number at the foot of the wall, take heed, no one likes living with a bastard's fist down their throat, take heed, lotteries won't answer everything just ask the Romans they had theirs, take heed, *fuck-you* can go both ways.

I remember the children on that day of gathering. They came with jars filled with coins, they came to save the Jets, giving all they had to keep the team in their home city. They wanted to make a difference. People gathered in their thousands wanting to make a difference. They weren't remembering a myth, they were living it for that moment, the worshippers had come out of the temple, stood under the open sky, they knew what they were up against, the modern world not just professional sports, up against the Game Masters a thousand miles away, the ones with penthouses in the clouds the ones with the taxman in their pockets the ones walking rainbow bridges the ones telling a city what it's worth squinting at ledgers to tell each person what they're worth, reduced to particles of labour or potential labour, what they're worth, not much. These are tidal forces sweeping the globe swim or drown, we'll watch from our yachts, we're the fuck-you people running the fuck-you governments. You're taking on the big-boys now, you won't win because you won't see us, we'll stay faceless, nowhere for you to focus your hate, your energy, and in the end you'll lose, feel as worthless as we know you are. It's important to teach children the lessons of the real world, reality's dose prepares them for adulthood.

I don't know, it's a tired hour full of tired thoughts and haunting memories. It seems breaking hearts is an acceptable consequence to the rules of money, those rules being the world's rules and maybe Jack's right, nothing has ever changed in the history of the species. Surplus equals wealth equals division equals haves and have-nots equals greed equals envy equals strife equals death. Jack's favourite irony *surplus equals death,* so in the end the game is everything, the battle of haves and have-nots starting there on the ice, the ones with talent, the ones with less, the winners the losers the fast the slow the smart the thick the hoarding of goals the struggle to get then stay ahead till the cosmic buzzer sounds, and in the stands the fans watching, filled with the witnessing and the sharing of the same struggle, all their own struggles reduced, simplified, the lessons of worth and justice played out for them over and over again. The arena is church school right wrong win lose live die and finally faith in next season it'll all come together then.

In Winnipeg there's no next season. The children look elsewhere, arms wrapped around their jars of coins. It'll be a little harder prying that money from them next time oh they've learned nice going Winnipeg but dammit I still dream the Jets will rise again, stupid isn't it. I wonder if the kids do the same it's bad getting burned so young or have they done what I can't do? Swallowed it all down got on with it go with Grandpa to the Moose games in the arena and never *think this is all we deserve we were worthy of more once* and Grandpa sits in winter-silence. He could say, *yes we were worthy of more once but the modern age caught up with us and there's not a chance in hell I'm going to say that out loud because then I'd have to say 'appreciate what you've got.' That minor league team crawling around down there on the ice. Someone decided that's all we're worthy of these days and I can't say don't let it eat you inside because it's eating me inside and I'm damned if this grown-up is going to lie to you* and maybe the popcorn tastes the same and the souvenirs sell and maybe the Moose win every now and then hell they're doing the best they can and there's ear-splitting music during face-offs and hotdogs fired out cannons all to keep anyone from thinking too much maybe and dear Winnipeg is it enough after all that fighting to save the Jets? Maybe it is.

The wall

Axel wanted to save England from itself. He'd lived in trees, in tunnels, in tents, in caravans; he'd fought new roads, strip malls, nuclear waste, over-fishing, fox-hunting, deregulation, privatization; he'd been beaten up, arrested, chased, he'd even been tarred and feathered; but he hung his head defeated when his favourite football team got demoted. Some realities you just have to bow to but there's always next year isn't there. He was taking his turn carrying the canoe on his own because it was good exercise. We could see Stonehenge finally, Jack pointing out burial mounds which we walked around and we got closer to the crowds some of them forgetting the stones and turning to watch us as if there was anything special about us worth staring at. Sophia had thrown a shoe or heel or whatever, so Jack carried her piggy-back. I had my equipment: our packs and the paddles, don't know which of us was struggling more.

Axel said he could rebuild my goaltending equipment, add some motors and gyrostabilizers, turn it into a self-propelled robot. Jack thought this was brilliant. I wasn't too sure. Something scary about that, so I thought instead about a football game we'd watched in a pub. Talk about a game of wimps, guys getting nudged in the thigh, tumbling like they'd been fired out of a cannon, writhing around in mortal agony. Out come the stretchers. These guys were the biggest wusses in professional sports – not like hockey players at all. What's twenty-two stitches over the eye, just get the sewing done before next period. What's with a broken leg, I can play on it, tape it up and watch me score the Stanley Cup-winning goal in overtime. What's a broken nose, cracked ribs, busted hand, sprained thumb? The only time you'll see a stretcher on the ice is when there's a compound fracture of the leg or a broken neck or someone's throat's been slit by a skate blade and even then he's better off standing at least until he's off the ice. Soccer's a damn good game if the players just played it and stopped all this Academy Award bullshit. Jack says it's just cynicism again, the players themselves cynical about the game they supposedly love and it's happening in hockey now too. Russians showed us how, I guess they got it from playing soccer but hockey fans are good at universal disgust. Fans need a clear eye to be good fans, need to be objective when the refs can't or won't. Name me one Jets fan who wasn't disgusted when Jimmy Mann cold-socked that Sabre or was it Penguin doesn't matter broke the guy's jaw. Jimmy may have been wearing a Jets jersey but he wasn't a hero in anybody's eyes in Winnipeg. I can handle watching rugby, it's just like hockey, tough as nails with movement, explosive flow. But watching those football players flop and twitch, it's bloody nauseating see what ten million over three years buys.

Stonehenge looked small and vulnerable surrounded by roads. People circled it along the fenced-in walkway, just sightseeing, not a pilgrimage. We decided not to pay the entrance fee so we stood the other side of the fence not saying much until Axel took it on himself to give us a lecture.

Merlin was the High Druid this was six thousand years ago and Caesar was leading his armies across England fighting Anglo Saxons and small hairy people who were the original Britons they weren't Celts they were Picts who'd fled the sinking of Atlantis which was called Lyonesse now called Lyon if you go to Lyon these days you'll see it's sunk down and six thousand years ago the water levels went up three hundred feet which is where the story of Atlantis comes from Plato and Merlin they talked it over at a secret meeting on Stonehenge on the Night of Celestial Chaos when Halley's Comet arrived Merlin had just built Stonehenge taking stones from Ireland where the Atlanteans lived though they had colonies in America and off the Bimiji coast the stones are actually from the capital of Atlantis which was called Santithera.

I thought it was Santiclausa.

You were wrong Jack don't interrupt. Anyway Merlin made Stonehenge as a magical portalway to the aliens living on Halley's Comet they were called the Hallatians after Halley.

Not the Hallitosians after garlic salad?

You're showing your ignorance Jack now shut the fuck up. Like I was saying Plato wrote down the conversation in his Dialogues because Merlin and Socrates were actually the same guy Caesar knew that's why he tried to poison him so Merlin had to retire his Socrates persona and didn't get his revenge until he enlisted Brutus and Cassius and they stabbed Caesar to death or at least that's how Shakespeare wrote it.

Jack nodded sagely. I glanced at Sophia who rolled her eyes. Axel was a born lecturer bound for a teaching career at Cambridge though probably not in history. Jack said he was another Sir Arthur Evans and had he heard of the American country western singer named Rosetta Stone?

No, said Axel putting into that word *why would I bother?*

But that's the problem isn't it, Axel, Jack went on, *you Brits are isolationist snobs. The centre of an Empire long gone though you'll never admit it's long gone. The rest of the world has moved on but you still can't produce a toilet that flushes properly you spend all day on the radio stations doing special exposes on American cults neofascists UFO-freaks school-kids with guns and under it all not very deep is your conviction of superiority that slightly mocking tone the sneer between the lines how does a country as fucked up as this one acquire such arrogance that's what I don't get.*

Comes from having had an empire, Sophia said with a smug smile.

That's your problem, Axel said to Jack, *not mine, mate.*

Classic response I salute you, Axel.

Anyway if you hate the place so much what are you doing here?

Running away.

Canada sucks?

In its own way every country sucks. Here and there this and that try drinking the water in Regina try finding a bus in Victoria after 6 p.m. try finding your way out of West Edmonton Mall.

The tourists were dancing around Stonehenge now hands linked and chanting. I don't know maybe they weren't tourists or maybe they were Americans line-dancing but I didn't see any confederate flags so I guess not. Now they were dancing in sinuous lines through the monuments and some guy with a bronze dagger the size of a sword was chasing a tour bus driver, caught him, dragged him screaming to a big flat stone where the others pinned him down and the knife went in with a collective *Oi!* So not tourists after all. Just a group of yobs having some fun, boys will be boys. They were eyeing us now, especially Axel, so we decided to make a strategic withdrawal back to River Avon. It was looking like we'd never get to Cardiff in time for my try-out but Jack just shrugged off my complaining and said, we'll make it don't worry. I said we needed to find a coast or another river or we'll have to canoe overland.

The family

A Norseman came down damn near on top of us, its pontoons slapping the water with a painful sound. The plane turned around ahead of us, the props slowing we paddled up. An RCMP officer looked down at us, eyes narrowing on Lester and Frank.

If you ask them if that canoe is theirs I'll lodge a complaint, Jack said with a big smile.

But he didn't, just gave us all shit for being out on the river; he said we'd have to pay our dues fighting the fire. He said head down another mile, you'll see the temp camp on the left. Pull in there, boys. Two hours later we were trudging through a black spruce bog heading for the firebreak, a powerline cut where we were making our stand. The air was thick with hot smoke and cinders, the water tanks on our backs weighed a ton along with the shovels walkie-talkies axes and brush-hooks. Our squad leader carried the oxygen and our masks. His name was Brig and he was wider than he was tall. He was the perfect squad leader for fighting forest fires; said he planned on putting out hell's fires when he got down there. Anyway we reached the cut and found ourselves facing a wall of flame. Brig stepped into the clearing, turned to us and said get out here you wimps. But his fire-retardant coat was smouldering so we said no way sir, this cut ain't holding, we'd better pull back. He said I'll rip the head off the first of you that runs, I swear it. Dig me a break line, use the water on each other, that's what it's for, now move it! So we dug our trench, what was supposed to be a straight line we ended up making a circle because the fire had jumped the cut. Brig walked into a wall of flame, swearing and cursing. That was the last we saw of him while we dug our trench, coughing our lungs out, no hair left on our faces. My cuffs caught fire and I shoved my hands into the ring of earth we'd mounded just as two nearby trees toppled, hooked onto each other right over us, raining down burning embers and twigs and sticks and blackened birch leaves. Lester and Frank lifted Jack between them and he reached up and kicked the offending trees to one side. Brig showed up at this moment, his eyes going wide and he bellowed out *Stonehenge!*

Then a plane dropped tons of water on us.

Looking back, it was a lucky thing we didn't drown in that forest fire. One second burning, the next deluged, staggering onto our feet covered in ashy muck. The break was re-established. Brig staggered up to us through a cloud of steam and said time to pull out.

The city

I was the lucky one. I wasn't there to see her sink into herself, to see her long past saying goodbye. Jack standing over her, his face ravaged by helplessness, the half-smile stripped away. Only in books can you point a finger and say *there that was the moment where my faith died, my faith in the world itself and life and humanity and civilization and justice.* Real life's not like that, the other side of Jack's face, the unsmiling half where he spent most of his time. It was his mystery, no solution in sight, just the way of things that's all. Jack pinned to the sarsen stone, layer after layer peeled away. If you've known thunder in your own heart, you know what I'm talking about. I only saw the aftermath, the drawn frozen mask, the imprint of Mom's death which he'd gone through alone. Jack had been alone but he managed some kind of control over the telephone, told me to meet him at home, *there was nothing of Mom left at the hospital, meet me at home, Mark, and bring Caroline of course. I'll meet you both there okay?*
Okay.
Jack fell into my arms in the living room. He sank down in my arms, the light in his eyes dimmed. I guess maybe he felt safe. It wasn't what I needed from him but it turned out Caroline was there to give me that. Jack only had me, his shoulders shaking, tears flooding down to soak my t-shirt. Then Caroline had her arms around both of us. I'd never imagined she could do that for not just me, for us, and her face that night was love. Only a child knows how to answer that, accepting the vulnerability without fear. We didn't do any giving that night just taking; we were children who'd lost their mother.
The next morning Caroline slept late. Me and Jack laced up our skates and went to the rink across the street. He played like magic, shot me full of holes, picking high glove-side the opening I'd give a player. I didn't close it up and he scored again and again because his talent stayed with him no matter how he ignored it and I accepted that, admired that, loved that with all my heart. Overhead the blue sky sparkled with ice crystals hanging suspended. It was brittle cold but we

steamed. Two ravaged boys playing hockey. Caroline came out all bundled up, leaned on the boards watching us till we finally stopped. We went back to the house, sat in the kitchen drinking coffee. Caroline offered Marlboros to us. I've no more words for that morning.

The arena

It was small as temples go with glass cases in the concessions area holding holy relics: the Avco Cup, the 8x10 colour shots of Hedberg and Nilsson and Hull and Sjoberg and the Duke and red-faced Bill Friday, the one referee we respected. Since the Jets left I haven't been back to it, maybe it's a shrine now, a Greek temple of Ilium on the ruins of Troy worshipping the Golden Age or the Trojan War, the one with the wooden horse full of rubbers. That was Jack's line. He's always full of obscure references he sees life everything in it in comparative terms, is that a good thing I wonder? There's something romantic in his eyes when he says things like that, as if for all his grim commentary he's in love with the species, with humans, but he says not love, Mark, just awe, the only sense of wonder I have left and it grows it just keeps growing.

You can look at the arena as just a building, a squat rectangular pile of iron girders and concrete or you can see it in such a way that it glows. You do that instinctively, Mark, that's your gift. I have to work at it, I have to use my brain finding echoes from all that I know, all that I've learned but it's what you understand without having to think about it. I stand here in awe because I'm outside it, I'm too jaded to feel without questioning, cursed as the eternal outsider. I'm outside the dance, you're in it. Call it hero worship.

He was confused that day, his feet were off the ground, he'd met a woman at university. She was only nineteen but you couldn't call her a girl, she had breeding, nothing born to but consciously worked at, a rare discipline Jack said. So he was happy and Jack talks too much when he's happy.

The first walls were raised nine thousand years ago, Mark, you can look at human history as a history of raising walls. More and more walls going on to this day. We partition, we partition our lives, partition for exclusion, for division, for secrecy, for defence, for segregation, confirming superiority enforcing inferiority, partitions for hoarding, for organizing, for imprisoning, for self-identification, for disguise, for cruelty for malice for shame for guilt for turning a blind eye and here in this city the walls keep going up. You see them behind the faces on the street, a city coming of age every horizon limited to something manageable reaffirming our delusion of control.

The arena was waiting for me, and people like me, waiting for us – our squat iron girder and concrete temple with its floor of ice that we tred with the sure-footedness of the faithful.

The hill

My equipment was assembled, my equipment rose up on its own, clicketyclack. Axel's red face beaming with triumph, his child animate, the gods looking down aghast. My equipment picked up the paddles, me and Jack picked up the canoe. Axel the packs Sophia herself and we portaged across Salisbury Plain under a light drizzle, the sky grey and low over us, mud clumping our boots, not quite as bad as Red River gumbo but close. Jack with Sophia looking behind us occasionally scanning in silence and Axel not saying much, my equipment nothing at all thankfully. I couldn't have stomached my equipment voicing opinions on this and that telling me to keep my glove-hand higher or whatever. Through the misty rain we could see more standing stones the occasional hamlet or village farms and roads and milestones and fencelines and footpath stiles trekkers stopping to stare. We concluded it was Sophia's orange hair that did it. We kept going pushing west ever west. There was a coast over that way somewhere and beyond it open water and on the other side of that water was Cardiff, the city of dreams, the city in the sky, the city of God and the Cardiff Devils.

We walked miles and miles the rain now a solid downpour smeared in mud stumbling staggering the canoe like lead on our shoulders. We nearly died in quicksand nearly fell to our deaths down gorges nearly got trampled by stampeding sheep nearly got shot by local primitives nearly died from bad cups of tea offered to us at rest-stops. We trudged on weighed down by soggy biscuits the canoe's canvas was torn frayed worn raw patched with birch bark and spandex and cling-film and wads of chewing gum, we rode the canoe down slopes of mud and wet grass we crashed it into a tree splintered the prow and through it all my equipment marched unceasing sightless and relentless and inexorable rain streaming down its plastic armour clumps of mud clinging to it like grey flesh a growing of muscles over its bone frame bulking up becoming gigantic bestial monstrous bigger than all of us marching shambling across the wasteland through sheets of rain. Jack gave it a name called it Armageddon. I gave it a name called it Fred.

You know, Sophia said after a time, *if we'd used the canal system we might have been able to actually canoe, I mean paddle, most of this way.*

Me and Jack stopped in our tracks. *What canals?*

The Family

Winter dragged on into May. We were busy dealing with insurance policies, two in a row, Dad's and Mom's. All of a sudden me and Jack had more money than we knew what to do with. Jack rented a place with his girlfriend, whose name was Calli, on Pembina Highway close to the university. I moved in with Caroline and applied for a passport and a visa. She was starting to show, gaining more weight after a couple months of throwing up. The doctors were concerned because she was forty and smoking a pack a day but the baby looked fine at least that's what the doctors said as they bent close to study the ultrasound image. The baby was grainy where it was supposed to be grainy, clear where it wasn't, and despite everything Caroline just seemed to be getting healthier-looking by the day. We didn't even slow down on our fucking, taking turns falling inside each other. The baby just kept on growing into our lives, a presence that would depend on us for everything. That brought us a different kind of happiness and seemed to fill up the gaps when I thought about my Mom who would never see her first grandchild.

Caroline got a letter from her parents written on a Japanese typewriter. They were offering a reconciliation while firing one last salvo. They were coming for a visit next month. By the beginning of the fourth week I had a peptic ulcer and was a wreck. Caroline just looked at me and laughed. She'd found happiness somewhere. It was as if the cosmic forces knew it and came into line, no hassles anywhere in her life – the divorce papers were finalized, Mack stopped dropping by or phoning, she wasn't spending much money, the bank account he'd set up for her was stuffed with cash, she turned it into an education fund for the baby. I said you don't need money to get your Grade Twelve diploma. She said for after that as in universities which got me scared. What if the baby was smarter than me, that wouldn't be hard being smarter than me, I was one rung above Yahooship – the highest grade I'd ever gotten was a B minus and that was for Physical Education.

For once Caroline didn't laugh. Somehow she understood though she hated hockey despite being a natural on skates. For her it wasn't part of the game, it was something else, a kind of freedom, a way to escape. It's nice when loving someone includes admiring them but it's depressing too since you then look at yourself and don't see much to admire so you wonder what's she doing with me? Hard to know because knowing means looking at yourself and I tried to never do that, but a kid on the way forces you to. And the doctor saying *no more coffee no more cigarettes stop taking after your wife you're on lowgrade antibiotics but it's stress that's manifesting itself you've got to find a healthy way of dealing with it* but what could I do I made saves that's all I could do the ones that got past me made holes in my stomach lining and hurt like hell.

We met her parents at the airport. They appeared wraith-like from the crowd, her father Sinji wearing a dark three-piece suit with brown Italian shoes, his hair silver military cut, her mother in a dark blue dress with small white flowers on it, pearls around her neck, wearing slippers from what I could see, her round face pale almost white. They stopped twenty feet away, eyes on Caroline. We had to walk up to meet them, not what you'd call halfway. There was a stiff hug with Father and cheek pecks with Mother, mumbled introductions with me. I escaped to take charge of collecting the luggage. We went out to the '89 Ford Bronco, the one I'd borrowed from Jack, his latest guzzling monstrosity accessorized to the gills, huge off-road Michelin boots on spoked alloy wheels. Turned out to be a real mistake as Father had to help Mother climb up into the backseat. He was frowning fierce and I got a bit ticked off. Started daydreaming of grabbing him, tying him to the roof-rack for the drive home. Then I blinked realizing they were all watching me standing there like some brainless twit. I guess I alarmed them even more when I shouted *All aboard!*. They got in, I climbed behind the wheel, fired it up and backed over their luggage.

The mood in the apartment, everyone seated sipping tea, wasn't too hot, nobody saying a damned thing. Father was an investment banker. Mother was mother a mother whose only child had run off with an Occidental businessman of untested honour who her daughter then cheated on and left to be with an Occidental hockey player half her age now living in sin until I learned that sin wasn't an issue with them not in the same way anyway since they were Buddhists and not serious ones at that. Things eased suddenly when Caroline then Father then Mother all lit Matinee Kings, some kind of subtle but vitally important continuity established. I was odd-man out again.

Impressive! Father barked.

I stared blankly, he was staring at my crotch or was he? I closed my legs suddenly splashing tea across Mother's lap. I babbled apologies, she pretended it never happened. Father frowned *This apartment. Very impressive. Clean. Swedish furniture. Teak. You're a hockey player. Goalie.*

Yes. For now. I plan to be a coach.

Excellent. Japan had a Canadian coach. Olympic team. Named King.

Calgary Flames.

What?

Before he went to Japan.

Oh yes.

And Canadian Olympic team.

What?

Before Calgary.

Oh yes. Excellent.

I won't be coaching in Japan.

Why not?

Too long a commute.

Oh yes. Of course.

I've got nothing against Japan.

Nothing?

No, nothing. I know nothing about Japan.

Olympic hockey team.

Right, I know that much.

Nothing else?

Sushi. Pearl Harbour. Sulu.

Sulu?

Star Trek.
Oh yes. Your finances?
Solid.
Good. From coaching?
Inheritance.
Good. Invest it.
Yes.
I will invest it. For you and Caroline. I will make you rich.
All right.
You're a very big man.
Yes.
Big babies. They will get stuck.
Stuck?
Caesarians.
I'm not very religious.
Oh.

Everybody was smoking up a storm; my eyes were watering. Mother went off to the spare bedroom where they'd be sleeping. Father went to the toilet. Caroline turned on me when they were gone, *Stop it!*

Stop what?

Mocking him, talking like him.

I'm not! I can't help it. It just comes out that way. I'm not mocking him I swear!

Father came back. *Make us coffee, Caroline.* She went out he smiled at me. *We love her very much we want what is best for her you understand? There have been ... disagreements.*

I understand, sir, I love her too. I loved her from the first time I saw her through my binoculars. I want to take care of her, be with her. I'm sorry about your luggage I didn't break anything did I? You didn't have a Ming vase in there or anything. I'll pay for it I swear a new set of luggage Italian leather or teak anything you want. I'm sorry about the Bronco too I should've rented a Toyota Landcruiser or a limo, a Honda limo if they make them. I don't know what got into me I wasn't thinking I've been so nervous about this, so stressed out. I haven't got a subtle bone in my body. Caroline says Japanese etiquette is very subtle. I'm completely at a loss I've probably insulted you a hundred times already. I didn't mean to. I stopped then turning to see Caroline at the kitchen entrance, her Mother at the bedroom entrance, both motionless staring at me. I wanted to scream run to the French windows fling myself through them and fall to my death but we were only on the second floor so I said to Caroline in a calm voice, *Darling have you got a large kitchen knife?*

At some point over the next six days we actually got to know each other. Things settled down. I tagged onto a Japanese investment banker's peculiar sense of humour, got a sense of what would make him smile, got a sense of detecting which part of his frown was actually a smile, got a sense of a mother who was pretty much the same as her daughter, the only thing making her distraught being her inability to see that. But what really swung the whole thing was taking Sinji fishing for lake trout in West Hawk Lake while Caroline and Mother went shopping for two days. We rented a boat and down-riggers. I told Sinji about when I'd gone drysuit diving one winter collecting pieces of meteorite. Then he hooked a thirty-pounder and brought the damn thing up after forty-five minutes, superb play on ten-pound test monofilament line. That was a real smile, never seen such a real smile. He posed for the picture, then wept with joy as he released it back into the lake, some Buddhist thing I guess. When I bowed to show my respect at his achievement he shook my hand and gave me a half-hug and everything was right for once. A huge weight slipped from my shoulders and when we got back Caroline and Mother had found communion of some kind with each other in Eaton's. We all said goodbye at the airport with genuine feeling and on the way home Caroline put a hand on my arm at a stoplight and said, *They really liked the new luggage.*

In July Jack's girlfriend Calli went crazy one night, some kind of crisis having to do with cellulite. She stormed out taking his CD player with her. Just showing her immaturity said Jack but he was glum for a week, saying it's the curse of men to suffer – not women but men specifically – suffer suffer suffer. He buried himself in books, didn't talk much, didn't smile much, not even his half-smile.

The NHL playoffs were dreadful, especially the final round, seriously dull clutch-and-grab trap-style games yawn-city. It was the only game in town and it stank. If not for Don Cherry, it would have been unwatchable. I had a dream once, one night, that the CBC fired Cherry and the whole nation went up in flames, every city from east to west burned to the ground; wholesale looting, martial law, thousands dead in the streets. Maybe the CBC execs have the same dream so the only way Don Cherry will go out is if he loses all credibility, god knows the games themselves aren't keeping Hockey Night in Canada afloat that's for sure.

In June the thunderstorms arrived, the sky ripping apart, going weird colours, rain dumped by the gallons on the streets, drains backing up in basements. Just the year before there'd been the city's biggest flood saved only by Duff's Ditch around Winnipeg's outskirts. But Fargo or was it Grand Forks in the States got flooded, then burned to the ground and pretty soon all of southern Manitoba was under water. We did the usual volunteering on the sandbag brigades busting ass like everyone else to keep towns and Winnipeg itself dry. But that flooding had been only the slow rise of violence, not like a good prairie thunderstorm and the twisters that sometimes came with it. They rolled up fast like demon elementals, energy sizzling the air. It was glorious going outside soaking it up and that's why on a Saturday night I got hit in the forehead by a bolt of lightning. I was in a coma for six days, hair falling out and a hard-on that wouldn't go away.

My line is I have no memory of those lost days but the truth is I dreamed.

Puck

Right up until that last leap into the unknown, the Madman of Wawa danced everywhere he went. He was short and rubbery and heard music no one else could hear and that might have caused problems with the townsfolk – being wilderness-fearing simple people out in the middle of a wilderness – but he danced with a broad smile and that smile couldn't help but make everyone who saw it smile as well.

Come winter he danced day and night, probably in an effort to keep warm because when the winds blow people climb into refrigerators to warm up and come winter in Wawa the Winds Shall Blow it was God's eleventh commandment the one He reserved for people who lived in the middle of nowhere.

If you check on a map of Ontario and find Wawa, you'll see.

It was the winter of 18– as they say, when the Madman of Wawa danced his last dance. His cavorting steps had taken him to the snow-heaped shore of Lake Superior which when you look at it could be a small sea, and upon seeing a score of boys and girls skating on the ice the Madman watched, dancing in place, for a long ten minutes.

Two teams had assembled out on the ice. Everyone had hockey sticks and they were skating around bodychecking each other and basically having a good time although the game if that was what it was seemed a little pointless.

The Madman of Wawa danced out of sight and returned a little later with a huge cauldron balanced on his head, a leather satchel slung from one shoulder, and bundles of firewood under each arm. He danced down onto the ice.

The kids played on, paying him little heed since he was a familiar figure around town.

Still dancing, the Madman built a fire out on the ice and lit it with a snap of his fingers. Still dancing, he filled the cauldron with snow and set it on the fire. He circled the now steaming cauldron and opened the flap on his leather satchel. He danced on, reaching into the satchel and withdrawing items one after another which he tossed each and every one into the cauldron.

There is magic in dancing, and whatever is held while dancing absorbs that magic like a wad of cotton absorbs blood. From the satchel in his hands the dancing Madman held frozen pine sap, birch bark, clay pipe stems and bowls, wolverine fur, steatitie pipes, pemmican, hot dogs, popcorn, ice cream bars. Each and every one he tossed into the cauldron.

By this time the children had stopped to watch. The Madman always danced, but never before had he conjured. Fearful yet fascinated, the children watched on.

Still dancing, the Madman circled the hissing, bubbling, steaming cauldron. The fire had melted down into the thick ice and he danced through knee-deep water that steamed in the frigid air.

Suddenly the Madman of Wawa leapt high and plunged headfirst into the cauldron.

The children screamed.

The cauldron rocked, then, the fire having melted completely through the lake's ice, plummeted out of sight in a vast cloud of steam.

The children screamed a second time.

The Madman of Wawa was never seen again, but that Spring, as the children played along the lakeshore, they came upon strange disc-shaped pieces of rubber. Playing with them, they found that they rolled well when on end, but were otherwise unpredictable given their peculiar shape. But the next winter, when the rubber discs froze hard, they slid like poetry across the lake's ice, and this, combined with sticks and skates and goal nets, proved a wonderful past-time in which to encompass as if within a single, chill, breath, the entire winter and indeed, winter eternal.

No one knows where the name 'puck' came from.

The wall

It's the night of truths, Jack said raising the bottle to his lips. *It's the night before the dawn of the Dark Ages the rising flood of humming electronic words to drown the world in confusion. The time of losing our way is upon us, Mark, let's celebrate the coming darkness we're young on life's cusp we're the looters of cities thirsty for blood and flame we've been cut loose there's nothing stopping us tell me our future, Mark, tell me what you see.*

I've got nothing to tell.

You mean you've sensed the options narrowing down but you've delayed your migration you've come with me not her and the little one. You gave her the unwanted option not to join you and you've taken for yourself this last rampage across the unsuspecting land where any direction is as good as another your last rite of passage in the company of your brother.

I watched him pull a bandana from his pocket, blue and white folded ready for the knot. *I've been only one step ahead of you all this time, Mark, in our growing up. I made every move took every shot I had. I used every ounce of my talent against you and you never buckled not once you kept getting up checking your goalposts and my heart bled watching those goalposts pulled wider and wider apart more net for you to cover more and more until you're defending the world left behind, the past, all of it, the country's past, the city's past and finally our own.*

I couldn't really understand what he was saying or maybe I didn't want to. It was too dark to see his face to search for the smiling half but I already knew I wouldn't find it. I looked up and the stars cascaded down but it was only water in my eyes.

You could coach in Cardiff. Kid's teams. You could contribute in no small way to the UK's nascent myth of ice hockey. The kids will fall into your heart, it's big enough to hold all of them. Think hard on this, Mark, is all I'm asking. You know some people said Winnipeg grew up at last in losing the Jets. Grew up not in a good way but a way nevertheless. Some people live a life that has no time for myths and if you step into them walk down the unlit passage of their soul you'll find their child selves small corpses flat on their backs on sarsen stone chests cut wide open and gaping. You have to walk back out to find the bloody hand that did it and it's the same with Canada you step out from it and look back see the blood on its hands the look of dumb confusion on the ageing face. To what god have we sacrificed our most precious myth? And who the hell said we had to and why the hell why in fucking hell did we listen to them? Oh grow up oh grow up it's just the way things are, face up to it and get on with it that's what we say as we cut ourselves open. As we kill all that we were once. As if a fifty-year-old man two hundred years ago was a child compared to a fifty-year -old man today. What bullshit. But we look back on the history of the species as if it was our own personal history and only now have we all grown up taking every sustaining myth and replacing it with a bloodsucking one that stands alone and monumental, a huge golden heel pressing down on all our necks and we take it like it was a fact of life but it isn't it's a choice our last option the narrowing down to one last option we've rewritten the worst of our natures into virtues.

That's just a way of seeing things, Jack, that's all it is you can choose to see it differently.

So tell me how you see it, brother. Please.

I didn't say I saw it any different from you but I'm thinking there has to be another way of looking at it and that's the way of saying 'just let me play, just let me dream, just let me give thanks to my memories.'

Even as you die inside?

The thing is we can all see what the fuck's gone wrong but we all feel helpless to stop it.

Helpless? Hell we've aided and abetted that's the point I'm making.

But maybe we felt we had no choice about it, it was happening all around us anyway unstoppable.

Then I welcome Armageddon good riddance to us all but not yet. I have to shake the Queen's white-gloved hand first.

And then what? Kill yourself?

Christ no, Mark, there's still so much more to do there's a niece I want to watch grow up isn't there. You'll guide her well you and Caroline she'll shine that girl. I'm certain of that and I like the thought of being the wild unpredictable uncle, the one wandering the world seeking what can't be found. Besides the end of the world needs an objective witness and that'll be me. I'll enjoy it, my self-appointed role and through it all I can think of you my brother and my sister-in-law and your little sharp-eyed daughter, my family once-removed the solid gentle love of you.

God you're drunk, Jack, what if she doesn't come to Cardiff? You've said it enough times it's a huge step to make especially with a baby in her arms.

He rose in the darkness, walked behind me along the spine of the ridge the bottle swishing loud, booze splashing. *You think I haven't read your secret fears? Hell nothing's much secret with your face. You give it all away all of it so I put it into words for you just to wake up your faith in her and as for big steps she started on one on her smoke-break at the arena years ago and she's been at your side all this time. You don't know half the strength in that woman, she defies everything in service to herself to her own inner course, that path she's aligned with yours. Mark you're the luckiest man on this planet so now you'd better choose.*

He pulled a lighter from his pocket, leaned forward and dropped it in my lap.

The city

For a week radio stations and television crews occupied the corner of Portage and Main. Crowds gathered, poured through, celebrities yelled into microphones. Someone had sliced the city's chest open, dismissive and contemptuous. The story spread like a stain across the nation. This was a city born of gathering, some faith remained with muscle to flex Portage and Main which had seen the Voyageurs take on the Métis and Natives which had seen a superstar hung from the neck until dead which had seen Lord Selkirk arrive with his team the Settlers which had seen immigrants arrive unfolding like butterflies which had seen fierce riots the Redcoats on horseback thundering down on crowds which had seen Bobby Hull accept his million dollar cheque which had seen Avco Cups and floods and blizzards.

And just a few blocks away, the Forks of the Red and Assiniboine rivers was another gathering place. Abandoned then retrieved, where we gathered in our thousands, all the children, all the immigrants, pockets stuffed with bills, jars rustling with coins, we wanted our team and we would buy it, give whatever it took to keep it the Jets. We would give what was necessary and the leaders who led from boardrooms and backrooms had no choice; they listened, they said yes maybe it's possible. We would have ripped their heads off if they'd turned their backs right then but for all their words, their hearts were dead inside. They relied on time, stretching it out with retracted rectums, bickering over words and lines of small print in whatever deals they had their lawyers concoct. The grey-haze confusion they created from clear hard diamond-sharp intent *we wanted our team and we were paying for it we were buying it* and the haze spread outward like exhaustion, poisoning us, sucking the strength from our limbs. The mayor had tears in her eyes, I think they were real, but giants had joined the game and maybe the question was asked *if they get their way on this one what will they demand next it's a bad precedent we'd better kill it before it kills us* or maybe the deadness inside was enough by itself and the gathering became a mockery, a fucking mime show.

Cynicism is self-fulfilling and it fulfilled itself. Took our will and dream and the belief that we were worth something, mangled it and handed back whispering *see told you didn't I?*

We came so close but we lost in the end. The team was gone and when she's gone she's gone for good. You know, when I was a kid I used to look forward to growing up.

The family

I never use public restrooms Axel said from the bushes *why go into a room where you have to smell other people's bowels?*

Because it's fun? Jack had stripped down naked again. It was warm enough, the sun blistering over us. Sophia stood beside him holding his penis instead of his hand like normal couples do. They were happy with each other arguing Greek Age Bronzology or whatever it was. We'd finally reached the coast, Cardiff somewhere across the water from where we were.

Axel was fouling the coastal path. The canoe waited down on the cobbles, the packs beside it. Fred stood like a colossal Rhodes scholar – one step would take him across the inlet or bay or whatever it was. Fred ticked and whirred his gears, awaiting the command to march to roar to destroy. We were still arguing the options when Axel stepped into view hitching up his pants and we all caught a fierce whiff of his bowels.

Fred! Jack screamed, *rend that man to pieces!*

I guess in some ways Axel got his wish, he was recycled reduced to bits scattered across the land or maybe he never existed anyway. There was no way to tell once Fred was done with him. Sophia found a plastic bag and went into the bushes to pick up after him and deposit the doodoo in a bin designed for that purpose. She was a brave lady got to hand it to her, though Jack made her wash her hands in the sea before he handed it back to her. At some point in all that she was impregnated. It's funny how these things just sort of happen, ask any topped-up fourteen-year-old girl.

Like a monster in a movie Axel reassembled himself. You don't get rid of Cambridge prodigies that easily. He was as apologetic as an engineer can get. We were surprised he apologized at all because most Brits never apologize for any brainless shit-stupid thing they do. We dithered a while before letting him rejoin our group. He was sort of a patched-up version closely resembling our canoe.

Sophia said Oh my God, we all turned to see her looking back inland. There was a mob of black people coming at us at a run, *My brothers.*

What all of them? There's hundreds!

They've brought their friends.

We'd better get moving.

We set out across the waves, the canoe leaking everywhere. I sent Fred on ahead to wait. I was heading for my try-out and behind us plunging into the surf was the mob of brothers and friends of brothers a little bit of sea wasn't stopping them. We set to paddling hard, real hard but they were gaining on us. *It's their whole swim team,* Sophia screamed.

The city

Caroline and the baby in her belly sat having a cigarette on the porch. The weather was hot, mosquitoes hiding in the grass, we were spending a week at Big Whiteshell Lake Resort had rented a cabin facing the rutted track that led down to the boat-launch the lake on our left. Caroline was big the baby was big they were both fine chilled-out and content and mildly buzzing. Jack and Lester had gone out in the canoe to fish all catch-and-release of course but I'd gone even soppier I didn't want to deliver pain and stress by hooking a fish. Lester said the excitement was good for them all I know is a hook through the lip wouldn't class as exciting for me especially with someone yanking on it so I'd given up fishing. My back was giving me trouble anyway. The chiropractor said my verts were pointing every which way, at least the ulcer had cleared up but I was worried about skin cancer now all those years as a kid canoeing under the sun *that's what babies do* Jack said *mortality creeping up on you.* Lester was twenty-two years old had three kids and two ex-wives and was cool with everything who knows what gentle spirits guided him, though I doubt his ex's were impressed. He painted a turtle on Caroline's belly for protection or maybe for the hell of it he just smiled when I asked him. We played poker late into the night Lester won six dollars I lost fifteen Jack asked me and Caroline when were we getting married? I said in Cardiff on centre-ice. Caroline smiled at him behind smoke he half-smiled back. Lester trimmed the deck offered her the cut she made it he showed us the bottom card it was the Queen of Hearts that man's hands were magic just ask his ex-wives *we'll skate up the aisle* I explained *with the baby in an Inuit papoose nestled under Caroline's breasts yes those are breasts you guys don't have to look just because I mention them.*

I can get you one, Lester said as he dealt the cards.
One what?
A papoose but a Cree one the softest deer-hide lots of beadwork.
Christ what a long sentence from you, Jack said.
It would have been longer but you interrupted me.
The suspense was killing me.
But the Inuit ones are chewed soft by Inuit grandmothers, I said.
We can import some Inuit grandmothers if Cree grandmothers aren't good enough for you.

I didn't say that.

I'll stack a Cree grandmother against an Inuit one any day.

What a chewing contest?

Fuckin' right nobody messes with Cree gums.

All right a Cree grandmother.

My grandmother scared off a Bigfoot once.

With her gums?

She was babysitting us it was late just like right now.

It got late back in those days too then did it? Jack asked.

It tried to get in through the cabin window.

Why didn't it use the door?

I said Bigfoot not Bigbrain.

It's still easier to get a big foot in the door than a window. How high was the window?

Ankle-high.

Well presumably Bigfoot had Wideankle.

She cursed it 'Gay yuh dai uh nha nha dun dun nananananana nyahnyah d'dun dun duh nananananananyaha' and it ran away.

Because it hated 'American Woman?'

Lester nodded.

I'm not surprised, Jack said.

He nodded again. *One card draw acey deucy wild card in the kitty over ten not diamonds earns us a second draw.*

So what did it look like?

What?

Bigfoot.

Well it was hairy with five toes I was only a baby you know.

Fair enough.

Wait a minute, I said, *it was just a big hairy foot sticking through the window?*

That's right that's what I said.

Well it could've been anybody's hairy foot couldn't it?

My Mum said it was probably Uncle Frank he lived in the bush.

See.

But he wasn't hairy.

It was winter?

Yeah.

Well he could've been wearing bear fur boots or something.

With five toes?

Bears have toes behind their claws.
Sure but bears have hair Frank didn't not on his feet anyway.
Oh … Yeah.
So, Jack said behind his cards, *it was probably a bear.*
Probably, Lester said.

Lester won the hand. None of the rest of us could figure out his rules, he made up new ones every time he dealt, always won those hands too. It'd been only a week since I'd woken up from my coma. I still went jittery on occasion but my hair was growing back the lightning bolt hadn't even burned me anywhere but it was still alive inside me. I had flashes behind my eyes as it raced around in my body and my brain I imagined becoming Lightning Man a superhero who could just point a finger and lightning would blast out incinerating careless drivers and other obnoxious people the world's cynical soul-rotten fat-cat assholes *ZAP!* nothing but ashes stirring in the wind *how's that for a bottom line, fellas?* We packed the game in a little after midnight. Jack and Lester went out for a paddle on the lake, Caroline took me by the hand to the bed we fucked slow and easy, her straddling me the big belly with its big baby inside resting heavy on my stomach shifting around every now and then. I luxuriated in the sheer mass of her solid and imposing pinning me down. The night was warm the air still everything quiet outside her tits were massive in my hands full to bursting she'd been focussing more and more into herself as the day neared it was magical to watch a little scary her dark depthless eyes rested on mine.

I thought I'd lost you.
You didn't you won't.
Everything fell to pieces.
It only seemed that way.
Then it came back together again I realized I could live without you me and the baby without you not how I wanted it but it would be possible.
I guess it would.
I think I'm happy with myself, Mark.
I think so too.
I'm immune to every outside pressure.
I know you are.
Does that scare you?
Sure but at the same time I love you for it.
Are you afraid I'm going to leave you? Not meet you in Cardiff?

All the time but it's out of my hands isn't it?

This child is yours, too, Mark.

I don't think you'd ever pretend otherwise.

Our last visit had been a little rough, the doctor seeing some other patient, us waiting in the waiting room, the nurse a prim puckered woman glaring across her desk at us. I finally said *What?* She scowled at Caroline.

You're making your child smoke twenty-five cigarettes a day, do you realize that?

Closer to thirty, Caroline said.

Good God that's ... evil.

The doctor appeared. He was young, tall, with red cheeks and a paunch. He had a file folder under one arm. His last patient wobbled out into the waiting room, looked a thousand years old, some character from the Bible, white bearded, every wrinkle immaculately tanned. He and the doctor stopped to listen as the nurse went on.

Do you intend to breast-feed your child?

Of course.

There will be even more nicotine in your milk.

Caroline shrugged, her hands in her lap, no expression on her face. The nurse rose from her seat, leaned over her desk and pointed *People like you should be arrested. It's evil what you're doing, an abomination.*

With the bearded guy there it was as if God who'd just come in for a check-up was right there with us I smelled brimstone knew it was brimstone even though I'd never smelled brimstone before. His huge rudder nose was swivelling back and forth. I saw a blistering halo form over the nurse, a burning sword in one hand now waving threateningly at Caroline.

An abomination I say! Spawn of the Devil! Antichrist!

I scowled at the doctor.

She's expressing a valid opinion, the doctor said puffing his cheeks.

This woman isn't the Antichrist, God said in a wheezy voice, *don't you think I'd know the Antichrist if I saw the Antichrist?*

Please Mr Candle your blood pressure.

Is just fine, son.

I pointed at the nurse, said to God, *Can't you just strike her down or something she's stressing the baby. It's begging for a smoke by now I guarantee it.*

If only I could, son. He shook his head tapped his chest *Doctor's orders* and out he marched both hands on the top of his head as if sizzling mana was raining down.

If you two will follow me, the doctor said exchanging one file for another and heading into the examination room. I thumbed my nose at the nurse whose eyes burned like Armageddon as we walked past. In the examination room the doctor fired up the ultrasound again ran a measuring tape across Caroline's belly peered between her legs and stuck a gloved hand up there then put gel on her belly and drew circles with the ultrasound pen while we all looked at the screen. *She looks fine, much to my surprise quite large in fact. I don't think she'll be underweight there's always the exception that proves the rule of course and there can always be undetectable defects which we'll only discover once she's born. There's doctors now who won't even treat you, you know.*

What about their hypocritic oath? I asked. *Will they stop treating alcoholics too? How about criminals?*

Well that's not the same.

Yes it is. How about obese people?

There's a medical —

And if there isn't? If it's just someone who eats too much? You guys going to stop treating them, too? Who made you fucking priests, judges, Inquisitors?

You know the Women's Movement should conscript Caroline as their Woman of the Century. Of course they never would disapproving as they would of her bad habit but she knew her own mind, was immovable, imperturbable, implacable, bullet-proof. They'd probably call her a psychopath. Now I won't deny our daughter was a little young to be taking up the habit though Jack always said it was priming her for pesticide-laced food, toxic atmosphere, the stress of unemployment, rebounding sexism, the widening poverty-gap, the fashion industry, radioactive waste, and the imminent genetic crossbreeding of beef with mango to achieve sexy meat. Jack saw Caroline as the official high priestess of the official Fuck You religion. For that you didn't wear a cross just a smile to answer every bit of self-righteous crap thrown at you looking at it that way Caroline's born-again faith was unassailable you could see it in her smile like the one she gave the doctor and the nurse on our way out, anyway I still had her enormous tits in my hands she was looking down on me the mystery there in her eyes,

Springsteen's Secret Garden territory here, I wasn't even at the gate. If I was the worshipping type I'd worship Mortal Woman meaning women in general no man on the planet can understand their ways their thoughts their motives their hungers their thirsts their degrees of satisfaction their discontent or what it's like being them inside those bodies with those tits those thighs those cheeks swaying to their own music. Don't get me wrong I'm not considering an operation to find out, wouldn't be the same anyway though I'd probably take masturbation to new heights. The point is women are beyond understanding the same way God is with His enigmatic 'Doctor's orders' twinkling mischief in his rheumy eyes exit stage left before shit hit the fan for real so I looked up into those unknowable eyes and did the only thing I could do which was surrender.

Hours later in the dark cabin, silence everywhere, I thought about Jack and Lester out on the lake. There's really nothing like canoeing at night with the water beneath you the same colour as the sky above you. You're drifting in the universe, the celestial stream, you can't see the shore even the insects are asleep. If you're away from everywhere you navigate by the stars and by sound and feel I don't know why I thought about all that right then but it seemed the sizzling lightning inside me was asleep or maybe it had gone out through the conduit of my cock and now raced inside Caroline lying on her side beside me and through the little baby too like something protective or maybe it had fizzled out entirely and the only mark of that strike that would stay with me was what I had dreamed while in the coma. My Dream of the Jerseys.

Forest

In the wilderness of Perry Sound, Ontario, a man stepped out from his log cabin and walked into the forest that would one day be one hundred and eighty acres of strawberries followed by a haphazard apple orchard then finally a suburb. In the cabin behind him was his young pregnant wife. Four miles to the east were their nearest neighbours, the Millers, who'd already cleared fifty acres of deciduous forest that was destined to become a landfill soaked in pcb's from discarded transformers culminating in the birth of a four-headed baby who would one day compose an entire team on CBC's Reach for the

Top which was a grade school copy of BBC's *University Challenge*, Canadian high-schoolers being as smart as British university students.

The man's name was Christian Churchill Mason and in his hands slept a sorcery waiting to be born.

He entered the forest, walked a short distance until he came to a glade. A basolith dome of Precambrian rock occupied the glade's centre, pushing up through the thin boreal soil. Ringing the clearing were aspen, silver birch, ash, elm, dogwood and hickory, as well poison ivy, a few Saskatoon berry bushes, choke-berry bushes, wintergreen, wild ginger, puffballs, juniper and blueberry bushes.

He strode forward until he stood on the quartz-veined rhyolite-veined gold-speckled bedrock that was already three billion years old, maybe older, that had already witnessed over a trillion sunrises, over a trillion sunsets – over a trillion days of baking heat and brittle cold, give or take a few centuries of absolute darkness when under a mile or ten of glacial ice. Bedrock that had looked up into a night sky without an orbiting moon. Bedrock that had felt the tred of dinosaurs and the pressures of vast oceans.

On that marred surface the man saw scraped scars, each ten inches long and repeating one after another across the exposed dome, two sets running parallel. He stared at these peculiar tracks a long, long time.

He did not know it but the bedrock was slowly lifting under him, a fact that would one day doom his thirsty strawberry plants. It had been bearing a lot of weight ten thousand years earlier, pushed down under tons and tons of ice, and it was still rebounding. And so, as he stood there, he rose a fraction closer to heaven.

Just enough for his invisible third eye in the middle of his forehead to intersect the invisible stream where God's secret river of revelations coursed. The revelation came to him as it must, and the sorcery in his hands came alive.

Looking upon the forest around him, Clayton Charles Masters saw not paper mills nor pulp mills, for a man on skates had once passed this way, and so he saw the country's future in its purest form: a forest of sticks. Hockey sticks.

To this day you can stand on Precambrian bedrock and as the minutes pass you will rise imperceptibly closer to heaven.

The wall

This is how I want it to be, Sophia said duffing in the middle of the canoe her brothers a quarter mile behind us the stars twinkling overhead a bitter cold wind sweeping crossways from the west every muscle in me and Jack screaming with pain Axel rigging up his fishing gear *for the rest of my days. I feel a squirming something in my belly down deep.*

You should never have washed your hands in the sea, Jack said.

It was fated to be. As soon as I saw your penis, Jack, it was like seeing my future right there complete all spelled out for me. Do you know what I mean?

I plan on travelling the world, Jack said.

I'm coming with you, we're coming with you.

I swore between gasps. *Haven't your brothers got anything better to do?*

Not them you twit. Jack understands don't you?

All too well.

Axel had his rig ready had one of those short unfolding fishing rods. He trailed the flashing lure into the black water let out line in arm-length sweeps.

I never used to be a penis-worshipper, Sophia went on, *but now everything's changed. It wasn't just the size it was the tattoo. I used to be a Feminist until the moment our eyes met across the crowded pub. I realized I was staring into my own destiny. Remember I didn't know about your penis then but some part of me must have. We just have to square it with Agamemnon that's all.*

Who the hell's Agamemnon? I asked.

My oldest brother.

Like hell she's talking bullshit, Jack snapped, *now she'll say another one's named Achilles and another one's named Odysseus yeah right.*

My oldest brother's nine years older than me. Do you think that's an accident, Jack?

Homer was not a prophet, Sophia.

It's the cycles of history, darling Jack, that's what it is. Look, I'm being spirited away and they're coming in pursuit and outside the walls of Cardiff the tragedy will come to fruition.

Cardiff has walls? I asked.

I got something nibbling, Axel whispered, *Nibbling ... nibbling ... nibbling ...* he yanked back on his little rod *Got him!*

We stopped going forward, we started going sideways south out toward open sea.

The family

In the end sports matters more than politics matters more than big business matters more than anything and everything and it always has. Used to be sports belonged to the commoner the game was outside all else. It stood outside and it stood for all that was outside. It was the goal that was uncorruption, that was rising into grace, that was holy and pure and unsullied. If sport had power it was power that couldn't be stolen by the politicians or by businessmen. Even Hitler found that out and because of that I guess it was a threat to people in power so the people in power set their sights on it and brought corruption into it poisoning the game and all it stood for until there was nowhere left to turn nowhere left to focus outside everything else and now the world's a poorer place a world of cynics and grafters and soul-sellers and soul-buyers. They came in and pissed on the altar and we didn't just watch we invited them in.

One day I'll come back to Winnipeg to see the slow gathering a gathering so slow no one will even notice it happening. The Jets jersey will reappear, worn by three young girls worn by the stats geek by little kids and their mothers and their grandmothers and grandfathers not in homage to the past but in avowal to the future, not nostalgia but a promise and the currents will pick up steam a will that'll start in silence not even noticed just building then building some more because what's possible is worth believing in believe hard enough and the possible becomes real and you can load on its back all the meaning you want or hardly any meaning at all. It can carry whim and determination wistful smiles and fierce threat. I dreamed, the lightning bolt circling and spreading spiralling outward touch one touch another, outward, gathering more and more, taking back what once belonged, taking it back because it's what's right *when she's gone she's gone but she's coming back she's coming back you just watch.* A mother in the greys, her two hulking sons with her as real as the game they've come to watch and claim for themselves for now for this moment of their lives. The spray of gold mist on ordinary lives, triumph and heartbreak yearning seeing wishing failing. And this is my dream, the dream I dreamed six days in a coma awakening on the seventh day.

Caroline decided on a midwife. Her name was Marie. She was big and round, a card-carrying lesbian with a brushcut and a Spitfire tattoo on the brawny arm she showed me when we arm-wrestled the first day. Beat me clean. I pleaded technique but not seriously. She announced she had a crush on Caroline so we could rest assured she would treat her right, maybe even steal her away if she could. I saw her then as a sorceress capable of anything, even transforming Caroline's gender preference in the sex department.

It could have been Marie slicking Caroline with her tits or maybe it was our fucking later that night but she started into labour next morning, the baby figuring it'd better get out if it wanted any uninterrupted sleep. I woke up to find Caroline sucking on one butt after another as if they were her version of that pain-numbing gas Marie swore was modern civilization's sole positive contribution to childbirth. I phoned Marie and she said she'd be there in twenty minutes.

The forest

The morning after we'd stood the fire break, we got out of our tents to find the entire western skyline ablaze. The wind had shifted twice, first blowing the fire south then tossing it westward, it was out of control we got airlifted out, dropped back down by helicopter into the fire's face, the Whiteshell Park's invisible demarcation line engulfed in flames, aspen parkland at our backs. If the wind kept blowing, if we couldn't stop the fire right here, there was nothing between it and Winnipeg except seventy miles of pocket forests, fields of crops at their driest and farmhouses. We were suddenly fighting to save Winnipeg, blasted in our faces by heat and ashes and cinders gouts of flame whirlwinds rising up in towering spouts, the crew shrieking and screaming as we were driven back step by step.

The word came that the army was on the way, fifteen hundred soldiers from CFB Shilo. We hacked at brush dug trenches, chopped down trees, dumped water, pissed into the flames, anything everything we could think but she kept on coming. Marie and Brig held hands chanting something pagan that sounded like the smell of blood. I boiled water, I boiled milk and orange juice, I poured a fifth of scotch and downed it but nothing helped. I sat down beside her, concentrated on lighting cigarettes for her, staring down at the quivering flickering conflagration. The army arrived, a German regiment in Leopard Tanks and Scorpions with the Canadians in WWII SPG's. Shells flew thick and furious, explosions, night-stars in dyed smoke, the thumping blades of helicopters, the cloying membrane-burning smell of napalm. The fire marched relentless westward, devouring everything in its path. We could see Winnipeg's skyline at our backs, there was no stopping it. Brig and Marie pulled us to one side *you're the only ones standing between the way things were and the way they're about to become, you've got to hold right here can you do it?* We nodded, us standing on a rise that wouldn't be called a hill anywhere else but in Manitoba, standing in the path of the avenue of flames reaching like Lucifer's arm straight for the city's heart. We pulled out our shovels, no one else in sight, the last ones left. The fire gusted heat against us. Jack turned to me, all falling silent for just that one moment.

Well, Mark?

I thought hard, all the history, all the surrendering, all the losses, all the failures. I thought about the glories the dreams the faded kids the winter-silent grandfathers, girls in jerseys, fuck-you governments, distant skeletal hands pulling strings. I thought about the schools I'd been to, the rinks I'd played in, the friends I'd made. I thought about Portage and Main, the Forks, Pembina Highway, polar bear migrations, lynched hockey players, massacres settlers traders middlemen Redcoats premiers and sweaters, mayors in red dresses, blizzards and floods and wind-chills, dust and gravel, mosquitoes and black flies, snowdrifts and ice, a dog dying in my arms, a father wrapping his car around a tree but already dead of a massive heart attack, a mother sinking away into herself. I thought of Caroline and Mack her ex with his rental cars and bank accounts and goaltending advice *keep your glove hand higher, son* and I met Jack's eyes. And said *Let it burn.*

159

The city

We climbed into our hockey gear, seemed a weird thing to be doing on a hot summer day, the whole Plains Cree hockey team, me and Jack and Mosley. Sweetgrass was burned, passed over us, cigarettes were smoked then we all descended into the sweatlodge.

I think Brett Hull could have been hockey's best player. He's got the brains and the talent. He just doesn't like hard work.

Great in interviews. He knows the game is fucked and he says so and everybody shrugs and says that's just Brett Hull and that's that.

The real problem is clutch and grab slows everything down to a crawl it comes with so many professional teams watering down the talent pool.

How can you water down a pool?

You know what I mean, shit.

But the game's at a level never seen before.

Maybe it only seems that way maybe it actually sucks.

It's all pretend anyway.

What do you mean?

I mean it doesn't mean shit.

Who is that I'll kill him.

None of us that's the Great Spirit talking.

You saying the Great Spirit's not a hockey fan? Get serious.

You always get one pessimist ... in every sweatlodge always one, why is that?

Must be a percentage thing.

Must be and it's probably this guy with his elbow in my face.

Ow you don't have to bite, shit, I'm not your pessimist.

Who brought in their hockey stick?

That's not my hockey stick, asshole.

So why's it taped up?

Funny now stop jerking on it.

Shouldn't there be a stipulation that we use deodorant?

You saying humans smell bad?

I'm saying humans stink.

Sorry I had beans for lunch.

So am I.

I just saw a little guy crawl out of someone's ear.

What did he look like?

Pierre Berton.

Oh God someone's leaking history.

You should be thankful considering what he could be leaking.

When I was six I saw God he was in a Habs' jersey Number 10.

Wrong that was Guy Lafleur.

No it was God, skated like lightning, beard flowing like flames in the wind.

I'm telling you that was Guy Lafleur but it wasn't a beard it was just his hair.

This was God. You think I couldn't tell the difference even at six? And He said to me: Frank, I shall give your life a mission and this mission shall be your life, your life in entirety shall be your mission.

Okay you're right that was God. No one else talks like that not even Guy Lafleur.

Unless he's giving a hundred and ten percent.

Even then Frank's right it was God. Wearing the Habs jersey was the clincher. God always backs a winner.

So what mission was this, Frank?

The one on the Reserve.

What? You mean that broken-up pre-fab trailer that crazy Jesuit lived in?

That's the one, or so I thought, I mean what would I want with that mission. The Jesuit was still living there must have been over a hundred years old by then.

He's still there.

No he isn't and neither is the mission.

They moved the mission, Frank. Towed it away with him inside it I was there I saw it you were at school or college or something I swear it, Frank.

That would make that Jesuit what, a hundred twenty-five years old.

Was God on skates, Frank?

Bauer skates, anyway I've since reconsidered His words to me and I think He didn't mean the mission on the Reserve, He meant some other mission.

Where, then? Swift Current?

Not where, but what.

All right so what is your mission, Frank?

Well I don't know now, is there one in Swift Current?

Wait wait wait ... Frank, what did you think your mission was, before Albert mentioned Swift Current?

To become the next Guy Lafleur.

You can't you haven't got thinning blonde hair.

Not to mention talent.

You're too old anyway, Frank.

And Guy's not dead you can't become the next Guy until the present Guy's dead.

No it's allowed Guy's retired from hockey so Frank can become the next Guy Lafleur.

All he has to do is retire?

No, you're not getting it. Mention Guy Lafleur and you mean Guy Lafleur the hockey player. Like Pele. Mention Pele and you don't mean Pele now, retired and all, you mean Pele the soccer player.

Football.

No, soccer. Pele never played in the NFL.

Or the CFL.

The rest of the world calls soccer football, you twit.

You mean like Italians?

Right.

Hey everybody I thought this was supposed to be a spiritual experience?

Some white guy said that.

Obviously.

This is a spiritual experience, dolt. We're talking hockey.

So was Gretzky the best ever?

The Kid Who Had It All

Here's the truest of stories. The month was August. The agent had flown up to a lake in Northern Alberta for one last fishing trip before resuming contract negotiations with a dozen teams on behalf of the dozen marquee players he represented, all of whom were in the Option Years of their contracts.

It was a fly-in lake, no roads, and packed shore to shore with Lake Trout. The agent spent the weekend reeling them in. He'd been dropped off with only a guide for company. Sunday afternoon the Norseman float-plane landed and they loaded their gear aboard. The pilot said get a move on there's a storm front rolling in.

They took off, the plane climbing into the clouds. The storm buffeted them about, loaded the wings with ice, filled the fuel lines with crystals of condensate. The Norseman's lone prop engine sputtered, died. The plane plummeted toward the thick forests below.

The crash was a nasty one, both the pilot and the guide being killed instantly, leaving the agent alone, abandoned. He stayed within the wreckage that night and the morning broke clear and cold. He stumbled outside, half in shock, and wandered off.

As anyone who knows the bush will tell you, that was a mistake. Should've stayed with the plane. Should've eaten the guide and pilot if necessary. The plane had a transponder. Rescue helicopters were warming up less than a hundred miles away. Instead, the agent wandered into the wildlands and was quickly lost.

Some people think the boreal forest is a place of plenty. No it ain't. You can walk all day and not see a single other living thing apart from plants. Not a squirrel, not a bird. If the season's past there's no blueberries, no mushrooms, no grubs. If you're lucky you'll stumble on a lake and if you've got fishing gear you'll catch yourself a supper, but sometimes you can walk within sixty feet of a lake and not even know it. The land's flat, the trees tall. It's hostile, unforgiving land.

The agent stumbled through the bush, exhausted, numbed, disorientated. And the air grew colder. Another storm coming in, this one bringing snow. He spent a night in the sinkhole left by a tree-fall, the wall of upturned roots at his back. His fingers turned blue; he couldn't feel his nose or the tips of his ears. Snow came down an inch every half-hour, the arctic wind howling.

He fought to keep himself awake, having read somewhere that sleep would kill under these conditions, and the hours slowly dragged on until the darkness began to fade, the wind dropping off, the clouds cracking open to reveal blue sky and a world frozen white.

The agent was in trouble and he knew it. He began walking once again, moving fast to warm himself up, selecting a direction and sticking to it as best he could.

The forest around him was perfectly still, the air bitter cold. He entered an expanse of marshy ground, the peat crunching underfoot, fog draped knee-high hiding stumps and sinkholes. Ahead he saw a clearing through the black spruce boles, and heard a strange sound. It was familiar, yet out of place. He listened more carefully, slowly

163

creeping up on the clearing, until the sound was unmistakable. He came to the clearing's edge.

The opening was a frozen pond, wreathed in fog, and on the pond a lone boy was playing hockey. He was of the First Nations – as the agent had learned to call Native Americans – a hulking youth of about seventeen, wearing fur-lined mukluk skates and shoulder-pads covered in tattered wolverine fur. He skated like a god. Though he couldn't see the puck through the fog, he stickhandled it effortlessly with a home-made straight-bladed stick.

The boy looked up as the agent stumbled onto the ice. And smiled.

Down in the agent's soul something burst into light, a conviction that here was not just a great hockey player: here was the greatest hockey player that ever lived. It was a conviction born of a sourceless faith – he'd not seen the kid take on other players, plunging into the fierce frenzy of an actual game – yet the agent knew. *He knew.*

The kid led the agent out of the wilderness, and once returned to civilization the agent in turn led the kid into the world of professional hockey. He got the boy signed onto a farm-team but that lasted only two games – the kid was too good for that, scoring thirty goals the first game, forty-five the next. No one could touch him, no goalie could stop him.

The agent decided to hold an auction on the boy's rights. The bidding was fierce, the bidding was like ripping nuggets of gold from the ground, the bidding tore a hole through the ceiling of sanity and common-sense, and the winning team signed the kid to a forty-year one billion dollar deal, resulting in a hike on ticket prices to five thousand bucks a seat in the arena's nosebleed section.

The boy was placed on a throne the throne carried in by four full-time servants devoted to his every whim and desire. He was then transferred to a solid gold Cadillac that was driven by the President of the United States out onto centre ice. There was no cheering, since every seat in the arena had been purchased by the media and corporate sponsors who'd filled their respective seats with product placement to be seen by the thirty thousand cameras beaming the scene to every household on the planet. There were no other players present either – they'd all decided to sit out demanding renegotiations on their contracts.

The Head of the United Nations opened the Cadillac's door and the kid stepped onto the ice, stick in his hands. He skated a few circles, then stopped and looked around. And around. And around. Up in one of the broadcast booths, the agent looked down on his prize with shining eyes. He'd done it. He'd swung the biggest deal in the history of sport, in the history of anything. He'd done it. The kid was his, all his, and already the agent was trying to work out a way of exploiting an ambiguous clause in the contract to leverage for more money.

Commentators and guests on the ice started getting restless. The boy was just standing there, looking around. Then he skated back to the car, tossed in his stick and gloves. He skated over to the boards, clambered over them and made his way into the dressing room.

Suddenly fearful, the agent bolted, rushing down the endless flights of stairs to finally arrive, heart pounding, at the dressing room door. He pushed it open, but the boy was gone. He was gone.

And was never seen again.

He was a fool, they said.

He wasn't that good anyway.

It was a scam, the biggest con-job in history.

He had no heart he had no soul he had no respect for the game.

Just a punk.

They said all those things and a lot more. For a while anyway, then the whole thing just faded away as such things do. The agent survived because agents always survive. The striking players went back to work after renegotiating their salaries. Ticket prices were readjusted accordingly. And it was as if the kid had never been.

And that is the truest of stories, I swear to God.

The Family

In all the excitement somebody forgot to call the doctor. Marie blamed me I blamed Marie. Caroline told us both to shut the fuck up, not loudly but quiet and dangerous-like. She was focused so far into herself that looking into her eyes was a scary experience, animal, nothing but animal, everything you could think of had spilled out of her. I'd changed the sheets three times then switched to towels and it just kept on gushing out, the thought of her thingy going wide enough so a baby could crawl out had me in a state of babbling awe and outside the apartment windows, flames were high in the sky flickering off the glass, there'd been lightning earlier reminded me of the night lightning struck the new Denny's on Pembina Highway hee hee burned it to the ground but it was just the forest fire come west to burn every bridge. I welcomed the heat, I felt purged though not purged the way Caroline was. It was like she was giving birth to her bowels and bladder as well as the baby whose head I could see taking my chances bending low and peeping between her legs when she wasn't squatting. She said she wasn't going to lie down didn't feel right lying down. Marie said that position was for the convenience of the doctors and nurses not the mother so fuck that, any position you want, love muffin. I said hey you're not allowed to call her love muffin if anyone was going to call her love muffin it was me. Marie just grinned, a triumphant gleam in her bullet-grey eyes. She said you've done your job, man, you're not needed any more. So I did the only thing I could do. I challenged her to another arm-wrestle, she agreed so we set to the coffee table between us Caroline groaning on the sofa-bed. We put our weight into it, our muscles creaking we grunted swayed bore-down the table shimmying under our elbows. Marie brought her face close to mine.

This is the one, male pig, I win this and she's mine. You walk away like a good little sperm-producer. Me and her will raise this little goddess who's on her way into the male-dominated paternalistic nightmare of a fucked-up world. We'll shelter her, raise her right, teach her empowerment.

Fuck that, I growled through gritted teeth, *you don't know what Caroline's done to me in bed during sex so don't talk to me about empowerment.*

You were just a wussy, Mark, letting her do that stuff.

Like hell I was.

God she was winning. Slowly edging my arm down. My muscles screamed in agony. If I lost this one I'd lose it all *Wow* I said.

What?

I just noticed your tits aren't tits. They're just muscle, they don't move at all. You're probably a man.

I gave it one last shot then her eyes wide with shock, as I angled up threw my weight down and pinned her arm onto the table top.

You bastard!

I win, I said, rocking back. *Hah.*

You called me a man!
No I didn't. I likened you to a man. Big difference.
I'm going to knock your teeth through to the back of your skull.
You're sounding just like a man only you're without a dick.
I'll kill you.
You call me a wussy, I call you a dickless man so we're even.
Caroline gasped, *She's coming, she's coming, she's coming!*
There's a science to winning arguments, just like there's a science to winning an arm-wrestling match. Most of the time women win arguments but not this time. There's winning and there's winning then there's winning when you lose and losing when you win and other times winning's just plain winning and losing's just plain losing. Marie lost but I couldn't yet be sure that she hadn't won.

The wall

Axel had hooked something big. We tried to paddle against it but no chance. Jack said *Cut the damn line, Axel. You've snagged a submarine or something!* but Axel shook his head *I won't, I won't, I won't.* It was inexorable, relentless, pulling us westward into open sea. Axel lashed his fishing line through the thwarts, under the seats, around his waist, his ankle, through Sophia's twig-entwined hair, looped it around his big toe, left foot, then right, *We're all in this all of us nobody cuts this line nobody.* The seas started heaving under us, spray whipping from the white manes of the waves. Big black clouds started blotting out the stars overhead. The world closed in glowering. We sweated with the paddles doing draws and ruddering and sweeps just trying to keep the canoe upright, Axel was screaming as he tugged on the line something about a philosopher's stone the engineer's original paradigm the lost science of alchemy and something that sounded like *beaucoup foucault* assuming it was French and me being unilingual I assumed everything I couldn't understand was probably French. He'd hooked something big, bigger than all of us so big the word big doesn't do it justice actually it could have been *Francois Truffault* or Frank Truffle in English now that I think on it, he was a player on the French National team a second tier team bad enough to get whupped by the Japanese though Axel knew nothing about hockey we'd say 'hockey' and he'd blink and say 'ice hockey you mean?' well no kidding what other hockey is there? And don't talk to me about field hockey that game's got so many stupid rules there's no flow to it at all, everybody stops for incomprehensible reasons turns over the ball to the other side I don't know why, didn't see any infractions worth mentioning, what a frustrating game to watch anyway the something big was rising swelling up thrashing under us not a submarine after all something animate, flesh and blood, muscle and bone, primeval primordial a behemoth a leviathan long and sinuous shimmering scales arcing out of the water our canoe yanked under the arc the next thing we knew we had a serpent's body across the canoe's beam between me and Axel astern and Sophia and Jack at the bow. It was bronze in colour and smelled of salty mud, pocked with barnacles, morays clinging to it gills gaping air. The beast's weight settled, an ominous cracking sound running the length of the canoe the cedar ribs shuddering then bowing outward canvas splitting *oh hell* Jack said.

Axel shrieked and flung himself onto the serpent, clambering up to ride it like a horse. The body slid into motion oozing across the gunnels *It's leaving!* I shouted as I reached out with my knife and sliced through the monofilament line just before Sophia had her hair ripped off her head *Wait!* We'd get to the tail sooner or later then we'd be fine already the mass had shifted but Jack shook his head *If we wait for the tail we'll get the head with it! We've got to work it off – now!*

Head? Tail? Made no sense to me but one look at his face I took him at his word, threw myself forward under the sliding length on my hands and knees, raised my back against the slimy body and heaved.

Later Sophia told me she last saw Axel still clinging to the serpent as it vanished under the waves. Anyway at the moment I was too busy to see for myself as I pitted my Canadian muscles against the beast from the depths, rose up bellowing, staggering back a step then shrugging the body off, past the stern. We were free of the damned thing and the canoe was sinking.

Bail Sophie bail!

The coast was a half-mile away, the lights of Cardiff twinkling. We paddled like fiends, Sophia bailing with our camp cookpot. The sun was blushing the eastern horizon, the keel was cracked, there were ribs jutting through the canvas to either side. Our canoe was dying gracefully and gamely. It was touch and go whether we could stretch that last gasp.

You'd be surprised what a player will go through to tryout for a team, but the myth of the walk-on earning a place in the line-up then becoming a superstar lives on still and all across the country. Where teams aren't so rule-bound that they don't accept walk-ons, there's strangers, complete unknowns, undrafted prospects, showing up at arena entrances quiet and determined but alone with their dreams. Come to show what they can do. So many dreams in this world are silent ones dreams held close until that moment when someone says *okay let's see what you can do*, it's the myth of sport but not just sport it's the power of mystery and human hearts and all they're capable of and capable of holding. We yearn for the innocent and the naïve, the unsullied, the pure talent to show us all what's inside, because the heart of sport is the human soul and sometimes just sometimes we need to see that soul come striding into the scene, onto the rink, onto the field. We sit and watch hoping they'll show the best not just in them but in all of us too.

It may be that humility is the most magical of all the virtues but it's also the most vulnerable and just as we look at a kid young enough to still be innocent and feel sad knowing the loss of that is ahead of them, so we look at the green rookie all bursting with talent and natural modesty and we feel sad even as we admire because the chances are high that corruption will come because like the Hollywood and rock stars always say, fame fucks you up. Some come through it most don't. If you ask me any movie star demanding twelve million per movie hasn't come through nothing and I don't care how modest and self-effacing they seem on the talk-shows it's all bullshit like putting your neighbour's homely face on the skull of greed don't buy the smile check the bloodless hunger in the eyes. The American dream has a postscript Jack always says and it's simple *and if you achieve it it'll destroy you.* The disease has long since spread to sports and it's the rare star who escapes it but even with them the truth remains that three months' salary from any one of them could rebuild every house in an African village, buy new school books and build a new school to boot. If something's not wrong here I'd like to be told because it's souring me something awful.

The family

Having the baby arrive, dropping down off the edge of the sofa into my hands probably wasn't part of the plan. I was pretty sure there was supposed to be a doctor involved at some point, at least a nurse and I'm pretty sure we talked about it happening in a hospital. I had this picture in my head from some movie I guess of looking through a glass window down onto a row of babies wondering which one was ours, the one with skates on her feet and blowing smoke-rings I guess. Jack said *just look for the one with blue eyes in epicanthic folds* meaning Japanese eyes. Anyway that scene never materialized. Instead I kneeled in front of Caroline's squatting legs and this baby's black-haired head showed in her impossibly big thingy, two more groaning pushes like a priestess before the altar of the Goddess of Constipation and out came the head, the smaller body slurping out after it. Basically giving birth means giving birth to a big brain inside a big skull, the body follows like an afterthought and the eyes are all squeezed shut, the face red and crusty and her mouth opens and out comes bleating sounds. I've got one hand on the umbilical like it was a pull-cord, the other is holding the entire baby head body, everything right there, an entire squalling creation with no penis and therefore an alien brain. She already scared me. Little pudgy fingers grasping mystery and cunning behind the eyes that Marie swabbed open blue as blue. I imagined invisible strings in her hands already pulling me this way and that with female instinct the natural assumption of power. Marie whispered *It's the Goddess reborn* I said *Oh no.*

The sweatlodge I guess was just one big artificial womb inside which we were lodged together sweating but I'd left the womb a long time ago without having any real desire to return to it so it all seemed kind of silly though I didn't say so since everyone else was taking it seriously conversation getting heated *was Guy Lafleur God or not?* Everyone had an opinion and if there'd been room it would've come to blows, as it was people kicked tweaked and pinched and occasionally bit to emphasize whatever point they were making. It had been unanimously agreed that Wayne Gretzky had engraved on his DNA *This Shall Be A Player of Hockey*, a collective acknowledgement of every spirit god and goddess that ever existed, even the ghost of Louis Riel smiled benignly at the proclamation, this was an Ontario farmboy who was Mr. Hockey just as his hero Gordie Howe had once been but when it came to Guy Lafleur there was controversy and ultimately schism not healed to this day. It wasn't that Guy had more talent than anyone else because he didn't he was talented sure but not the most talented not by a long shot but Guy might still have been the second coming because the time was right for him when he arrived and it's this confluence that whispered *magic* not to mention his waving hair as he flew down the wing now personally since I'd never been much of a Canadiens' fan *sacre bleu!* and *Numero Dix* was just another number in my books, I couldn't have cared less about the argument and so said nothing, just laid there like a corpse jammed in the hold of a slave ship with Spartacus muttering revolution beside me, being jabbed by his cleft chin till I clicked and realized he was checking to see if I was still alive and asking me to roll over, not Spartacus at all not even Kirk Douglas I groaned something to ease his concern. I closed my eyes again and saw a thousand angels descending from a brilliant sky all wearing Jets jerseys, pristine, blinding white, those jerseys with that crappy but glorious logo. I saw God's finger behind them turning back the wheel of time or maybe forward, it was a massive blunt yellowed finger with a battered nail and shiny ridged calluses, this was the working stiff's God, the herder's God, the winter-silence God, God the immigrant, God the death-camp survivor, God the pioneer the sodbuster the itinerant farmer fruit-picker, God the silent watcher with red-rimmed eyes, a face wrinkled into infinity, with every life taken every path chosen the ravaged lines of human history, but in His eyes I saw the eyes of our newborn baby and that was that wasn't it.

There were dark blotches in the city of Winnipeg and one of them was a neighbourhood called Wolseley, a place with more than it's share of whining smug middle-class guppies, guppies being granola-eating yuppies. They wore khaki and sandals with socks, produced hordes of obnoxious children, rode their mountain bikes on the streets every Sunday. Other people lived in that neighbourhood but I'm not talking about them right now. The guppies were the ones who during the entire Jets crisis waved their pale plucked wings saying *it's just a hockey team what about the homeless the substance-abused the stalked the storked the deprived the deranged the fatherless children? Our hearts bleed when we think about them on our way to the Fort Whyte Centre to look at the ducks and geese, all that money raised by those kids, those people from all walks of life, that money should be put to better use. New housing projects, new community self-help empowerment programs for the underprivileged, this isn't real city spirit it's nothing but paying through the nose for a bunch of overpaid hockey players* but you know it's easy bleating for a holy cause when it costs you nothing, when your expectation is always for someone else to do the dirty work to make the real commitment. I'm sick of self-righteous twits packed full of meatless words, it's just the easy cheap virtue words from a dreamworld nothing to do with reality. The real source of their complaints, as they watched the city's people rise to the cause, was resentment *not their cause,* and besides down deep they resented seeing anyone caring enough about something to dig down into their pockets and put hard cash behind their dreams, hell that's an alien notion as far as they're concerned, for them there is no down deep just pond-scum, those who gathered at the Forks with their scraped-together savings weren't the city's guppies they were the city's poor and the city's just-getting-by and some of the city's well-off who remembered they had hearts after all and personal memories that meant something, those who gathered weren't stupid, weren't ignorant, weren't misled, weren't to be looked down from superior heights, they were and this is the truth, they were the best of Winnipeg. They were the resurrection of the city's spirit, Winnipeg's glory, its beauty and its strength and its pride. There'll always be ones who resent all of that and put it down, ones whose sense of pride only goes as far as the new Volvo in their garage, but my memory remains, the vision burns behind my eyes, that gathering, the people of the city rising up to pay to keep their dream alive, and my rage now has the face of those smug guppies who won in the end and the Winnipeg with the Jets, the Winnipeg with homeless people substance-abused people the downtrodden and the deprived, is now Winnipeg with homeless people substance-abused people the downtrodden and the deprived. What's changed? Simple: no Jets. Nothing else, not a goddamned thing except another layer of loss, another scar to carry, a little less hope, a little less optimism, a little less faith, *we can't change things why try?* and that dear guppies will come home to roost.

Sitting in the dark, Caroline and baby sleeping, Marie gone home and the flicker of flames in the street, I found myself looking into the future because the future is my little girl's and already I grieve for her and I am frightened down to the core.

From that darkness came memories. All the children I've known, worked with, took care of, and how they've changed, how they seem to have grown up quicker than when I was a kid but was it really growing up quicker? Children today got attitude, they're cynical sceptical they trust nothing, it was one thing when priests and politicians started falling, the exposure of perversion and corruption, not many of them were heroes anyway but then the sports stars started falling not just from greed but taking bribes, taking drugs, beating up their wives, the works. Who's left to look up to, who's left to worship, what's left to strive for except looking out for yourself, grab what you can and fuck the rest, the players are sour, the teams pack up and go or fold, every star out for themselves, bigger contracts, more money, selling their feet their smiles their hairstyles the burgers they eat the cars they drive, they've sold every part of their bodies, every part of their brains, every aspect of their lives, nothing can't be bought, here's your role model, kids, is it any wonder the global fuck-up's getting worse?

It's just the way of the world. Is that what I tell my daughter? Is that my only answer to every disgusting thing she will see? Switch on the news and watch stations selling murder, wars and disaster between commercials *here's the world, girl and if you survive clawing your way through the poisons maybe you'll find something that isn't for sale but don't count on it.* In the love of the game it's the love that counts and that love is the currency the players and owners are using in their mad buy and sell frenzy, how long will that love last? Not long. Problem is, love is the currency for everything else that's worthwhile in this life, bleed it here and it dies there and there and there. In the end she'll grow up with only herself to hold onto and like Jack says we weren't built that way, isolation turns us rotten just look around for proof of that.

We didn't let it burn no matter what we said. Like battling against the flood, we remembered the spirit that used to be, remembered it well enough to answer it once again but I'm scared because the next generation might be a generation not of savers but of looters, as the fires arrive, as the water rises, they'll just grab what they can and run.

Some people can look at anything and call it a small, meaningless kill, a barely felt absence, one less bird in the sky, one less animal underfoot, one less store in the town-centre, one less team, one less place to escape to, one less dream to tug at your heart. Some people are so used to giving up and turning their backs it's become a way of life, the total sum of the lessons taught their children, the *tsk tsk it's a damn shame but nothing we can do about it*, the line repeated over and over again in one situation after another until life itself is a journey of ducking and dodging, vision shuttered to take in only what can be grabbed and clutched to chest along the way, there's no solving the world's problems when you refuse to see them.

These midnight hours dragged on and on Jack's Armageddon came camping out with endless horror stories around the dying fire of my soul. I felt sticky, grim, weighed down blood-heavy and goddamned old that night with Caroline and our baby girl asleep in the other room. I guess there's a lot of people who would laugh at that since all I've stirred in them is cold ashes but I don't care, I've had my say. It was a bloody awful night that ended with a hungry cry in the dark.

The wall

You left me behind years ago, Mark, you always pushed that little bit harder, something I never did. I had all this talent but it stopped mattering to me so instead of pushing that extra bit I turned away. Is it a failure of the soul, I don't know. I think it's more like a loss of fearlessness. You sometimes see it in professional players, they take a nasty injury and when they come back from it something's missing, that hunger isn't there, the willingness to take punishment to get what you're going for, it's a metaphor for life itself, Mark, if you walk down the same alley every night and someone comes up and punches you in the face one night then the next then the next every damn night, pretty soon you stop walking down that alley, pretty soon you think you'd rather stay home, not go out at all because that fist might be waiting, not just in that one alley but in every alley, so you don't go out at all and that not going out kills something inside you because that alley was the way you had to go to get to the glory and maybe the glory's just a game but maybe it's something else entirely, maybe it's believing in yourself, maybe it's faith, maybe it's finding maturity or wisdom or knowledge, but now it's all a million miles away, getting farther away by the minute, and before you even realize it you've lost sight of it, then you lose even the memory of it and one night years later, you've lived a life and you're sitting in the dark and something stirs inside you, something draws a breath for the first time in decades, down in your soul and if you're into deceiving yourself you say 'that was just a kid's dream better off without it, it's all a part of growing up' and that's that but sometimes that breath brings clarity and your heart pounds, you sweat, there's tears in your eyes and afterward you feel old, wasted because you see it was all supposed to mean something, you were sure of that back then, the child within you knew it for a certainty, but now it comes to you with the choices you made, the choices you didn't make, that in the end it meant nothing, forty years in the same company either assembly line the one you work with your hands or the one you work with your brain, it's all the same, it meant nothing, your wife's bored, your kids don't respect you, you don't know any of your neighbours, you're drinking too much smoking too much or you've started jogging until that addiction replaces the others, and you're as likely to drop dead of that one as the other two because the body wears out in the end, no escaping it, the body wears out, I'll never do the nine-to-five and neither will you. We've set out on different paths, the only similarity between them is what they're both avoiding, but I think you're on a better path. I'm still caught up in the avoiding, I can't find a destination, but you've got Caroline and your little girl and that little girl is going to grow up and you'll get to watch that day by day and I know that scares you because we've handled so many kids and so many of them are fucked up, disrespectful insolent little shits, and you're thinking this messed-up world we've created made them that way but think back, Mark, remember those kids' faces, remember how every now and then we got past the cynical masks and saw the child still there, hiding inside, you think kids are growing up faster but they aren't, they're just learning to cope faster, they're learning defence mechanisms before they learn anything else, and the problem is those defence mechanisms can end up keeping them from learning anything else, but no one's chained the child in you, Mark, or even in me I guess. Our parents gave us the room and you and Caroline will do the same with Hannah, she was born smiling and she'll keep smiling, so don't worry about any of that, Mark, and don't worry about what I said an hour ago saying it was time for you to make a choice, a time for you to grow up, that was my fear and jealousy talking so give me back that lighter, this night needs no beacon of flame, can I have it back now, please, thanks. Sorry, Mark. You don't have to take on the entire world just your small part of it, those are the battles that count.

I don't know. Those small battles need to be won, sure, but only to show to yourself that it's possible after all which gives you the strength you need to fight the bigger battles. Do I want to change the world? Of course I do, what would be the fucking point otherwise?

I can't imagine there'd be many parents out there who'd admit they're teaching their kids how to rob banks since robbing banks is illegal and people often die in the process but from what I can see there's parents out there busy teaching their kids the sentiment of robbing banks, the art of grabbing what you can for yourself as much as you can grab, the hoarding of wood to keep the flames high and all the security that comes with that fire. But as any caveman will tell you life's a lot more secure when you share that fire, life's better when you push your hoards together. You use less, you don't have to risk going out into the dark nearly as often to collect more, you don't have to watch your own back, is that changing the world I guess it is and that's a pretty sad fact isn't it.

It's probably an instinct in parents to want to make things better for their children than they had themselves. So they do all they can to make life easier for them but easier isn't necessarily better, in fact easier may turn out to be worse. What I learned out on the rinks as a kid was easier never worked, it's easier tripping a guy on a near breakaway than it is skating like mad to catch him legally, so you trip the guy and he ends up getting a penalty-shot. A hard lesson and one you'd rather not make again. What I learned, what every kid playing a game for real learns, is working hard makes things better, being lazy or going easy makes things worse but then you step off the ice and it's like your parents have made it their task in life to clear every potential obstacle in front of you, to ease every struggle, to commit every foul possible on your behalf and that lesson is a lesson in dependency. On those canoe trips when we took kids out the hardest things those kids had to swallow was our insistence on them solving their own problems, on them actually having to work to get somewhere, on them doing their own dishes, washing their own clothes, pulling their own weight, cooking their own food, me and Jack were there to guide and support, not be their goddamned servants. We didn't buy into their whining or their demands, there were things that had to be done so get on with it. I guess sociologists would label us tyrants but fuck that because the truth was we led by example, we pulled our own weight, cooked our own food, washed our own clothes, and we did it all with jokes and laughs and three weeks later those were different kids from when they started. But three weeks is just three weeks, then it was back to the real world and all those self-sufficient habits fell away, but I have one story to tell about that – I was walking down Portage Avenue one day just a week or so before I left for Cardiff and this big pimpled kid with arms like a gorilla's stepped in front of me forcing me to stop. I eyed him and his glare thinking what the fuck now? Then he smiled and said, *You don't recognize me do you?* So I took a second look saw something familiar and said, *I think I do, only I still can't place you,* and he grinned. *Every summer I wear a bandana, every summer I take twelve kids across Lake of the Woods and near the end I gather them around and we do a voyageur ceremony and they get bandanas of their own. I'm Rick. Rickie,* and he held out his hand *Hi, Mark, seen any more wolves?*

Rickie. Rick. Shit, wolf sign, yeah, but no more wolves, they're too shy these days. How about you?

Sign, that's all. But you know once was enough. I've got that Alpha Male's eyes still burning in my head.

Me too.

We always will, eh?

Yeah I think so.

Shit you and Jack were bastards on that trip.

Yeah.

Just like I'm a bastard on mine.

Is it working?

He shrugged. *How can you tell? Could you? I mean, like, with me.*

No. I guess if it works at all it works years later.

But you never know.

I do now, Rick.

He nodded and that nod was thanks and it did me good, it still does and that's my story. I hope to make life better for Hannah but not easier, but if I think on it, even that's not right. I hope for Hannah life can be as good as mine was and is and that might be hard because the world's changed, so her life will be different, but even different I hope it'll be as good.

I guess if every parent has one fear this is it, isn't it?

The night on the wall was almost done. Ghost hands sweated real sweat on spear hafts the rustle of armour showing nerves as the painted savages gathered below for the assault. For a while we watched in silence.

I still think on everything we give up each day in our lives and the way things build, weighing you down on your back. It'd be nice to win just once, a real win that no one can take away and if that's not possible it'd be nice to watch a team win, a team without holdout players, without short-term owners, without performance-enhancing drugs, without all the cheating and all the rest that lures people into the realm of the big buck, but I'm not being romantic about the past because the spirit of things always had a way of going sour. I remember the '72 series against the Russians, they had a player No. 17 named Kharmalov, he wasn't just good he was devastating, he could skate like the wind, he was single-handedly beating Team Canada and our boys knew it and talked about him on the bench and someone said *we gotta do something about that guy,* so Bobby Clarke next shift stepped onto the ice and did Kharmalov good, did him permanently. Clarke did it to help his team win, *by God what spirit that man had,* yeah well not in my books. He ruined another player's career with a dirty cheap shot, he's no hero in my books, what he did wasn't what the game's about, only somehow he thought it was and that's a fucked-up way of thinking as far as I'm concerned and I was ashamed to be a Canadian then and the memory still shames me to this day. I remember switching allegiance in that game because of that one incident, the Russians were a marvel to watch and I chose the beauty of their game over the nasty cheapshots and the clutch and grab of the Canadian game. I tossed nationalism away then and there, I guess that made me a purist, at least until the Russians started the soccer-style bullshit of writhing around all over the ice every time someone hit them with a clean check, because that's as cynical as what Bobby Clarke did to Kharlamov. I watched hockey because of its beauty, but I don't see much beauty in the game anymore, and I've tried with soccer, with rugby, with basketball, with baseball, but it all seems shot through with the same rot, so what's left, well what's left is getting it back, only I can't do that by myself.

Jack says his dreams haunt him, dreams of skating like mad but getting nowhere, trying to escape something, trying to get to something. He says his dreams belong in a world without sports, where it's all fixed like professional wrestling, all for cheap show, spectacle, just do away with the pretence of a true contest of skills, better off choreographing the whole thing, the best actors get the most money and leave it all at that, me and Jack have watched so many games together and most of what I remember from doing that, at least lately, is how disgusted those games made us. If being a fan means living with disgust about the thing you love, well, I think I'll do without.

Jack has his dreams, but I have mine and I think I'll hold onto mine just a while longer because a part of me wants to believe. I want to keep thinking that things are still possible. I guess that makes me a fool but hell I could be worse things than a fool.

The family

Hannah was big, loud, demanding, smiling with gas, ill-tempered, a black-haired dark-eyed bitch desperate for a smoke, sweet and beautiful. I was exhausted after that first hour, Caroline having the nerve to actually sleep, me fumbling with a bottle of breast-milk pumped out of Caroline's tits forty minutes ago, until Hannah closed her little mouth around the plastic nipple and sighed, suckled, and breathed all at once nice trick that. God there was going to be years of this. I was already longing for the day she could carry an eighty pound foodpack and a canoe on her shoulders, humping a three mile portage all on her own, this dependency stuff felt like chains and shackles. I spent ten minutes panicking before settling down, accepting that weight forever I guess it was going to be oh well.

Suddenly I was thinking career, stability, security, responsibilities, being a role model, setting an example, showing discipline, being supportive, basically an endless list of adult things I was now going to have to accept as parts of my life.

I heard the flick of a lighter in the bedroom, gathered up suckling Hannah and hurried in there seeing the glow of the cigarette end brightening showing Caroline's lovely round face she was sitting up in bed I hissed: *What do we do now? This is a baby it's a real baby eight and a half pounds of want. What if you run out of milk what if she needs her diaper changed what happens when she can't just wear blankets anymore she needs clothes what happens when she gets tits starts wearing tight jeans going out with hormone-soaked teenaged walking penises what happens when she needs help with homework like math and geography and art what happens Caroline what happens now?*

She shrugged, took another drag.

I stared down at Hannah's liquid black eyes staring up at me. *She understands every word I'm saying. She's already got a list made up of my inadequacies to exploit for the rest of our lives. I'm doomed, Caroline.*
Probably.
What will I do?
Suffer.
You're not much help.
Sorry. Do you want to run away?
I couldn't even if I wanted to. She's got her hooks in me.
You mean you love her.
Yeah. We made her.
Yes.
It's the three of us.
Yes.
You'll both come to Cardiff?
She took another drag, studying me through the smoke.

The wall

Spears sailed out through the dawn air as we reached the seawalls of Cardiff, plunging into the waves on either side of the sinking canoe. We'd run the gauntlet of breakwaters moles piers pylons rusty tankers hawlers lock-gates and river mouth and now the denizens were throwing iron-headed spears at us. Some welcome.

An official event was under way. We saw people dressed in Roman armour, we saw a Saxon longship pulled up on the dark sand to the north, we saw hairy savages we took to be Welsh capering around with spears and wicker shields, the media was there, too. Standing ankle deep offshore was Fred the mechanized effigy, the hollow samurai.

My brothers are getting closer, Sophia said and she was right, there they were, a half mile out heads bobbing in the waves arms thrashing the water.

We were blocked, no way into the city with the locals wanting to skewer us or worse, manning the battered Roman walls like they once did centuries ago

No choice, said Jack light in his eyes some flickering amusement. *We've got to follow it through to the letter, the modern world is the*

ancient world, every core of being is in disguise, with reporters and news moguls and critics all chewing like maggots trying to get in, it's all packaging don't you see.

I see, said Sophia, *it's the pregnant metaphor, allusions of birth and rebirth, the deceit of the wrapper, what does it all mean? Well it's hidden there, don't let the packaging fool you.*

You've both lost your minds, I said, ducking another clattering spear. *It's the yobs on the walls we have to worry about. All this hostility.*

Here in the ashes of a burnt-out empire, Jack said nodding, *the laminations of centuries of pomposity combined with studied indifference pumped and preening puffed and prancing, the smirk is the national smile, I'm left wanting to punch a whole country in the face.*

Jack took the lead, Sophia following, then me, back out into the water, back around Fred the effigy, up one leg, through the butt-hatch then inside the hollow monstrosity where we settled in to wait for who knows what.

The city

It was the day of leavetaking, long after the thousands had gathered at the Forks, long after those days of hope and wonder followed by betrayal, long after the fires rushed through leaving nothing but ashes.

Every season saw an old sport rise anew, a little more tarnished, a little more beaten and salty, a few more players holding out in brutally obvious brandished almost boastful proclamation of greed, another hike in ticket prices, rumours of strikes, pending millionaire athletes versus millionaire businessmen side by side mutually feasting on the fans of the game, the followers, the purveyors, the consumers as the puckered penny counters call them but who's doing the consuming? Watch them bickering over the scraps of meat. Those scraps are you and me, the blood smearing their mouths is our blood, another season rising, the game encrusted and scarred, dripping money maggots well fuck that fuck that from now on.

We'd taken to the bush that summer to find out if what we'd miss was worth missing. It was, it was the wild lands, blistering heat and thunderstorms, star-crowded skies over black lakes, it was friends and it was over by August and I waited and then Hannah was born and then it was time to leave.

I hold in my mind the people of Winnipeg gathering to save their hockey team. I hold it because I was there among them, seeing the children's faces, the faces of old fans, the faces of everyone and I wrapped around me their desires, their feelings, their memories, because we all shared them then and every cynical fucker mocking that is mocking humanity, but humanity lost that day. Jack's society of fans, a true society he says, it was stabbed through the heart left for dead, and the seasons roll round again and again, each time we're less than what we were, our power getting further away.

For the city itself I held no regrets leaving. Barring the fans, barring what used to be there, barring my friends I wish it could be otherwise.

And maybe the dream isn't dead, maybe that speared-through body is but moments away from resurrection wouldn't that fuck the cynics over wouldn't it just.

We were at Winnipeg International Airport which sounds like a big place but isn't. Because the place had gone nonsmoking the group stood outside near the taxis, Lester and Frank helping with our bags while I carried Hannah, and Caroline stood to one side, two police officers walked up eyeing Frank and Lester.

Those your bags?

Jack said, *Actually they're ours, they just helped carry them.*

You shouldn't let other people carry your bags.

They're our friends.

You can never be sure even the best of friends might take advantage of you to smuggle contraband.

Maybe your friends, sir, but not ours.

Was that a crack?

No sir.

Lester and Frank handed our bags to us. I handed Hannah to Caroline, she dropped and ground out her butt, the policemen watched, one said, *Where are you flying to?*

United Kingdom, Jack said.

Vacation?

Are you guys Customs? You do Customs interviews outside the doors like this?

No we're not Customs, it was just a friendly question.

Actually we were thinking of sneaking these two Natives aboard so they could apply for refugee status in England, and given the endless fucking harassment these guys receive I'm all for it. Look, they're our friends, they came here to say goodbye to us. What drew you to us, to this group of people over, say, that group of people standing over there? You won't answer that but we know the answer, everyone standing here.

One of the policemen got on his radio, called in airport security. The guy in charge started asking us questions and after a minute he gave the policemen a strange look, pulled them to one side said something, turned back to us and said *go get your baggage checked in.*

Now I've got nothing against cops, how they behave just reflects how society behaves, so looking at them is looking at ourselves and I've heard about South Africa and the treatment of non-whites there back when the whites were in power, and all I'll say is from what I've experienced, Canada is just a north version of the same thing, racism and segregation of the *indigenous peoples,* and from what I've heard it's maybe even worse in the States but my only point is there's no point in getting high and mighty about South Africa, not in Canada, not in the States, not in the UK, that kind of bullshit goes on everywhere and that's that.

We'll come visit, Lester said. We were having coffee, the bags checked in forty minutes before we had to board the plane, *in Cardiff, maybe we'll canoe across the Atlantic.*

That'd be a helluva trip, Jack said.

Our dongs are long enough, Lester assured us. *We could do it, maybe we will next summer, take the south route down the Yank coast then out to Cuba then across to the Azores then up to Gilbraltar, up the Portuguese coast then across the Channel then south along the English coast then up and around, paddle into Cardiff's harbour on a misty morning to discover a New World and we'll push through the crowds and plant a Plains Cree flag.*

New Creedonia.

That's it, New Creedonia, sounds good, we'll be Founding Fathers founding lots of children by local women.

I won't, said Frank, *I've got my vows to consider.*

Have you considered them?

All the time.

During fornication?

Especially then but what I have to consider is if it really counts, I mean those locals are just ignorant savages, right? It probably doesn't count with them in the eyes of God. I'll have to think a bit on that.

183

Jack frowned, *You'd do better if you sailed across, rigged a sail for the canoe I mean, and I've got the perfect sail to use, it just came to me, you have to steal the Queen's portrait from the arena, that would make a good sail, thick canvas, the right proportions. What do you think?*

Could do, Lester nodded. *Not a bad idea that. It'd make a nice picture for the newspapers and National Geographic. I'm thinking National Geographic because we'll want sponsors, think we can get National Geographic, Frank?*

Absolutely.

Okay, next summer then. We'll see you guys then.

We got up, all shook hands, Lester, Frank and Jack went off to one side. I gathered Caroline and Hannah in a hug, held them tight, the baby was fidgeting, looking up at me, frowning, Caroline said she was pooing, she wasn't memorizing my face, I figure she was doing both and then everything went by real fast and before we knew it we were heading down the passage to the plane, handing over our boarding passes, sitting down, staring out at the sunbleached tarmac. If either of us said goodbye to our country it wasn't out loud.

The family

Seven days, in seven days I'll be at the arena in Cardiff.

Hannah in her arms, Caroline just nodded, she was tired, I was tired, babies make you tired and Hannah was going to be a baby for months maybe even years, we got tired just thinking about it.

We're flying to Edinburgh then we'll visit Hadrian's Wall then we'll canoe down to Cardiff. It's all worked out or if it isn't it will be, we'll wing it, that's what we'll do but I'll be at the arena when I said.

Okay, she nodded.

I've got to leave. Leave Winnipeg. I've got to find a new place, a city in the clouds, clean ice, a team of players playing the game for the game and for the screaming fans. I want to be a foreigner, someone with odd sensibilities and an accent. Winnipeg's like a shroud of defeat. I want to shrug it off, does that make any sense? I don't want to drive past an empty arena or go to minor league games and pretend it's good enough. I don't want to watch highlights or games on CBC or

TSN. I don't want my being a fan of the game to be exploited by people who don't give a shit about what I think so long as I keep paying over the bucks. I want to give them all the finger and walk away and that's all I want to do.

Okay.

The city

The locals got curious as Jack and Sophia knew they would. They came down with cranes and cables, picked up Fred and wheeled him in through the city gates just in time since we could hear the slap of hands on water and the grunts of Sophia's brothers. It was just two hours before the noon deadline. We climbed out and found ourselves in the heart of Cardiff, old buildings mostly run-down and abandoned along the waterfront, the scent of lost industry a century old hanging like a drunk's breath, one long street that had probably once felt the trod of African slaves, leading into the downtown area, council blocks on the left warehouses on the right. The street was crowded with some kind of festival, celebration, people dancing, policemen on horseback, cameras flashing and whirring .

I repacked Fred, threw the duffel bag over a shoulder, then the three of us pushed our way along the street. I could see the arena ahead, that solid temple of functional architecture, there was a grandstand set up with blue red and white bunting, the crowds thick around it except for an aisle of royal purple carpet lined by Roman soldiers, horsetail plumes flickering in the breeze, and near the grandstand steps a small figure was descending, a woman with a sky blue hat and sky blue dress and white gloves on her hands. Jack went perfectly still.

It's her, it's the Queen. My God I can't believe it here's my chance, and he plunged into the crowd, Sophia turning on me a luminous beaming smile of triumph. I focused again on the arena, the game awaited, and in the stands she waited, we'd arrived.

Jack had vanished, the only sign a rustling ripple through the crowd making a bee-line for the Queen as she walked down the carpeted aisle. He was closing fast and then the paths intersected.

I saw Jack's head. I saw the Queen smile graciously and reach out one gloved hand.

185

A sudden commotion, a scream, then soldiers closed in, frenzied as they leapt on Jack's back, bore him to the ground. Plainclothes bodyguards hustled the Queen toward a waiting limo, only her sky blue hat visible, cameras flashed, more people screamed, others shouted. I grabbed Sophia. *She didn't shake his hand did she? What did she shake, Sophie, what did she shake?*

Sophia just smiled, they were carting Jack away, somewhere inside a mob of soldiers. I caught a flash of my brother's face, it was glowing, satisfied, content, both sides of that mouth smiling, he was all in the visible, I'd never seen that before, he was all there.

The wall

The savages came over the wall there was no stopping them this time. Picts and Scots and Attacotti and Saxons and Angles and Danes and Frisians and Geats, they came to burn civilization to the ground. We stood on the wall jumping up and down cheering like animals, it was all coming down, good riddance, flames and screams, the game's done, the game's over, done with for all time, money has killed us, it had promised that from the start now it killed us it killed us all.

Fuck the train, let's canoe to Cardiff, Jack said.

How the hell would we do that?

I'll explain in a minute. The point is Canadians don't make enough waves, not enough waves at all, the basic truth is history isn't there to be ignored, every lesson of our demise not only as a civilization but as a species is there in what's gone before, the problem is the eternal one of point-of-view, we're convinced we're distinct from all the rest, like children convinced we're immortal not individually but in all that surrounds us, the computers the planes the stock market the cars the oil the paper the plastics the pulp the political parties taxes television movie stars the American dream guns and missiles and medicines and sports gear and quiz shows and books and newspapers and jobs and education it'll all go on, impervious, never to face the threat of extinction, only change through evolution, endless improvements, transformations but basically going on and on. I guarantee you Mayan high-priests figured the same for their civilization, the endless surplus from the farmers, the endless blood sacrifices, the political intrigues, soap opera lives, they had a calendar that measured time in millennia. They were all as certain of continuity as they were the sun was going to rise day after day, but they were fooling themselves, which is what our species does best day in day out, we assure ourselves of continuity. Civilization will continue, will overcome all, will go on and on, the few people saying 'hey, looks like the end-run here, fellas' just get mocked 'oh yeah we've heard that before' said the last Mayan high-priest, says most everybody these days, but you know it's all catching up to us, we decry brutality and mayhem in small war-torn nations but we ain't seen nothing yet, what do you think will happen when we all get desperate?

So why are we canoeing to Cardiff?

Why not?

Huh, good enough.

Jack handed me the bottle. *One last drink, brother, to destiny.*

To destiny, and so I drank, the numbness spreading inside like a hint of what was to come.

We stood side by side on the battered wall that in the end held nothing back, nothing at all.

The city

Jack got quietly told to leave the UK but he didn't much care, he was content. Sophia decided to go with him, what with her brothers laying siege to Cardiff and settling down for a long winter, maybe more than one. I heard all this later, Sophia was already showing, not sure how that happened, I was going to be an uncle.

I sat in the dressing room. It was quiet and peaceful as I strapped on my equipment. My back felt good, my muscles were primed. I could see in my mind's eye the rink, the skaters, the other Canadians, the Finns, the Swedes, the Italians, the Germans, the home-grown Brits, all skating, snapping pucks against the boards, playing tic tac toe with the puck, blades slid smooth and cut deep into the ice, the rituals of preparation were going on out there like the seeds of a dream.

The world's fastest team sport here and now. I tied my skates on, one of the trainers had just honed the blades. I stood up, feeling my weight on these two slivers of steel on a rubber floor, the knee pads tight on my legs feeling solid and warm.

187

I checked the tape on my fingers, my knuckles, then slid my hands into the gloves, the trapper and blocker, reached down and collected my stick, studying the dressing room, the pegs, the numbers, the name tags from last season all etching in my memory through the wire cage of my mask.

The bristle on my chin rubbed at the worn padding lining the base of the cage and I took a deep breath. My future was out there on the ice. And in the stands she was there, sitting on her edge of her seat, hands in her lap.

And propped at her side was Hannah, all wrapped up against the chill, a bandana tied around her neck like a scarf, her dark magical eyes taking it all in.

I walked through the dressing room, strode into the aisle leading to the rink. Pucks on boards echoed, a breath of cool air flowed past. I reached the ice, a world of white topped with rows of seating like heaven's crown, and took my first stride, carrying me out to join with the other players, circling the rink. Sometimes a life reduces down to gestures, the time for explanations is past, a life's bulk is only there in the end to give meaning to the gestures riding it. That's a lesson every professional sports hero should heed, doesn't matter what you've done. The day you grab for the hoard of gold bleating 'if they're gonna offer me one hundred million over six years I'm gonna take it who wouldn't' or 'this strike means I'll have to sell one of my eight cars' boo hoo or 'the player's union of hockey solidly backs the striking basketball players because it's life or death for all of us' is the day the real team's colours are worn and they're dollar green through and through, so I stayed mindful that when you're left to gestures, you just get on with making them.

Shrugged my shoulders loose, rotated my head, then scanned the seats. And she was there, Hannah propped on her lap. She was there and that was that.

Cardiff Arena's a no-smoking building. Caroline lasted twenty minutes before bundling Hannah up and heading out. I tipped my stick blade to her then got ready to stop every shot including closing the hole upper glove-hand corner. It takes a while but good advice eventually sinks in.

The family

In my mind Mom will always be sitting there, right on the edge of her seat, proud of her team, her sons, hands folded in her lap, there in winter-silence, there a solid memory, there ravaged by life but a presence always at my side, small and earning every hug my imagination creates. She's sitting there in the arena, in the temple that mapped out parallel lives, dreams, aspirations, hopes, glories and all the rest. Hannah knows how I feel.

And in my mind he's there as well, with all the lessons he represents, what a father puts into the lives of his children. I can hold onto this continuity even though so much else has been broken and, just like the team that left us, I can keep it alive.

The ghost

Somewhere in the Canadian bush, on a frozen pond surrounded by trees where the mist hangs knee-deep, a kid plays hockey. He plays the game against the forces of nature, turning the laws of physics into poems.

Occasionally some passer-by stumbles into view, and watches in reverence, the slow realization that the kid is more than just a kid, the game more than just a game, the love more than just love. The witness sees sport without a coin to its name.

The passer-by moves on after a time, because like staring into the burning bush you shouldn't look too long, and never tell anyone anything, ever. But the rest of that person's day is measured from that single point, and it's there in the eyes of the chosen at every game, in every arena, every stadium, a shimmering glimmer of sadness.

People say perfection doesn't exist in the real world. Only in our minds, that memory that Plato talked about, the ghost world of perfection we all use as a point of reference.

Legends of that kid remain. Skating on clouds, the perfect ghost playing the perfect game. We all had our chance at seeing it, seeing him. I guess there are just some things money can't buy.

I'll say it again. There are just some things money can't buy.